Praise for the Novels of

CHRISTINA LAUREN

"Heartfelt and funny, this enemies-to-lovers romance shows that the best things in life are all-inclusive and nontransferable as well as free."

—*Kirkus Reviews* on *The Unhoneymooners* (starred review)

"A funny, sexy page-turner that warns: Keep your friends close and their avatars closer."

—*Kirkus Reviews* on *My Favorite Half-Night Stand*

"This is a messy and sexy look at digital dating that feels fresh and exciting."

—*Publishers Weekly* on *My Favorite Half-Night Stand* (starred review)

"You can never go wrong with a Christina Lauren novel . . . a delectable, moving take on modern dating reminding us all that when it comes to intoxicating, sexy, playful romance that has its finger on the pulse of contemporary love, this duo always swipes right."

—*Entertainment Weekly* on *My Favorite Half-Night Stand*

"With exuberant humor and unforgettable characters, this romantic comedy is a standout."

—*Kirkus Reviews* on *Josh and Hazel's Guide to Not Dating* (starred review)

"The story skips along . . . propelled by rom-com momentum and charm."

—*New York Times Book Review* on *Josh and Hazel's Guide to Not Dating*

"Lauren has penned a hilariously zany and heartfelt novel . . . the story is sure to please readers looking for a fun-filled novel to escape everyday life with."

—*Booklist* on *Josh and Hazel's Guide to Not Dating*

"From Lauren's wit to her love of wordplay and literature to swoony love scenes to heroines who learn to set aside their own self-doubts . . . Lauren writes of the bittersweet pangs of love and loss with piercing clarity."

—*Entertainment Weekly* on *Love and Other Words*

"A triumph . . . a true joy from start to finish."

—Kristin Harmel, internationally bestselling author of *The Room on Rue Amélie* on *Love and Other Words*

"Lauren's standalone brims with authentic characters and a captivating plot."

—*Publishers Weekly* on *Roomies* (starred review)

"Delightful."

—*People* on *Roomies*

"At turns hilarious and gut-wrenching, this is a tremendously fun slow burn."

—*Washington Post* on *Dating You / Hating You*
(A Best Romance of 2017 selection)

"Truly a romance for the twenty-first century. . . . A smart, sexy romance for readers who thrive on girl power."

—*Kirkus Reviews* on *Dating You / Hating You*
(starred review)

"Christina Lauren hilariously depicts modern dating."

—*Us Weekly* on *Dating You / Hating You*

"A passionate and bittersweet tale of love in all of its wonderfully terrifying reality . . . Lauren successfully tackles a weighty subject with both ferocity and compassion."

—*Booklist* on *Autoboyography*

"Perfectly captures the hunger, thrill, and doubt of young, modern love."

—*Kirkus Reviews* on *Wicked Sexy Liar*

"The perfect summer read."

—*Self* on *Sweet Filthy Boy*

"Christina Lauren's books have a place of honor on my bookshelf."

—Sarah J. Maas, bestselling author of *Throne of Glass*

"In our eyes, Christina Lauren can do no wrong."

—*Bookish*

Also by Christina Lauren

Dating You / Hating You

Roomies

Love and Other Words

Josh and Hazel's Guide to Not Dating

My Favorite Half-Night Stand

The Beautiful Series

Beautiful Bastard

Beautiful Stranger

Beautiful Bitch

Beautiful Bombshell

Beautiful Player

Beautiful Beginning

Beautiful Beloved

Beautiful Secret

Beautiful Boss

Beautiful

The Wild Seasons Series

Sweet Filthy Boy

Dirty Rowdy Thing

Dark Wild Night

Wicked Sexy Liar

Young Adult

The House

Sublime

Autoboyography

THE UNHONEYMOONERS

CHRISTINA LAUREN

GALLERY BOOKS

New York London Toronto Sydney New Delhi

G

Gallery Books
An Imprint of Simon & Schuster, Inc.
1230 Avenue of the Americas
New York, NY 10020

This book is a work of fiction. Any references to historical events, real people, or real places are used fictitiously. Other names, characters, places, and events are products of the author's imagination, and any resemblance to actual events or places or persons, living or dead, is entirely coincidental.

First Gallery Books trade paperback edition May 2019

GALLERY BOOKS and colophon are registered trademarks of Simon & Schuster, Inc.

For information about special discounts for bulk purchases, please contact Simon & Schuster Special Sales at 1-866-506-1949 or business@simonandschuster.com.

The Simon & Schuster Speakers Bureau can bring authors to your live event. For more information or to book an event, contact the Simon & Schuster Speakers Bureau at 1-866-248-3049 or visit our website at www.simonspeakers.com.

Interior design by Michelle Marchese

Manufactured in the United States of America

30

Library of Congress Cataloging-in-Publication Data

Names: Lauren, Christina, author.
Title: The unhoneymooners / Christina Lauren.
Description: First Gallery Books trade paperback edition. | New York : Gallery Books, 2019.
Identifiers: LCCN 2018052888| ISBN 9781501128035 (trade pbk.) | ISBN 9781501128042 (ebook)
Subjects: | GSAFD: Love stories. | Humorous fiction.
Classification: LCC PS3612.A9442273 U54 2019 | DDC 813/.6—dc23
LC record available at https://urldefense.proofpoint.com/v2/url?u=https-3A__lccn loc.gov_2018052888&d=DwIFAg&c=jGUuvAdBXp_VqQ6t0yah2g&r=jOP_-C gRZWvBrDdCwa8xatiC6xfq_b-txHvQ-EzzwapJfII4Aa7gU5HEQRlR4PPw&m= mtdYo0ghmtYIRo54SWyOv5r7km-cEZ2OR2vS_JaOb4o&s=c4RsM3yoMFy7r 7mZEmMkSPi0EjwAr_i8RpbjYL2mdkU&e=

ISBN 978-1-5011-2803-5
ISBN 978-1-5011-2804-2 (ebook)

For Hugues de Saint Vincent.
Work like a captain, play like a pirate.

THE
UNHONEYMOONERS

chapter **one**

In the calm before the storm—in this case, the blessed quiet before the bridal suite is overrun by the wedding party—my twin sister stares critically down at a freshly painted shell-pink fingernail and says, "I bet you're relieved I'm not a bridezilla." She glances across the room at me and smiles generously. "I bet you expected me to be *impossible*."

It is a statement so perfectly dropped in the moment, I want to take a picture and frame it. I share a knowing look with our cousin Julieta, who is repainting Ami's toes ("It should be more petal pink than baby pink, don't you think?"), and gesture to the bodice of Ami's wedding gown—which hangs from a satin hanger and on which I am presently and painstakingly ensuring that every sequin is lying flat. "Define 'bridezilla.' "

Ami meets my eyes again, this time with a half-hearted

glare. She's in her fancy wedding-bra contraption and skimpy underwear that I'm aware—with some degree of sibling nausea—her dudebro fiancé, Dane, will positively destroy later. Her makeup is tastefully done and her fluffy veil is pinned in her upswept dark hair. It's jarring. I mean, we're used to looking identical while knowing we're wholly different people inside, but this is something entirely unfamiliar: Ami is the portrait of a bride. Her life suddenly bears no resemblance to mine whatsoever.

"I'm not a bridezilla," she argues. "I'm a perfectionist."

I find my list and hold it aloft, waving it to catch her attention. It's a piece of heavy, scalloped-edged pink stationery that has *Olive's To-Do List—Wedding Day Edition* written in meticulous calligraphy at the top, and which includes seventy-four (*seventy-four*) items ranging from *Check for symmetry of the sequins on the bridal gown* to *Remove any wilted petals from the table arrangements.*

Each bridesmaid has her own list, perhaps not quite as long as my maid-of-honor one but equally fancy and handwritten. Ami even drew checkboxes so that we can record when each task is completed.

"Some people might call these lists a little overboard," I say.

"Those are the same 'some people,'" she replies, "who'll pay an arm and a leg for a wedding that is half as nice."

"Right. They hire a wedding planner to—" I refer to my

list. "'Wipe condensation off the chairs a half hour before the ceremony.'"

Ami blows across her fingernails to dry them and lets out a movie-villain laugh. "Fools."

You know what they say about self-fulfilling prophecies, I'm sure. Winning makes you feel like a winner, and then somehow . . . you keep winning. It has to be true, because Ami wins everything. She tossed a ticket into a raffle bowl at a street fair and walked home with a set of community theater tickets. She slid her business card into a cup at The Happy Gnome and won free happy hour beers for a year. She's won makeovers, books, movie premiere tickets, a lawnmower, endless T-shirts, and even a car. Of course, she also won the stationery and calligraphy set she used to write the to-do lists.

All this to say, as soon as Dane Thomas proposed, Ami saw it as a challenge to spare our parents the cost of the wedding. As it happens, Mom and Dad could afford to contribute—they are messy in many ways, but financially is not one of them—but for Ami, getting out of paying for anything is the best kind of game. If pre-engagement Ami thought of contests as a competitive sport, *engaged* Ami viewed them as the Olympics.

No one in our enormous family was surprised, then, when she successfully planned a posh wedding with two hundred guests, a seafood buffet, a chocolate fountain, and multicolored roses spilling out of every jar, vase, and goblet—and has shelled out, at most, a thousand dollars. My sister works her ass off to find the best promotions and contests. She reposts every Twitter and Facebook giveaway she can find, and even has an email address that is aptly named *AmeliaTorresWins@xmail.com*.

Finally convinced there are no misbehaving sequins, I lift the hanger from where it's suspended from a metal hook attached to the wall, intending to bring the gown to her.

But as soon as I touch it, my sister and cousin scream in unison, and Ami holds up her hands, her matte pink lips in a horrified O.

"Leave it there, Ollie," she says. "I'll come over. With your luck, you'll trip and fall into the candle and it'll go up in a ball of sequin-scented flames."

I don't argue: she isn't wrong.

WHEREAS AMI IS A FOUR-LEAF clover, I have always been unlucky. I don't say that to be theatrical or because I only seem unlucky in comparison; it is an objective truth. Google Olive Torres, Minnesota, and you'll find dozens of articles and comment threads dedicated to the time I climbed into one of those claw crane arcade games and got stuck. I was six, and when the stuffed animal I'd captured didn't drop directly into the chute, I decided to go in and get it.

I spent two hours inside the machine, surrounded by a lot of hard, coarse-furred, chemical-smelling toy bears. I remember looking out through the handprint-smudged plexiglass and seeing an array of frantic faces shouting muffled orders to each other. Apparently, when the owners of the arcade explained to my parents that they didn't actually own the game and therefore didn't have the key to get inside, the Edina fire department was called, followed quickly by a local news crew, who diligently documented my extraction.

Fast-forward twenty-six years and—thank you, YouTube—there's still video floating around. To date, nearly five hundred thousand people have watched it and discovered that I was stubborn enough to climb in, and unlucky enough to catch my belt loop on the way out, leaving my pants behind with the bears.

This is but one story of many. So yes, Ami and I are identical twins—we are both five foot four with dark hair that misbehaves when there's even a hint of humidity, deep brown eyes, upturned noses, and matching constellations of freckles—but that's where the similarities end.

Our mother always tried to embrace our differences so we'd feel like individuals rather than a matching set. I know her intentions were good, but for as long as I can remember, our roles were set: Ami is an optimist who looks for the silver lining; I tend to assume the sky is falling. When we were three, Mom even dressed us as Care Bears for Halloween: Ami was Funshine Bear. I was Grumpy.

And it's clear the self-fulfilling prophecy works in both directions: From the moment I watched myself picking my nose behind a piece of grimy plexiglass on the six o'clock news, my luck never really improved. I've never won a coloring contest or an office pool; not even a lottery ticket or a game of Pin the Tail on the Donkey. I have, however, broken a leg when someone fell backward down the stairs and knocked me over (they walked away unscathed), consistently drew bathroom duty during every extended family vacation for a five-year stretch, was peed on by a dog while sunbathing in Florida, have been crapped on by innumerable birds over the years, and when I was sixteen I was struck by lightning—yes, really—and lived to tell the tale (but had to go to summer school because I missed two weeks of classes at the end of the year). Ami likes to sunnily remind me that I once guessed the correct number of shots left in a half-empty bottle of tequila.

But after drinking most of them in celebratory glee and subsequently throwing it all back up again, that win didn't feel particularly fortunate.

AMI REMOVES THE (FREE) DRESS from the hanger and steps into it just as our mother comes into the room from her (also free) adjoining suite. She gasps so dramatically when she sees Ami in the gown, I'm sure both Ami and I share the thought: *Olive somehow managed to stain the wedding dress.*

I inspect it to make sure I haven't.

All clear, Ami exhales, motioning for me to *carefully* zip her up. "*Mami*, you scared the crap out of us."

With a head full of enormous Velcro rollers, a half-finished glass of (you guessed it: free) champagne in hand, and her lips thick with red gloss, Mom is managing an impressive impersonation of Joan Crawford. If Joan Crawford had been born in Guadalajara. "Oh, *mijita*, you look beautiful."

Ami glances up at her, smiles, and then seems to remember—with immediate separation anxiety—the list she left all the way across the room. Hitching her billowing dress up, she shuffles to the table. "Mom, you gave the DJ the thumb drive with the music?"

Our mother drains her glass before daintily taking a seat on the plush couch. "*Sí*, Amelia. I gave your little plastic stick to the white man with cornrows in the terrible suit."

Mom's magenta dress is impeccable, her tan legs crossed at the knee as she accepts another flute of champagne from the bridal suite attendant.

"He has a gold tooth," Mom adds. "But I'm sure he's very good at his job."

Ami ignores this and her confident check mark scratches through the room. She doesn't really care if the DJ isn't up to our mother's standards, or even her own. He's new in town, and she won his services in a raffle at the hospital where she works as a hematology nurse. Free beats talented, every time.

"Ollie," Ami says, eyes never straying from the list in front of her, "you need to get dressed, too. Your dress is hanging on the back of the bathroom door."

I immediately disappear into the bathroom with a mock salute. "Yes, ma'am."

If there's one question we're asked more than any other, it's which one of us is the oldest. I would think it's fairly obvious, because although Ami is a mere four minutes older than me, she is without a doubt the leader. Growing up, we played what she wanted to play, went where she wanted to go, and while I may have complained, for the most part I happily followed. She can talk me into almost anything.

Which is exactly how I ended up in this dress.

"*Ami.*" I throw open the bathroom door, horrified by what I've just seen in the small bathroom mirror. *Maybe it's the light*, I think, hiking up the shiny green monstrosity and making my way to one of the larger mirrors in the suite.

Wow. It's definitely not the light.

"Olive," she answers back.

"I look like a giant can of 7UP."

"Yes, girl!" Jules sings. "Maybe someone will finally crack that thing open."

Mom clears her throat.

I glower at my sister. I was wary of being a bridesmaid in a Winter Wonderland–themed wedding in January, so my only request as the maid of honor was that my dress wouldn't have a scrap of red velvet or white fur. I see now that I should have been more specific.

"Did you actually choose this dress?" I point to my abundance of cleavage. "This was intentional?"

Ami tilts her head, studying me. "I mean, intentional in the sense that I won the raffle at Valley Baptist! *All* the bridesmaids dresses in one go—just think of the money I saved you."

"We're *Catholic*, not Baptist, Ami." I tug on the fabric. "I look like a hostess at O'Gara's on St. Paddy's Day."

I realize my primary error—not seeing this dress until today—but my sister has always had impeccable taste. On the day of the fittings, I was in my boss's office, pleading, unsuccessfully, to not be one of the four hundred scientists the company was letting go. I know I was distracted when she sent me a photo of the dress but I don't remember it looking this satiny or this green.

I turn to see it from another angle and—dear God, it looks even worse from the back. It doesn't help that a few weeks of stress-baking have made me, let's say . . . a little fuller in the chest and hips. "Put me in the back of every picture, and I could be your green screen."

Jules comes up behind me, tiny and toned in her own shiny green ensemble. "You look hot in it. Trust me."

"*Mami*," Ami calls, "doesn't that neckline show off Ollie's collarbones?"

"And her *chichis*." Mom's glass has been refilled once more, and she takes another long, slow drink.

The rest of the bridesmaids tumble into the suite, and there is a loud, collective, emotional uproar over how beautiful Ami looks in her dress. This reaction is standard in the Torres family. I realize this may sound like the observation of a bitter sibling, but I promise, it's not. Ami has always loved attention, and—as evidenced by my screaming on the six o'clock news—I do not. My sister practically glows under the spotlight; I am more than happy to help direct the spotlight her way.

We have twelve female first cousins; all of us in each other's business 24/7, but with only seven (free) dresses included in Ami's prize, hard decisions had to be made. A few cousins are still living on Mount Passive-Aggressive over it and went in on their own room together to get ready, but it's probably for the best; this room is way too small for that many women to safely maneuver themselves into Spanx at the same time, anyway.

A cloud of hair spray hangs in the air around us, and there are enough curling and flat irons and various bottles littering the counter to keep a decent-sized salon going.

Every surface grows either tacky with some sort of styling product or hidden beneath the contents of someone's overturned makeup bag.

There's a knock at the suite door, and Jules opens it to find our cousin Diego standing on the other side. Twenty-eight, gay, and better groomed than I could ever manage, Diego cried sexism when Ami told him he couldn't be part of the bridal party and would have to hang with the groomsmen. If his expression as he takes in my dress is any indication, he now considers himself blessed.

"I know," I say, giving up and stepping away from the mirror. "It's a little—"

"Tight?" he guesses.

"No—"

"Shiny?"

I glare at him. "No."

"Slutty?"

"I was going to say *green*."

He tilts his head as he steps around me, absorbing it from every angle. "I was going to offer to do your makeup, but it'd be a waste of my time." He waves a hand. "No one will be looking at your face today."

"No slut-shaming, Diego," my mother says, and I notice she didn't disagree with his assessment, she just told him not to shame me for it.

I give up on worrying about the dress—and how much

boob I'm going to have on display for the entire wedding and reception—and turn back to the chaos of the room. While cousins Static Guard each other and ask opinions on shoes, a dozen conversations are happening at once. Natalia dyed her brown hair to blond and is convinced she has ruined her face. Diego agrees. The underwire popped out of Stephanie's strapless bra, and Tía María is explaining how to just tape up her boobs instead. Cami and Ximena are arguing over whose Spanx are whose, and Mom is polishing off her glass of champagne. But amid all the noise and chemicals, Ami's attention is back on her list. "Olive, have you checked in with Dad? Is he here yet?"

"He was in the reception hall when I got here."

"Good." Another check.

It might seem strange that the job of checking in with our dad fell to me, and not his wife—our mother—who is sitting *right here*, but that's how it works in our family. The parentals don't interact directly, not since Dad cheated and Mom kicked him out but then refused to divorce him. Of course we were on her side, but it's been ten years and the drama is still just as fresh for both of them today as it was the day she caught him. I can't think of a single conversation they've had that hasn't been filtered through me, Ami, or one of their combined seven siblings since Dad left. We realized early on that it's easier for everyone this way, but the lingering sense I have from all of it is that love is exhausting.

Ami reaches for my list, and I scramble to get to it before she does; my lack of check marks would send her reeling into panic. Scanning down, I am thrilled to see the next to-do requires me to leave this foggy den of hair spray.

"I'll go check with the kitchen to make sure they're making a separate meal for me." The free wedding buffet came with a shellfish spread that would send me to the morgue.

"Hopefully Dane also ordered chicken for Ethan." Ami frowns. "God, I hope. Can you ask?"

All chatter in the room comes to a deafening halt, and eleven pairs of eyes swing my way. A dark cloud shifts across my mood at the mention of Dane's older brother.

Although Dane is firmly adequate, if not a bit bro-y for my tastes—think yelling at the television during sports, vanity about muscles, and a real effort to match all of his workout gear—he makes Ami happy. That's good enough for me.

Ethan, on the other hand, is a prickish, judgmental asshole.

Aware that I am the center of attention, I fold my arms, already annoyed. "Why? Is he allergic, too?" For some reason, the idea of having something in common with Ethan

Thomas, the surliest man alive, makes me feel irrationally violent.

"No," Ami says. "He's just fussy about buffets."

This jerks a laugh from me. "About *buffets*. Okay." From what I've seen, Ethan is fussy about literally everything.

For example, at Dane and Ami's Fourth of July barbecue, he wouldn't touch any of the food I spent half the day making. At Thanksgiving, he switched chairs with his dad, Doug, just so he wouldn't have to sit next to me. And last night at the rehearsal dinner, every time I had a bite of cake, or Jules and Diego made me laugh, Ethan rubbed his temples in the most dramatic show of suffering I'd ever seen. Finally I left my cake behind and got up to sing karaoke with Dad and Tío Omar. Maybe I'm still furious that I gave up three bites of *really good* cake because of Ethan Thomas.

Ami frowns. She's not the biggest fan of Ethan either, but she's got to be tired of having this conversation. "Olive. You barely know him."

"I know him well enough." I look at her and say two simple words: "Cheese curds."

My sister sighs, shaking her head. "I swear to God you will never let that go."

"Because if I eat, laugh, or breathe I'm offending his delicate sensibilities. You know I've been around him at least fifty times, and he still makes this face like he's trying to place who I am?" I motion between us. "We're *twins*."

Natalia speaks up from where she's teasing the back of her bleached hair. How is it fair that *her* big boobs manage to fit inside her dress? "Now's your chance to make friends with him, Olive. *Mmm*, he's so pretty."

I give her the Displeased Torres Brow Arch in reply.

"You'll have to go find him anyway," Ami says, and my attention whips back to her.

"Wait. Why?"

At my baffled expression, she points to my list. "Number sev—"

Panic sets in immediately at the suggestion that I need to talk to Ethan, and I hold up my hand for her to stop speaking. Sure enough, when I look at my list, at spot seventy-three—because Ami knew I wouldn't bother reading the entire list ahead of time—is the worst assignment ever: *Get Ethan to show you his best man's speech. Don't let him say something terrible.*

If I can't blame this burden on luck, I can absolutely blame it on my sister.

chapter **two**

As soon as I'm out in the hallway, the noise, chaos, and fumes of the bridal suite seem to be vacuum-sealed away; it is beautifully silent out here. It's so peaceful, in fact, that I don't want to leave the moment to go find the door down the hall with the cute little groom caricature hanging above the peephole. The tranquil figurine hides what is no doubt a weed-and-beer-fueled pre-wedding rager happening inside. Even party-loving Diego was willing to risk his hearing and respiratory health to hang with the bridal party instead.

I give myself ten deep breaths to delay the inevitable.

It's my twin's wedding, and I really am so happy for her I could burst. But it's still hard to buoy myself fully, especially in these solo, quiet moments. Chronic bad luck aside, the last two months have genuinely sucked: my roommate moved out, so I had to find a new, tiny apartment. Even then, I overextended what I thought I could afford on my own and—as my patented bad luck would have it—got laid off from the pharmaceutical company where I'd worked for six years. In the past few weeks, I've interviewed at no fewer than seven companies and haven't heard back from a single one of them. And now here I am, about to come face-to-face with my nemesis, Ethan Thomas, while wearing the shiny, flayed pelt of Kermit the Frog.

It's hard to believe there was a time when I couldn't wait to meet Ethan. Things between my sister and her boyfriend were starting to get serious, and Ami wanted to introduce me to Dane's family. In the parking lot at the Minnesota State Fairgrounds, Ethan climbed out of his car, with astonishingly long legs and eyes so blue I could see them from two car-lengths away. Up close he had more eyelash than any man has a right to. His blink was slow and cocky. He looked me squarely in the eye, shook my hand, and then smiled a dangerous, uneven smile. Suffice to say, I felt anything but sisterly interest.

But then apparently I made the cardinal sin of being a curvy girl getting a basket of cheese curds. We had stopped just past the entrance to make a game plan for our day, and I slipped away to get a snack—there is nothing more glorious than the food at the Minnesota State Fair. I came back to find the group near the livestock display. Ethan looked at me, then down to my delicious basket of fried cheese, frowned, and immediately turned away, mumbling some excuse about needing to go find the homebrew competition. I didn't think all that much of it at the time, but I didn't see him for the rest of the afternoon, either.

From that day on, he's been nothing but disdainful and prickly with me. What am I to think? That he went from smile to disgust in ten minutes for some other reason? Obviously my opinion of Ethan Thomas is: he can bite me. With the exception of today (wholly because of this dress), I like my body. I'm never going to let someone make me feel bad about it *or* about cheese curds.

Voices carry from the other side of the groom's suite—some fratty cheer about man sweat or beer or opening a bag of Cheetos with the force of a hard stare; who knows, it's Dane's wedding party we're talking about. I raise my fist and knock, and the door opens so immediately that I startle back, catching my heel on the hem of my dress and nearly falling.

It's Ethan; of course it is. He reaches out, his hands easily catching me around the waist. As he steadies me, I feel my lip curl, and watch the same mild revulsion work its way through him as he pulls his hands away and tucks them into his pockets. I imagine he'll rip open a disinfectant wipe the moment he has the chance.

The movement draws my attention to what he's wearing—a tuxedo, obviously—and how well it fits his long, wiry frame. His brown hair is neatly combed off his forehead; his eyelashes are as preposterously long as they always are. I tell myself that his thick, dark brows are obnoxious overkill—*settle down, Mother Nature*—but they do look undeniably great on his face.

I really don't like him.

I've always known Ethan was handsome—I'm not blind—but seeing him dressed in black tie is a bit too much confirmation for my liking.

He gives me the same perusal. He starts with my hair—maybe he's judging me for wearing it clipped back so plainly—and then looks at my simple makeup—he probably dates makeup-tutorial Instagram models—before slowly and methodically taking in my dress. I take a deep breath to resist crossing my arms over my midsection.

He lifts his chin. "That was free, I'm assuming."

And *I'm* assuming driving my knee right into his crotch would feel fantastic. "Beautiful color, don't you think?"

"You look like a Skittle."

"Aw, Ethan. Stop with the seduction."

A tiny grin twitches the side of his mouth. "So few people can pull off that color, Olivia."

From his tone, I can tell I am not included in this few. "It's Olive."

It amuses my extended family to no end that my parents named me Olive, not the eternally more lyrical Olivia. Since

I can remember, all my uncles on Mom's side call me *Aceituna* just to rankle her.

But I doubt Ethan knows that; he's just being a dick.

He rocks back on his heels. "Right, right."

I am tired of the game. "Okay, this is fun, but I need to see your speech."

"My *toast*?"

"Are you correcting my wording?" I wave a hand forward. "Let me see."

He leans a casual shoulder against the doorframe. "No."

"This is really for your safety. Ami will murder you with her bare hands if you say something dickish. You know this."

Ethan tilts his head, sizing me up. He's six foot four, and Ami and I are . . . not. His point is made, very clearly, with no words: *I'd like to see her try.*

Dane appears over his shoulder, his face falling as soon as he sees me. Apparently I'm not the beer wench they were both hoping for. "Oh." He recovers quickly. "Hey, Ollie. Everything okay?"

I smile brightly. "Fine. Ethan was just getting ready to show me his speech."

"His toast?"

Who knew this family was such a stickler for labels?

"Yeah."

Dane nods to Ethan and motions back inside the room.

"It's your turn." He looks at me, explaining, "We're playing Kings. My big brother is about to get *owned*."

"A drinking game before the wedding," I say, and let out a little chuckle. "Sounds like a prudent choice."

"Be there in a minute." Ethan smiles at his brother's retreating form before turning back to me, and we both drop the grins, putting our game faces back on.

"Did you at least write something?" I ask. "You're not going to try to wing it, are you? That never goes well. No one is ever as funny off the cuff as they think they are, especially you."

"*Especially* me?" Although Ethan is the portrait of charisma around nearly every other human, with me he's a robot. Right now his face is so controlled, so comfortably blank, that I can't tell whether I've genuinely offended him or he's baiting me into saying something worse.

"I'm not even sure if you could be funny . . ." I falter, but we both know I'm committed to this horrific rim shot: ". . . *on* the cuff."

A dark eyebrow twitches. He has successfully baited me.

"Okay," I growl, "just make sure your *toast* doesn't suck." I glance down the hall, and then remember the other bit of business I had with him. "And I assume you checked with the kitchen to make sure you don't have to eat the buffet for dinner? Otherwise I can do it when I'm down there."

He drops the sarcastic grin and replaces it with something resembling surprise. "That's pretty considerate. No, I hadn't asked for an alternative."

"It was Ami's idea, not mine," I clarify. "She's the one who cares about your aversion to sharing food."

"I don't have a problem *sharing food*," he explains, "it's that buffets are literal cesspools of bacteria."

"I really hope you bring that level of poetry and insight to your speech."

He steps back, reaching for the door. "Tell Ami my *toast* is hilarious, and not at all dickish."

I want to say something sassy, but the only coherent thought that comes to mind is how insulting it is that eyelashes like his were wasted on Satan's Errand Boy, so I just give a perfunctory nod and turn down the hall.

It's all I can do to not adjust the skirt while I walk. I could be paranoid, but I think I feel his critical eyes on the tight sheen of my dress the entire way to the elevators.

THE HOTEL STAFF HAVE REALLY taken Ami's Christmas-in-January theme and run with it. Thankfully, instead of red velvet Santas and stuffed reindeer, the center aisle is lined with fake snow. Even though it's easily seventy-five degrees in here, the reminder of the wet, slushy snow outside makes the entire room feel cold and drafty. The altar is decorated with white flowers and holly berries, miniature pine wreaths are hung from the back of each chair, and tiny white lights twinkle from inside the branches. In truth, it's all very lovely, but even from the back where we've lined up, I can see the little placards attached to each chair encouraging guests to *Trust Finley Bridal for your special day*.

The wedding party is restless. Diego is peeking into the banquet hall and reporting back the location of hot male guests. Jules is valiantly trying to get the phone number of one of the groomsmen, and Mom is busy telling Cami to tell Dad to make sure his zipper isn't down. We are all waiting for the coordinator to give the signal and send the flower girls down the aisle.

My dress seems to be growing tighter with each passing second.

Finally Ethan takes his spot next to me, and when he holds a breath and then releases it in a slow, controlled stream, it sounds like a resigned sigh. Without looking at me, he offers his arm.

Although I'm tempted to pretend I don't notice, I take it, ignoring the sensation of his curved bicep passing under my hand, ignoring the way he flexes just a bit, gripping my arm to his side.

"Still selling drugs?"

I clench my teeth. "You know that's not what I do."

He glances behind us and then turns back around, and I hear him take a breath to speak, but then he holds it, wordless.

It can't be about the size, volume, or general insanity of our family—they broke him in long ago—but I know *something* is bugging him. I glance up at him, waiting. "Whatever it is, just say it."

I swear I am not a violent woman, but at the sight of his wicked smile aimed down at me, the urge to dig my pointy heel into the toe of his polished shoe is nearly irresistible.

"It's something about the line of Skittle bridesmaids, isn't it?" I ask. Even Ethan has to acknowledge that there are some pretty amazing bodies in the bridesmaid lineup, but still, none of us can really pull off spearmint-green satin.

"Mind-reading Olive Torres."

My sarcastic smile matches his. "Mark the moment, people. Ethan Thomas remembered my name three years after we first met."

He turns his face back to the front, smoothing his features. It's always hard to reconcile the restrained, biting Ethan I get with the charming one I've watched make his way through a room, and even the wild one I've heard Ami complain about for years. Independent of how he seems determined to never remember a thing I tell him—like my job, or my *name*—I hate knowing that Ethan is a terrible influence on Dane, pulling him away for everything from wild weekends in California to adrenaline-soaked adventures on the other side of the world. Of course, these trips conveniently coincide with events deeply cherished by contest-hunters such as my sister, his fiancée: birthdays, anniversaries, Valentine's Day. Just last February, for example, when Ethan had whisked Dane off to Vegas for a guys' weekend, Ami ended up taking me to a romantic (and free) couple's dinner at the St. Paul Grill.

I've always thought the basis for Ethan's coldness toward me was just that I'm curvy and physically repulsive and he's a bigoted, garbage human—but it occurs to me, standing here, holding on to his bicep, that maybe *that's* why he's such an ass: Ethan resents that Ami has taken such a big part of his brother's life, but can't show that to her face without alienating Dane. So he takes it out on me instead.

The epiphany washes cool clarity through me.

"She's really good for him," I say now, hearing the protective strength to my voice.

I feel him turn to look down at me. "What?"

"Ami," I clarify. "She's really good for Dane. I realize you find me completely off-putting, but whatever your problem is with *her*, just know that, okay? She's a good soul."

Before Ethan can respond, the (free) wedding coordinator finally steps forward, waves to the (free) musicians, and the ceremony begins.

EVERYTHING I EXPECTED TO HAPPEN happens: Ami is gorgeous. Dane seems mostly sober and sincere. Rings are exchanged, vows are spoken, and there is an uncomfortably raunchy kiss at the end. That was definitely not church tongue, even if this isn't a church. Mom cries, Dad pretends not to. And throughout the ceremony, while I hold Ami's massive bouquet of (free) roses, Ethan looms like a silent cardboard cutout of himself, moving only when he has to duck a hand into his coat pocket to produce the rings.

He offers his arm to me again as we retreat down the aisle, and he's even stiffer this time, like I'm covered in slime and he's afraid it's going to rub off on his suit. So I make a point of leaning into him and then giving him a mental bird-flip when we're off the aisle, allowed to break contact to disperse in different directions.

We have ten minutes until we need to meet for wedding party photos, and I'm going to use that time to go remove wilted petals from the dinner table flower arrangements. This Skittle is going to cross some things off her list. Who cares what Ethan is going to do?

Apparently he's going to follow me.

"What was all that about?" he says.

I look over my shoulder.

"What was what about?" I ask.

He nods toward the wedding aisle. "Back there. Just now."

"Ah." Turning, I give him a comforting smile. "I'm glad that when you're confused, you feel comfortable asking for help. So: that was a wedding—an important, if not required, ceremony in our culture. Your brother and my—"

"Before the ceremony." His dark brows are pulled down low, hands shoved deep into his trouser pockets. "When you said I find you off-putting? That I have a problem with Ami?"

I gape up at him. "Seriously?"

He looks around, like he needs a witness to corroborate my stupidity. "Yeah. Seriously."

For a beat, I am speechless. The last thing I expected was for Ethan to need some sort of clarifying follow-up on our constant wave of snarky comments.

"You know." I wave a vague hand. Under his focus, and away from the ceremony and the energy in the full room, I am suddenly less confident in my earlier theory. "I think you resent Ami for taking Dane away from you. But you can't, like, take it out on *her* without him getting upset, so you're a chronic dick to me."

When he simply blinks at me, I barrel on: "You've *never* liked me—and we both know it goes way past the cheese curds, I mean you wouldn't even eat my *arroz con pollo* on the Fourth of July, which is fine, your loss—but just so you know, she's great for him." I lean in, going for broke. "*Great.*"

Ethan lets out a single, incredulous laugh-breath and then smothers it with his hand.

"It's just a theory," I hedge.

"A theory."

"About why you clearly don't like me."

His brow creases. "Why I don't like you?"

"Are you just going to repeat everything I say?" I produce my list from where I'd rolled it into my small bouquet and shake it at him. "Because if you're done, I have things to do."

I get another few seconds of bewildered silence before he seems to surmise what I probably could have told him ages ago: "Olive. You sound legitimately insane."

MOM PUTS A FLUTE OF champagne in Ami's hand, and it appears to be on someone else's to-do list to keep it filled to the brim because I see her drinking, but I never see it empty. It means that the reception goes from what was arguably a perfectly scheduled, slightly rigid affair, to a true party. Noise levels go from polite to frat house. People swarm the seafood buffet like they've never seen solid food before. The dancing hasn't even started yet, and Dane has already thrown his bow tie into a fountain and taken his shoes off. It's a testament to Ami's inebriation that she doesn't even seem to care.

By the time the toasts roll around, getting even half of the room to quiet down seems like a monumental task. After gently tapping a fork against a glass a few times and accomplishing nothing by way of noise control, Ethan finally just launches into his toast, whether people are listening or not.

"I'm sure most of you will have to pee soon," he begins, speaking into a giant fuzzy microphone, "so I'll keep this short." Eventually, the crowd settles, and he continues. "I don't actually think Dane wants me to speak today, but considering I'm not only his older brother but also his only friend, here we are."

Shocking myself, I let out a deafening cackle. Ethan pauses and glances over at me, wearing a surprised smile.

"I'm Ethan," he continues, and when he picks up a remote near his plate, a slideshow of photos of Ethan and Dane as kids begins a slow scroll on a screen behind us. "Best brother, best son. I am thrilled we can share this day with not only so many friends and family, but also with alcohol. Seriously, have you looked at that bar? Someone keep an eye on Ami's sister because too many glasses of champagne, and there's no way that dress is staying on." He smirks at me. "You remember the engagement party, Olivia? Well, if you don't, I do."

Natalia grips my wrist before I can reach for a knife.

Dane shouts out a drunk, "Dude!" and then laughs at this an obnoxious amount. Now I wish that the Killing Curse were a thing. (I didn't *actually* take my dress off at the engagement party, by the way. I just used the hem to wipe my brow once or twice. It was a hot night, and tequila makes me sweaty.)

"If you look at some of these family photos," Ethan says, gesturing behind him to where teenage Ethan and Dane are skiing, surfing, and generally looking like genetically gifted assholes, "you'll see that I was the quintessential big brother. I went to camp first, drove first, lost my virginity first. Sorry, no photos of that." He winks charmingly at the crowd and a flutter of giggles passes in a wave around the room. "But Dane found love first." There is a roar of collective *awwws* from the guests. "I hope I'll be lucky enough to find someone half as spectacular as Ami someday. Don't let her go, Dane, because none of us has any idea what she's thinking." He reaches for his scotch, and nearly two hundred other arms join his in raising their glasses in a toast. "Congrats, you two. Let's drink."

He sits back down and glances at me. "Was that sufficiently on the cuff for you?"

"It was quasi-charming." I glance over his shoulder. "It's still light out. Your inner troll must be sleeping."

"Come on," he says, "you laughed."

"Surprising both of us."

"Well it's your turn to show me up," he says, motioning that I should stand. "It's asking a lot, but try not to embarrass yourself."

I reach for my phone, where my speech is saved, and try to hide the defensiveness in my voice when I say, "Shut up, Ethan," before standing.

Good one, Olive.

He laughs as he leans in to take a bite of his chicken.

A smattering of applause carries across the banquet hall as I stand and face the guests.

"Hello, everyone," I say, and the entire room startles when the microphone squawks shrilly. Pulling the mic farther away from my mouth, and with a shaky smile, I motion to my sister and new brother-in-law. "They did it!"

Everyone cheers as Dane and Ami come together for a sweet kiss. I watched them dance earlier to Ami's favorite song, Peter Cetera's "Glory of Love," and managed to ignore the pressure of Diego's intense efforts to catch my eye and nonverbally commiserate about Ami's famously terrible taste in music. I was genuinely lost in the perfection of the scene before me: my twin in her beautiful wedding dress, her hair softened by the hours and movement, her sweet, happy smile.

Tears prick at my eyes as I tap through to my Notes app and open my speech.

"For those of you who don't know me, let me reassure

you: no, you aren't that drunk yet, I am the bride's twin sister. My name is Olive, not Olivia," I say, glancing pointedly down at Ethan. "Favorite sibling, favorite in-law. When Ami met Dane—" I pause when a message from Natalia pops up on my screen, obscuring my speech.

FYI your boobs look amazing up there.

From the audience, she gives me a thumbs-up, and I swipe her message away.

"—she spoke about him in a way I had never—"

What size bra are you wearing now?

Also from Natalia.

I dismiss it and quickly try to find my place again. Honestly, whose family texts them during a speech they are obviously reading *from a phone*? My family, that's who.

I clear my throat. "—She spoke about him in a way I'd never heard before. There was something in her voice—"

Do you know if Dane's cousin is single? Or could be . . . ;)

I give Diego a warning look and aggressively swipe back to my screen.

"—something in her voice that told me she knew this was different, that she felt different. And I—"

Stop making that face. You look constipated.

My mother. Of course.

I swipe it away and continue. Beside me, Ethan smugly laces his hands together behind his head, and I can feel his satisfied grin without even having to look at him. I push on—because he can't win this round—but I'm only two words deeper into my speech when I'm interrupted by the sound of a startled, pained groan.

The attention of the entire room swings to where Dane is huddled over, clutching his stomach. Ami has just enough time to place a comforting hand on his shoulder and turn to him in concern before he claps a hand over his mouth, and then proceeds to projectile-vomit through his fingers, all over my sister and her beautiful (free) dress.

chapter **three**

Dane's sudden illness can't be from his alcohol intake because one of the bridesmaids' daughters is only seven, and after Ami retaliates and throws up all over Dane, little Catalina loses her dinner, too. From there, the sickness starts to spread like wildfire through the banquet hall.

Ethan stands and drifts away to hover near one of the walls. I do the same, thinking it's probably best to watch the chaos from higher ground. If this were happening in a movie, it would be comically gross. Here in front of us, happening to people we know and who we've clinked glasses with and embraced and maybe even kissed? It's terrifying.

It goes from seven-year-old Catalina, to Ami's hospital administrator and her wife, to Jules and Cami, some people in the back at table forty-eight, then Mom, Dane's grandmother, the flower girl, Dad, Diego . . .

After that, I am unable to track the outbreak, because it snowballs. A crash of china tears through the room when a guest loses it all over an unlucky waiter. A few people attempt to flee, clutching their stomachs and moaning for a toilet. Whatever this is, it appears to want to exit the body through any route available; I'm not sure whether to laugh or scream. Even those who aren't throwing up or sprinting for the restrooms yet are looking green.

"Your speech wasn't *that* bad," Ethan says, and if I weren't worried he might vomit on me in the process, I'd shove him out of our little safe zone.

With the sound of retching all around us, a heavy awareness settles into our quiet space, and we slowly turn to each other, eyes wide. He carefully scans my face, so I carefully scan his, too. He is notably normal-colored, not even a little green.

"Are *you* nauseated?" he asks me quietly.

"Beyond at the sight of this? Or you? No."

"Impending diarrhea?"

I stare at him. "How are you single? Frankly, it's a mystery."

And instead of being relieved he's not sick, he relaxes his expression into the cockiest grin I've ever seen. "So I was right about buffets and bacteria."

"It's too fast to be food poisoning."

"Not necessarily." He points to the ice trays where the

shrimp, clams, mackerel, grouper, and about ten other fancy varieties of fish used to be. "I bet you . . ." He holds up a finger as if he's testing the air. "I bet you this is ciguatera toxin."

"I have no idea what that is."

He takes a deep breath, like he's soaking in the splendor of the moment and cannot smell how ripe the bathroom has grown just down the hall. "I have never in my life been more smug to be the eternal buffet buzzkill."

"I think you mean, 'Thank you for procuring my plate of roasted chicken, Olive.' "

"Thank you for procuring my plate of roasted chicken, Olive."

As relieved as I am to not be barfing, I am also horrified. This was Ami's dream day. She spent the better part of the last six months planning this, and this is the wedding day equivalent of a road full of advancing, flaming zombies.

So I do the only thing I can think to do: I march over to her, reach down to loop one of her arms over my shoulders, and help her up. No one needs to see the bride in a state like this: covered in vomit—hers *and* Dane's—and clutching her stomach like she might lose it out the other end, too.

We're lurching more than walking—really, I'm half dragging her—so we're only halfway to the exit when I feel the back of my dress rip wide open.

• • •

AS MUCH AS IT PAINS me to admit it, Ethan was right: the wedding party has been demolished by something known as ciguatera, which happens when one eats fish contaminated with certain toxins. Apparently the caterer is off the hook because it isn't a food preparation issue—even if you cook the living daylights out of a contaminated piece of fish, it is still toxic. I close out Google when I read that the symptoms normally last anywhere from weeks to months. This is a catastrophe.

For obvious reasons, we cancelled the *tornaboda*—the enormous wedding after-party that was going to be held at Tía Sylvia's house late into the night. I already see myself spending tomorrow wrapping and freezing the ungodly amount of food we spent the last three days cooking; no way will anyone want to eat for a long time after this. A few guests were taken to the hospital, but most have just retreated home or to their hotel rooms to suffer in isolation. Dane is in the groom's suite; Mom is next door curled over the toilet in the mother-in-law suite, and she banished Dad to one of the bathrooms in the lobby. She texted me to remind him to tip the bathroom attendant.

The bridal suite has become a triage unit of sorts. Diego is on the floor in the living room, clutching a garbage can to his chest. Natalia and Jules each have a bucket—compliments of the hotel—and are both in the fetal position on opposite ends of the living room couch. Ami whimpers in agony and tries to wiggle her way out of her completely saturated dress. I help her and immediately decide she's fine in her underwear, for a while anyway. At least she's out of the bathroom; I'll be honest, the noises coming from inside had no place on a wedding night.

Careful to watch my step as I move around the suite, I wet washcloths for foreheads and attempt to rub backs, emptying buckets as needed and thanking the universe for my shellfish allergy and constitutionally solid stomach.

As I step out of the bathroom with rubber gloves pulled up to my elbows, my sister zombie-moans into an ice bucket. "You have to take my trip."

"What trip?"

"The honeymoon."

The suggestion is so exceedingly random that I ignore her and grab a pillow to put under her head instead. It is at least two minutes before she speaks again.

"Take it, Olive."

"Ami, no way." Her honeymoon is an all-inclusive ten-day trip to Maui that she won by filling out over a thousand entry forms. I know because I helped her put the stamps on at least half of them.

"It's nonrefundable. We're supposed to leave tomorrow and . . ." She has to take a break to dry-heave. "There's no way."

"I'll call them. I'm sure they'll work around this situation, come on."

She shakes her head and then hurls up the water I made her sip. When she speaks, she sounds froggy, like she's the victim of a demon possession. "They won't."

My poor sister has turned into a swamp creature; I've never seen anyone this shade of gray before.

"They don't care about illness or injury, it's in the contract." She falls back onto the floor and stares up at the ceiling.

"Why are you even worried about this right now?" I ask, though in reality I know the answer. I adore my sister, but even violent illness won't get between her and redeeming a prize fairly won.

"You can use my ID to check in," she says. "Just pretend you're me."

"Ami Torres, that's illegal!"

Rolling her head so she can see me, she gives me a look so comically blank, I have to stifle a laugh.

"Okay, I realize it isn't your priority right now," I say.

"It is, though." She struggles to sit up. "I will be so stressed out about this if you don't take it."

I stare at her, and conflict makes my words come out tangled and thick. "I don't want to leave you. And I also don't want to be arrested for fraud." I can tell she isn't going to let this go. Finally, I give in. "Fine. Just let me call them and see what I can do."

Twenty minutes later, and I know she's right: the customer service representative for Aline Voyage Vacations gives zero damns about my sister's bowels or esophagus. According to Google and a physician the hotel called in who is slowly making the rounds to each guest room, Ami is unlikely to recover by next week, let alone tomorrow.

If she or her designated guest doesn't take the trip on the allotted days, it's gone.

"I'm sorry, Ami. This feels monumentally unfair," I say.

"Look," she begins, and then dry-heaves a few times, "consider this the moment your luck changes."

"Two hundred people threw up during Olive's speech," Diego reminds us all from the floor.

Ami manages to push herself up, supporting herself against the couch. "I'm serious. You should go, Ollie. *You* didn't get sick. You need to celebrate that."

Something inside me, a tiny kernel of sunshine, peeks out from behind a cloud, and then disappears again.

"I like the idea of good luck better when it isn't at someone else's expense," I tell her.

"Unfortunately," Ami says, "you don't get to choose the circumstances. That's the point of luck: it happens when and where it happens."

I fetch her a new cup of water and a fresh washcloth and then crouch down beside her. "I'll think about it," I say.

But in truth, when I look at her like this—green, clammy, helpless—I know that not only am I not taking her dream vacation, I'm not leaving her side.

I STEP OUT INTO THE hall before remembering that my dress has an enormous tear all down the back. My ass is literally hanging out. On the plus side, it's suddenly loose enough that I can cover my boobs. Turning back to the suite, I swipe the key card against the door, but the lock flashes red.

I go to try again and the voice of Satan rings out from behind me. "You have to—" An impatient huff. "No, let me show you."

There is nothing in the world I wanted less in this moment than for Ethan to show up, ready to mansplain how to swipe a hotel key.

He takes the card from me and holds it against the black circle on the door. I stare at him in disbelief, hear the lock disengage, and begin to sarcastically thank him, but he's already preoccupied with the view of my tan Spanx.

"Your dress ripped," he says helpfully.

"You have spinach in your teeth."

He doesn't, but at least it distracts him enough that I can escape back into the room and close the door in his face.

Unfortunately, he knocks.

"Just a second, I need to get some clothes on."

His reply is a lazy drawl through the door: "Why start now?"

Aware that no one else in the suite is remotely interested in watching me change, I toss my dress and Spanx onto the couch and reach for my underwear and a pair of jeans in my bag, hopping into them. Tugging on a T-shirt, I move to the door and open it only a crack so he can't see Ami inside, curled into a ball in her lacy wedding underwear.

"What do you want?"

He frowns. "I need to talk to Ami real quick."

"Seriously?"

"Seriously."

"Well, I'm going to have to do, because my sister is barely conscious."

"Then why are you leaving her?"

"For your information, I was headed downstairs to look for Gatorade," I say. "Why aren't you with Dane?"

"Because he hasn't left the toilet in two hours."

Gross. "What do you want?"

"I need the info for the honeymoon. Dane told me to call and see if they can get it moved."

"They can't," I tell him. "I already called."

"Okay." He exhales long and slow, clawing a hand through hair that is thick and luscious for no good reason. "In that case, I told him I'd go."

I actually bark out a laugh. "Wow, that is so generous of you."

"What? He offered it to me."

I straighten to my full height. "Unfortunately, you're not her designated guest. Dane is."

"She only had to give his last name. Incidentally, it's the same as mine."

Damn it. "Well . . . Ami offered it to me, too." I'm not planning on taking the trip, but I'll be damned if Ethan is getting it.

He blinks to the side and then back to me. I've seen Ethan Thomas blink those lashes and use that dangerously uneven smile to sweet-talk Tía María into bringing him freshly made tamales. I know he can charm when he wants. Clearly he doesn't *want* right now, because his tone comes out flat: "Olive, I have vacation time I need to take."

And now the fire is rising in me. Why does he think *he* deserves this? Did he have a seventy-four-item wedding to-do list on fancy stationery? No, he did not. And come to think of it, that *speech* of his was lukewarm. Bet he wrote it in the groom suite while he was chugging back a plastic pitcher of warm Budweiser.

"Well," I say, "I'm unemployed against my will, so I think I probably need the vacation more than you do."

The frown deepens. "That makes no sense." He pauses. "Wait. You were laid off from Bukkake?"

I scowl at him. "It's Butake, dumbass. And not that it's any of your business, but yes. I was laid off two months ago. I'm sure that gives you an immeasurable thrill."

"A little."

"You are Voldemort."

Ethan shrugs and then reaches up, scratching his jaw. "I suppose we could both go."

I narrow my eyes and hope I don't look like I am mentally diagramming his sentence, even though I am. It sounded like he suggested we go . . .

"On their honeymoon?" I ask incredulously.

He nods.

"*Together?*"

He nods again.

"Are you high?"

"Not presently."

"Ethan, we can barely stand to sit next to each other at an hourlong meal."

"From what I gather," he says, "they won a suite. It'll be

huge. We won't even really have to see each other. This vacation is packed: zip-lining, snorkeling, hikes, surfing. Come on. We can orbit around each other for ten days without committing a violent felony."

From inside the bridal suite, Ami groans out a low, gravelly "Gooooo, Olive."

I turn to her. "But—it's *Ethan*."

"Shit," Diego mumbles, "if I can take this garbage can with me, *I'll* go."

In my peripheral vision, Ami lifts a sallow arm, waving it limply. "Ethan's not that bad."

Isn't he, though? I look back at him, sizing him up. Too tall, too fit, too classically pretty. Never friendly, never trustworthy, never any fun. He puts on an innocent smile—innocent on the surface: a flash of teeth, a dimple, but in his eyes, it's all black-souled.

Then I think of Maui: crashing surf, pineapple, cocktails, and sunshine. Oh, sunshine. A glance out the window shows only dark sky, but I know the cold that lies out there. I know the car-grime-yellowed snow lining the streets. I know the days that are so cold my wet hair would freeze if I didn't completely dry it before leaving the apartment. I know that by the time April comes and it still isn't consistently warm, I will be hunched over and resigned, Skeksis-like.

"Whether you're coming or not," he says, cutting into my rapid spiral down the mental drainpipe, "I'm going to Maui."

He leans in. "And I'm going to have the best fucking time of my life."

I look back over my shoulder at Ami, who nods encouragingly—albeit slowly—and a fire ignites in my chest at the thought of being here, surrounded by snow, and the smell of vomit, and the bleak landscape of unemployment while Ethan is lying poolside with a cocktail in his hand.

"Fine," I tell him, and then lean forward to press a finger into his chest. "I'm taking Ami's spot. But you keep to your space, and I'll keep to mine."

He salutes me. "I wouldn't have it any other way."

chapter **four**

Turns out I'm willing to take my sick sister's dream honeymoon, but I have to draw a line at airline fraud. Because I am essentially broke, finding a last-minute flight from the freezing tundra to Maui in January—at least one that I can afford—requires some creativity. Ethan is no help at all, probably because he's one of those highly evolved thirtysomething guys who has an actual savings account and never has to dig in his car's ashtray for change at the drive-through. Must be nice.

But we do agree that we need to travel *together*. As much as I'd like to ditch him as soon as possible, the travel company did make it abundantly clear that if there is any fraud afoot, we will be charged the full balance of the vacation package. It's either the proximity of probable vomit or the proximity of me that sends Ethan halfway down the hall toward his own room with a muttered "Just let me know what I owe you," before I can warn him exactly how little that might be.

Fortunately, my sister taught me well, and in the end I have two (so cheap they're practically free) tickets to Hawaii. I'm not sure why they're so cheap, but I try not to think too much about it. A plane is a plane, and *getting* to Maui is all that really matters, right?

It'll be fine.

SO MAYBE THRIFTY JET ISN'T the flashiest airline, but it's not that bad and certainly doesn't warrant the constant fidgeting and barrage of heavy sighs from the man sitting next to me.

"You know I can hear you, right?"

Ethan is quiet for a moment before he turns another page in his magazine. He slides his eyes to me in a silent *I can't believe I put you in charge of this.*

I'm not sure I've ever seen anyone aggressively flip through a copy of *Knitting World* before now. It's a nice touch to keep magazines in the terminal like we're at the gynecologist's office, but it's a little disconcerting that this one is from 2007.

I tamp down the ever-present urge to reach over and flick his ear. We're supposed to pass as newlyweds on this trip; might as well start trying to fake it now. "So, just to close the loop on this stupid squabble," I say, "if you were going to have such a strong opinion about our flights, you shouldn't have told me to take care of it."

"If I knew you were going to book us on a Greyhound with wings, I wouldn't have." He looks up, and glances around in horrified wonder. "I didn't even know this part of the airport existed."

I roll my eyes and then meet the gaze of the woman sitting across from us, who is clearly eavesdropping. Lowering my voice, I lean in with a saccharine smile. "If I knew you were going to be such a nitpicker, I would have happily told you to shove it and get your own damn ticket."

"Nitpick?" Ethan points to where the plane is parked outside what I think is a plexiglass window. "Have you seen our aircraft? I'll be amazed if they don't ask us to pitch in for fuel."

I take the magazine from his hand and scan an article on *Summer Sherbet Tops and Cool Cotton Cable Pullovers!* "Nobody is forcing you to take a free dream trip to Maui," I say. "And for the record, not all of us can buy expensive same-day airplane tickets. I told you I was on a budget."

He snorts. "Obviously I didn't know what kind of budget you meant. Had I known, I would have loaned you the cost."

"And take money from your sexual companion fund?" I press a horrified hand to my chest. "I wouldn't dare."

Ethan takes the magazine back. "Look, Olivia. I'm just sitting here reading. If you want to bicker, go up there and ask the gate agents to move us to first class."

I move in to ask how it's possible that he's headed to Maui and yet *somehow even more unpleasant than usual* when my phone vibrates in my pocket. It's most likely one of the following: A) Ami with a vomit update, B) Ami calling to remind me about something I've forgotten and don't have time to get now anyway, C) one of my cousins with gossip, or D) Mom wanting me to ask Dad something, or tell Dad something, or *call* Dad something. As unpleasant as all of these possibilities sound, I'd still rather listen to any of them than have a conversation with Ethan Thomas.

Holding up my phone, I stand with a "Let me know if we board," and get nothing but a noncommittal grunt in return.

The phone rings again but it's not my sister on the screen, it's an unfamiliar number with a Twin Cities area code. "Hello?"

"I'm calling for Olive Torres?"

"This is Olive."

"This is Kasey Hugh, human resources at Hamilton Biosciences. How are you?"

My heart bursts into a gallop as I mentally flip through the dozens of interviews I've had in the past two months.

They were all for medical-science liaison positions (a fancy term for the scientists who meet with physicians to speak more technically than sales folk can about various drugs on the market), but the one at Hamilton was at the top of my list because of the company's flu vaccine focus. My background is virology, and not having to learn an entirely new biological system in a matter of weeks is always a bonus.

But to be frank, at this point I was ready to apply to Hooters if that's what it would take to cover rent.

With the phone pressed to my ear, I cross to a quieter side of the terminal and try not to sound as desperate as I'm feeling. After the bridesmaid dress fiasco, I am far more realistic about my ability to pull off the orange Hooters shorts and shimmcry panty hose.

"I'm doing well," I say. "Thanks for asking."

"I'm calling because after considering all thc applications, Mr. Hamilton would like to offer you the medical scientist liaison position. Arc you still interested?"

I turn on my heel, looking back toward Ethan as if the sheer awesomeness of these words is enough to set off a flare gun of joy over my head. He's still frowning down at his knitting magazine.

"Oh my God," I say, free hand flapping in front of my face. "Yes! Absolutely!"

A paycheck! Steady income! Being able to sleep at night without fear of impending homelessness!

"Do you know when you can start?" she asks. "I have a memo here from Mr. Hamilton that reads, 'The sooner, the better.' "

"Start?" I wince, looking around me at all the cheapo travelers wearing plastic leis and Hawaiian print shirts. "Soon! Now. Except not *now* now. Not for a week. Ten days, actually. I can start in ten days. I have . . ." An announcement plays overhead, and I look to see Ethan stand. With a frown, he gestures to where people are starting to line up. My brain goes into excitement-chaos overdrive. "We just had a family thing and—also, I need to see a sick relative, and—"

"That's fine, Olive," she says calmly, mercifully cutting me off. I squeeze my forehead, wincing at my stupid lying babble. "It's just after the holidays and everyone is still crazy. I'll put you down for a tentative start date of Monday, January twenty-first? Does that work for you?"

I exhale for what feels like the first time since I answered the phone. "That would be perfect."

"Great," Kasey says. "Expect an email soon with an offer letter, along with some paperwork we'll need you to sign ASAP if you choose to officially accept. A digital or scanned signature is fine. Welcome to Hamilton Biosciences. Congratulations, Olive."

I walk back to Ethan in a daze.

"Finally," he says, with his carry-on slung over one

shoulder and mine over the other. "We're the last group to board. I thought I was going to—" He stops, eyes narrowing as they make a circuit of my face. "Are you okay? You look . . . smiling."

My phone call is still playing on a loop in my ears. I want to check my call history and hit redial just to make sure Kasey had the right Olive Torres. I was saved from terrible food poisoning, managed to snag a free vacation, *and* was offered a job in a single twenty-four-hour span? This sort of luck doesn't happen to me. *What is going on?*

Ethan snaps his fingers and I startle to find him leaning in, looking like he wishes he had a stick to poke me with. "Everything okay there? Change of plans, or—?"

"I got a job."

It seems to take a moment for my words to sink in. "Just *now*?"

"I interviewed a couple weeks ago. I start after Hawaii."

I expect him to look visibly disappointed that I'm not backing out of this trip. Instead he lifts his brows and offers a quiet "That's great, Olive. Congratulations," before herding me toward the line of people boarding.

I'm surprised he didn't ask me whether I would be joining their janitorial team, or at least say he hopes my new job selling heroin to at-risk children treats me well. I did not expect *sincere*. I'm never on the receiving end of his charm, even if the charm just now was diluted; I know how to handle Sincere Ethan about as well as I would know how to handle a hungry bear.

"Uh, thanks."

I quickly text Diego, Ami, and my parents—separately, of course—to let them know the good news, and then we're standing at the threshold to the Jetway, handing over our boarding passes. Reality sinks in and blends with joy: With the job stress alleviated, I can really *leave* the Twin Cities for ten days. I can treat this trip like an actual vacation on a tropical island.

Yes, it's with my nemesis, but still, I'll take it.

THE JETWAY IS LITTLE MORE than a rickety bridge that leads from our dinky terminal to the even dinkier plane. The line moves slowly as the people ahead of us try to shove their oversize bags into the miniature overhead compartments. With Ami, I would turn and ask why people don't simply check their bags so we can get in and out on time, but Ethan has managed to go a full five minutes without finding something to complain about. I'm not going to give him any bait.

We climb into our seats; the plane is so narrow that, in each row, there are only two seats on each side of the aisle. They're so close together, though, they're essentially one bench with a flimsy armrest between them. Ethan is plastered against my side. I have to ask him to lean up onto one butt cheek so I can locate the other half of my seat belt. After the disconcertingly gravelly click of metal into metal, he straightens and we register in unison that we're touching from shoulder to thigh, separated only by a hard, immobile armrest midway down.

He looks over the heads of the people in front of us. "I don't trust this plane." He looks back down the aisle. "Or the crew. Was the pilot wearing a parachute?"

Ethan is always—annoyingly—the epitome of cool, calm, and collected, but now that I'm paying attention I see that his shoulders are tense, and his face has gone pale. I think he's sweating. *He's scared*, I realize, and suddenly his mood at the airport makes a lot more sense.

As I watch, he pulls a penny from his pocket and smooths a thumb over it.

"What's that?"

"A penny."

My goodness, this is delightful. "You mean like a good luck penny?"

With a scowl, he ignores me and slips it back into his pocket.

"I never thought I had good luck," I tell him, feeling magnanimous, "but look. My allergy kept me from eating the buffet, I'm going to Maui, and I got a job. Wouldn't it be hilarious"—I laugh and roll my head in his direction—

"to have a streak of good luck for the first time in my life, only to go down in a fiery plane crash?"

Judging by his expression, Ethan does not see the humor at all. When a member of the flight crew walks by, he shoots an arm out in front of me, stopping her.

"Excuse me, can you tell me how many miles are on this plane?"

The flight attendant smiles. "Aircraft don't have miles. They have flight hours."

I can see Ethan swallowing down his impatience. "Okay, then how many flight hours are on this plane?"

She tilts her head, understandably puzzled by his question. "I'd have to ask the captain, sir."

Ethan leans across me to get closer and I push back into my seat, scrunching my nose against the obnoxiously pleasant smell of his soap.

"And what do we think of the captain? Competent? Trustworthy?" Ethan winks, and I realize he's no less anxious than he was a minute ago, but he's coping via flirtation. "Well-rested?"

"Captain Blake is a great pilot," she says, tilting her head and smiling.

I look back and forth between the two of them and dramatically fidget with the gold wedding band I borrowed from Tía Sylvia. No one notices.

Ethan gives her a smile—and wow, he could probably ask her for her social security number, a major credit card, and to bear his children, and she'd say yes. "Of course," he says. "I mean it's not like he's ever crashed a plane or anything. Right?"

"Just the once," she says, before straightening with a wink of her own and continuing on down the aisle.

FOR THE NEXT HOUR, ETHAN barely moves, doesn't speak, and holds himself as if breathing too hard or somehow jostling the plane will make it fall out of the sky. I reach for my iPad before realizing that of course we don't have Wi-Fi. I open a book, hoping to get lost in some delicious paranormal fun, but can't seem to focus.

"An eight-hour flight, and there's no movie," I say to myself, glaring at the screenless seat back in front of me.

"Maybe they're hoping your life flashing in front of your eyes will be distraction enough."

"It lives." I turn and look at him. "Won't speaking upset the barometric pressure in the cabin or something?"

Reaching into his pocket, he pulls out the penny again. "I haven't ruled it out."

We haven't spent much time together, but from stories

I've heard from both Dane and Ami, I feel like I've built a pretty accurate picture of Ethan in my head. Daredevil, adventure hound, ambitious, cutthroat . . .

The man clinging to the armrest as if his very life depends on it is . . . not that guy.

With a deep breath, he rolls his shoulders, grimacing. I'm five foot four and mildly uncomfortable. Ethan's legs have to be at least ten feet long; I can't imagine what it's like for him. After he speaks, it's like the stillness spell has broken: his knee bounces with nervous energy, his fingers tap against the drink tray until even the sweet old lady wearing a Day-Glo muumuu in front of us is giving him a dirty look. He smiles in apology.

"Tell me about that lucky penny of yours," I say, motioning to the coin still clutched in his fist. "Why do you think it's lucky?"

He seems to internally weigh the risk of interacting with me against the potential relief of distraction.

"I don't really want to encourage conversation," he says, "but what do you see?" He opens his palm.

"It's from 1955," I note.

"What else?"

I look closer. "Oh . . . you mean how the lettering is doubled?"

He leans in, pointing. "You can really see it right here,

above Lincoln's head." Sure enough, the letters that read IN GOD WE TRUST have been stamped twice.

"I've never seen anything like that before," I admit.

"There's only a few of them out there." He rubs his thumb over the surface and slips it back into his pocket.

"Is it valuable?" I ask.

"Worth about a thousand dollars."

"Holy shit!" I gasp.

We hit some mild turbulence, and Ethan's eyes move wildly around the plane as if the oxygen masks might deploy at any moment.

Hoping to distract him again, I ask, "Where did you get it?"

"I bought a banana just before a job interview, and it was part of my change."

"And?"

"And not only did I get the job, but when I went to have some coins rolled the machine spit the penny out because it thought it was a fake. I've carried it around ever since."

"Don't you worry you're going to drop it?"

"That's the whole point of luck, isn't it?" he says through gritted teeth. "You have to trust that it's not fleeting."

"Are *you* trusting that right now?"

He tries to relax, shaking out his hands. If I'm reading his expression correctly, he's regretting telling me anything. But the turbulence intensifies, and all six-plus feet of him stiffen again.

"You know," I say, "you don't strike me as someone who'd be afraid of flying."

He takes a series of deep breaths. "I'm not."

This doesn't really require any sort of rebuttal. The way I have to pry his fingers from my side of the armrest communicates it plainly.

Ethan relents. "It's not my favorite."

I think of the weekends I spent with Ami because Dane was off on some wild adventure with his brother, all the arguments those trips caused. "Aren't you supposed to be like, Bear Grylls or something?"

He looks at me, frowning. "Who?"

"The trip to New Zealand. The river rafting, death-defying bro trip? Surfing in Nicaragua? You fly for fun all the time."

He rests his head back against the seat and closes his eyes again, ignoring me.

As the squeaky wheels of the beverage cart make their way down the aisle, Ethan crowds into my space again, flagging down the flight attendant. "Can I get a scotch and soda?" He glances at me and amends his order. "Two, actually."

I wave him off. "I don't like scotch."

He blinks. "I *know*."

"Actually, we don't have scotch," she says.

"A gin and tonic?"

She winces.

His shoulders slump. "A beer?"

"That, I have." She reaches into a drawer and hands him two cans of generic-looking beer. "That's twenty-two dollars."

"Twenty-two *American* dollars?" He moves to hand back the cans.

"We also have Coke products. They're free," she says. "But if you'd like ice that's two dollars."

"Wait," I say, and reach into my bag.

"You're not buying my beer, Olive."

"You're right, I'm not." I pull out two coupons and hand them over. "Ami is."

"Of course she is."

The flight attendant continues on down the aisle.

"Some respect, please," I say. "My sister's obsessive need to get things for free is why we're here."

"And why two hundred of our friends and family were in the emergency room."

I feel a protective itch for my sister. "The police already said she wasn't responsible."

He cracks his beer open with a satisfying pop. "*And* the six o'clock news."

I mean to glare, but am momentarily distracted by the way his Adam's apple moves as he drinks. And drinks. And drinks.

"Okay."

"I don't know why I'm surprised," he says. "It was doomed anyway."

The itch flares to a full-on blaze. "Hello, Ethan, that's your brother and sister-in—"

"Calm down, Olive. I don't mean *them*." He takes another gulp and I stare. "I meant weddings in general." He shudders and a note of revulsion coats the next word: "*Romance*."

Oh, he's one of those.

I admit my parental model of romance has been lacking, but Tío Omar and Tía Sylvia have been married for forty-five years, Tío Hugo and Tía María have been married for nearly thirty. I have examples of lasting relationships all around me, so I know they exist—even if I suspect they might not exist for me. I want to believe that Ami hasn't started something doomed, that she can be truly happy with Dane.

Ethan drains at least half of the first beer in a long chug, and I try to piece together the extent of my Ethan knowledge. He's thirty-four, two years older than us and Dane. He does some sort of . . . math thing for a living, which explains why he's such a laugh a minute. He carries at least one form of personal disinfectant on his person at all times, and he won't eat at buffets. I think he was single when we met, but not long after he entered into a relationship that seemed at least semiserious. I don't think his brother liked her because I distinctly recall Dane ranting one night about how much it would suck if Ethan proposed to her.

Oh my God, am I going to Maui with someone's fiancé?

"You're not dating anyone now, right?" I ask. "What was her name . . . Sierra or Simba or something?"

"Simba?" He almost cracks a smile. Almost.

"No doubt it shocks you when someone doesn't keep close track of your love life."

His forehead scrunches up in a frown. "I wouldn't go on a fake honeymoon with you if I had a girlfriend." Sinking back in his seat, he closes his eyes again. "No more talking. You're right, it shakes the plane."

WITH LEIS AROUND OUR NECKS and the heavy ocean air adhering our clothing to our skin, we catch a cab just outside the airport. I spend most of the ride with my face pressed to the window, taking in the bright blue sky and the glimpses of ocean visible through the trees. I can already feel my hair frizzing in the humidity, but it's worth it. Maui is stunning. Ethan is quiet beside me, watching the view and occasionally tapping something into his phone. Not wanting to disturb the peace, I snap a few blurry photos as we drive down the two-lane highway and send them to Ami. She replies with a simple emoji.

☹

I know. I'm sorry.

Don't be sorry.

I mean, I have Mom with me for the foreseeable future. Who's the real winner here?

Enjoy yourself or I'll kick your ass.

My poor sister. It's true that I'd rather be here with Ami or . . . anyone else, for that matter, but we're here and I'm determined to make the most of it. I have ten beautiful, sun-drenched days ahead of me.

When the taxi slows and makes a final right turn, the hotel grounds unfurl in front of us. The building is massive: a towering tiered structure of glass, balconies, and greenery spilling everywhere. The ocean crashes *right there,* so close that someone standing on one of the higher floors could probably throw a rock and make it into the surf.

We drive down a wide lane lined on both sides with full-grown banyan trees. Hundreds of lanterns sway in the breeze, suspended from branches overhead. If it's this gorgeous during the day, I can't imagine the sight once the sun goes down.

Music filters through speakers hidden in the thick foliage, and next to me even Ethan is sitting forward, eyes trained on the grounds as we pass.

We come to a stop, and two valet attendants appear out of nowhere. We climb out, stumbling a bit as we look around, eyes meeting over the roof of the car. It smells like plumeria, and the sound of the waves crashing nearly drowns out the sound of engines idling at the valet. I'm pretty sure Ethan and I have reached our first, enthusiastic consensus: *Holy shit. This place is amazing.*

I've been so distracted that I startle when the first valet pulls out a handful of luggage tags and asks for my name.

"My name?"

The valet smiles. "For the luggage."

"The luggage. Right. My name. *My* name, is—well, it's a funny story—"

Ethan rounds the car and immediately takes my hand.

"Torres," he says. "Ami Torres-soon-to-be-Thomas, and husband." He leans in, pressing a stiff kiss to the side of my head for realism. "She's a bit wiped from the trip."

Stunned, I watch as he turns back to the valet and looks like he's resisting the urge to wipe his lips with his hand.

"Perfect," the attendant says, scribbling the name on a few of the tags and attaching them to the handles of our luggage. "Check-in is through those doors there." He smiles and points to an open-air lobby. "Your bags will be brought up to your room."

"Thank you." Ethan presses a few folded bills into the valet's palm and steers me toward the hotel. "Smooth," he says as soon as we're out of earshot.

"Ethan, I'm a terrible liar."

"Really? You hid it so well."

"It's never been my strength, okay? Those of us who aren't summoned by the Dark Mark consider honesty to be a virtue."

He curls his fingers toward his palm, beckoning. "Give me both IDs—yours and Ami's—so you don't accidentally hand them the wrong one at the front desk. I'll put my credit card down for incidentals, and we'll square it up later."

An argument bubbles up in my chest, but he has a point. Even now, with a bit of mental rehearsal, I am sure the next time someone asks my name, I will shout, "I AM

NAMED AMI." Better than nearly spilling our entire cover story to a valet attendant, but not by much.

I reach into my purse for my wallet and pull out both IDs. "But put them in the safe when we're in the room."

He slips them in his wallet next to his own. "Let me do the talking at reception. From what Dane told me, the rules of this vacation are really strict, and even just looking at you, I can tell you're lying about something."

I scrunch my face, and then frown and smile in quick succession to try to clear it.

Ethan watches, expression mildly horrified. "Get it together, Olive. I'm sure it was on my bucket list at some point, but I don't really want to sleep on the beach tonight."

"Mele Kalikimaka" plays quietly overhead as we enter the hotel. Holiday festivity lingers post–New Years: massive Christmas trees flank the entrance to the lobby, their branches dripping with twinkling lights and the weight of hundreds of red and gold ornaments. Gauzy garlands and more ornaments hang from the ceiling, wrap around columns, and sit in baskets and bowls decorating every flat surface. Water from a giant fountain splashes into a pool below and the scents of plumeria and chlorine intermingle in the humid air.

We're greeted almost immediately at reception. My stomach twists and my smile is too bright as a beautiful Polynesian woman takes Ami's ID and Ethan's credit card.

She enters the name and smiles. "Congratulations on winning the sweepstakes."

"I love sweepstakes!" I say, too brightly, and Ethan elbows me in the side.

And then, her eyes linger on Ami's photo a moment before slowly blinking up to me.

"I've put on a little weight," I blurt.

Because there is no good response to this, she gives me a polite smile and begins entering the information.

I don't know why I feel compelled to continue, but I do. "I lost my job this fall, and it's been one interview after another." I can feel Ethan tensing at my side, the casual hand on my lower back clutching at my shirt until his grip must resemble a bird of prey trying to put a struggling field mouse out of its misery. "I tend to bake when I'm stressed, which is why I look a little different in the photo. The photo of me. But I did get a job. Today, actually, if you can believe it. Not that it's unbelievable or anything. The job or the wedding."

When I finally come up for air, both the woman and Ethan are just staring at me.

Smiling tightly, she slides a folder filled with various maps and itineraries across the counter. "It looks like we have you in our honeymoon suite."

My brain trips on the phrase *honeymoon suite* and fills with images of the room Lois and Clark Kent share in *Superman II*: the pink fabrics, the heart-shaped tub, the giant bed.

"The romance package is all-inclusive," she continues, "and you can choose from a number of amenities, including candlelit dinners in the Molokini Garden, a couple's massage on the spa balcony at sunset, turn-down service with rose petals and champagne—"

Ethan and I exchange a brief look.

"We're really more the outdoorsy types," I cut in. "Are there any activities available that are a little more rugged and a lot less . . . naked?"

Cue the awkward pause.

She clears her throat. "You can find a more comprehensive list in your room. Take a look, and we can schedule anything you like."

I thank her and chance a peek over at Ethan, who is now gazing at me lovingly—which means he's planning the nonbuffet menu for my funeral reception, after he's murdered me and hidden my body.

With a final swipe of our room keys to activate them, she hands them to Ethan and smiles warmly. "You're on the top floor. Elevators are around that corner there. I'll have your bags sent up immediately."

"Thank you," he manages easily, without spilling the details of the past year of his life.

But I'm pleased to see him falter in his smooth footsteps as she calls out after us: "Congratulations, Mr. and Mrs. Thomas. Enjoy your honeymoon."

chapter **five**

The lock chimes and the double doors swing open. My breath catches in my throat. Never in my life have I stayed in a suite, let alone one this opulent. I pour one out for Ami's dream honeymoon and try not to feel grateful that she's back in St. Paul suffering so that I can be here. But it's hard; objectively this has turned out very well for me.

Well, mostly. I look up at Ethan, who gestures for me to lead us inside. Ahead of us is an absurdly spacious living room, with a couch, love seat, two chairs, and low glass coffee table on a fluffy white rug. The table is topped with a beautiful violet orchid in a woven basket, a complicated remote that looks like it probably operates a bionic housekeeper, and a bucket with a bottle of champagne and two flutes that have *Mr.* and *Mrs.* etched in the glass.

I meet Ethan's eyes only long enough for both of our instinctive sneers to take root.

Just to the left of the living room is a small dining nook, with a table, two brass candlesticks, and a tiki-themed bar cart covered in all manner of ornate cocktail glasses. I mentally gulp down about four margaritas and get an anticipatory buzz from all the upcoming free booze I'm about to enjoy.

But at the far end is the true beauty of the room: a wall of glass doors that open to a balcony overlooking the crashing Maui surf. I gasp, sliding them to the side and stepping out into the warm January breeze. The temperature—so balmy, so *not* Minnesota—shocks me into a surreal awareness: I'm in Maui, in a dream suite, on an all-inclusive trip. I've never been to Hawaii. I've never done anything dreamlike, period. I start to dance but only realize I'm doing it when Ethan steps out onto the balcony and dumps an enormous bucket of water on my joy by clearing his throat and squinting out across the waves.

He looks like he's thinking, *Eh. I've seen better.*

"This view is *amazing*," I say, almost confrontationally.

Slowly blinking over to me, he says, "As is your propensity to overshare."

"I already told you I'm not a good liar. I got nervous when she was looking at Ami's ID, okay?"

He holds his hands up in sarcastic surrender. With a

scowl, I escape Mr. Buzzkill and head back inside. Just to the immediate right of the entry, there's a small kitchen I completely bypassed on my way to the balcony. Past the kitchen is a hallway that leads to a small bathroom, and, just past it, the opulent master bedroom. I step inside and see there's another huge bathroom here with a giant tub big enough for two. I turn to face the gigantic bed. I want to roll in it. I want to take off my clothes and slip into the silky—

I feel the tires come to a screeching halt inside my brain.

But . . . *how*? How have we come this far without discussing the logistics of sleeping arrangements? Did we both truly assume that the honeymoon suite would have two bedrooms? Without a doubt, we both would happily die on the *Not Sharing a Bed with You* hill, but how do we decide who gets the only bedroom? Obviously, I think I should—but knowing Ethan, he probably thinks he'll take the bed and I'll happily build my little troll fort under the dining table.

I step out of the bedroom just as Ethan is closing the wide double doors, and then we are sealed into this awkward moment of unprepared cohabitation. We turn in unison to gaze at our suitcases.

"Wow," I say.

"Yeah," he agrees.

"It's really nice."

Ethan coughs. A clock ticks somewhere in the room, too loud in the awkward silence.

Tick.

Tick.

Tick.

"It is." He reaches up, scratching the back of his neck. Ocean waves crash in the background. "And, obviously you're the woman. You should take the bedroom."

Some of those words are the ones I want to hear, and some of them are just terrible. I tilt my head, scowling. "I don't get the bedroom because I'm a *woman*. I get the room because my sister won it."

He gives a douchey little wince-shrug and says, "I mean, if we're going by those standards, then I should get the room, since Ami got it partly using Dane's Hilton status."

"She still managed to organize it all," I say. "If it was up to Dane, they'd be staying at the Doubletree in Mankato this week."

"You realize you're just arguing with me for the sake of arguing, right? I already told you you could have the room."

I point at him. "What you're doing right now isn't arguing?"

He sighs like I am the most irritating person alive. "Take the bedroom. I'll sleep on the couch." He gazes at it. It looks plush and nice, sure, but it is still a couch and we're here for ten nights. "I'll be fine," he adds with a hefty spoonful of martyrdom thrown in.

"Okay, if you're going to act like I'm beholden to you, then I don't want it."

He exhales slowly, and then walks over to his suitcase, lifting it and carrying it to the bedroom.

"Wait!" I call. "I take that back. I do want the bedroom."

Ethan stops without turning to look at me. "I'm just going to put some things in the drawers so I'm not living out of my suitcase in the living room for ten days." He glances at me over his shoulder. "I presume that's okay?"

He is so carefully balancing being generous with being passive-aggressive that I am all mixed up about how big an asshole he really is. It makes it impossible to measure out the correct dose of snark.

"It's fine," I say, and add magnanimously, "take all the dresser space you want."

I hear his bemused snort as he disappears from view.

The bottom line is that we don't get along. But the other bottom line is that we don't really need to! Hope fills me like helium. Ethan and I can move around each other without having to interact, and do whatever we like to make this our individual dream vacations.

For me, this slice of heaven will include the spa,

zip-lining, snorkeling, and every manner of adventure I can find—including adventures of the alcoholic variety. If Ethan's idea of a perfect vacation is brooding, complaining, and sighing exasperatedly, he can surely do that anywhere he wants, but I don't have to endure it.

I quickly check my email and see a new one from Hamilton. The offer is . . . well, suffice it to say I don't need to look through anything else to know I'll take it. They could tell me my desk was perched on the lip of a volcano, and I would accept in a heartbeat for this kind of money.

Pulling out my iPad, I digitally sign everything and send it off.

Practically vibrating, I thumb through the list of hotel activities and decide that the first order of business is a celebratory facial and body scrub down at the spa. Solo. I don't think Ethan is much of a pampering type, but the worst thing would be to have him lift a cooling cucumber slice off my eyelid and glare down at me while I'm lounging in a robe.

"Ethan," I call, "what are you up to this afternoon?"

In the answering silence, I sense his panic that I might be requesting his company.

"I'm not asking because I want to hang," I add quickly.

He hesitates again, and when he finally answers, his voice comes out tinny, like he's actually climbed into the closet. "Thank God."

Well. "I'm probably going to head down to the spa."

"Do whatever you want. Just don't use all the massage credits," he tacks on.

I scowl, even though he can't see me. "How many times do you think I'm going to get rubbed down in a single afternoon?"

"I'd rather not contemplate."

I flip the bird in his general direction, consult the directory to confirm that the spa has showers I can use, grab my key card, and leave Ethan to his surly unpacking.

GUILT EDGES IN A TINY bit when I am being pampered and indulged for nearly three hours using Ami's name. My face is exfoliated, massaged, and moisturized. My body is covered in clay, scrubbed until I'm red and tingly all over, and then covered with warm eucalyptus towels.

I make a silent promise to put aside money from each paycheck for a while so that I can send my sister to a lavish spa back home when she no longer feels "like a freshly reanimated corpse." It may not be Maui, but any little bit I can pay her back for this, I'm committed to do. All I have to do this entire week is tip the staff; it seems so preposterous. This type of blissful, transcendent spa experience isn't for me. I'm the one who gets a fungal infection from a pedicure in the Cities and a bikini wax burn at a spa in Duluth.

Limp as a jellyfish all over and drunk on endorphins, I look up at my therapist, Kelly. "That was . . . amazing. If I ever win the lottery, I'm going to move here and pay you to do that every day."

She probably hears that daily, but she laughs like I am exceedingly clever. "I'm glad you enjoyed yourself."

Enjoyed myself is an understatement. Not only was it dreamy, but it was a full three hours away from Ethan.

I'm led back to the lounge, where I'm told to take as much time as I want. Diving into the plush couch, I pull my phone from the pocket of my robe. I'm unsurprised to see messages from my mom *(Tell your dad to bring us some toilet paper and Gatorade)*, my sister *(Tell Mom to go hooooome)*, Diego *(Is this punishment for making fun of Natalia's terrible bleach job? I'd say I'm sorry but I've seen mops with fewer split ends)*, and Jules *(Do you care if I stay at your place while you're gone? This thing is like the plague and I might have to burn down my apartment)*.

Too tired and blissed out to deal with any of it now, I pick up a well-loved copy of *Us Weekly*. But not even celebrity gossip or the latest *Bachelor* drama can keep me awake, and I feel my eyelids closing under the weight of happy exhaustion.

"Ms. Torres?"

"Hmm?" I hum, groggy.

"Ms. Torres, is that you?" Eyes bolting open, I nearly

overturn the cucumber water I've got precariously perched on my chest. When I sit, I look up and nearly all I see is an enormous white mustache.

And *oh*. I know this mustache; I first met this mustache at a highly important interview. I remember at the time thinking, *Wow, a Sam Elliott doppelgänger is the CEO here at Hamilton Biosciences! Who knew?*

My eyes move up. Yes, the Sam Elliott doppelgänger—Charles Hamilton, my new boss's boss—is right in front of me at the Spa Grande in Maui.

Wait . . . what?

"Mr. Hamilton! Hi!"

"I *thought* that was you." He looks tanner than when I saw him a few weeks ago, his white hair a touch longer, and he definitely wasn't wearing a fluffy white robe and slippers.

He crosses the room, arms outstretched for a hug.

Oh. Okay, we're going to do this. I stand, and he catches my expression of discomfort—because I don't usually hug my bosses, especially not when naked under a robe—and then I see when he registers that his brain is on vacation and he doesn't hug his employees, either, but we're committed now and come together in an awkward side hug that ensures our robes don't gape anywhere.

"If this isn't a small world," he says once he's pulled away. "Recharging the batteries before starting your new adventure at Hamilton? That's exactly what I like to see. Can't take care of others if you don't take care of yourself first."

"Exactly." My nerves have dumped buckets of adrenaline into my veins; going from Zen to New Boss Alert is jarring. I pull the tie on my robe a little tighter. "And I want to thank you again for the opportunity. I am beyond excited to be joining the team."

Mr. Hamilton waves me off. "The minute we spoke I knew you'd be a great fit. Your dedication to Butake was commendable. I always say that Hamilton is nothing without the good people working there. Honesty, integrity, loyalty—those are our hallmarks."

I nod; I like Mr. Hamilton—he has an impeccable reputation in the biosciences field and is known for being an incredibly involved and hands-on CEO—but I can't help but note that this line is an almost exact replica of the one he gave me as we shook hands at the end of the interview. Now that I've lied to about twenty people on the hotel's staff, hearing it here feels more ominous than inspiring.

The sound of quickened footsteps can be heard on the other side of the door before a panicked Kelly bursts through. "Mrs. Thomas."

My stomach drops.

"Oh, thank God you're still here. You left your wedding ring in the treatment room." She offers an outstretched hand and places the simple band in my palm.

I let out a deranged silent scream inside my cranium while I manage to give her a muted thanks.

" 'Mrs. Thomas?' " Hamilton prompts.

The therapist looks between us, obviously confused.

"You mean Torres," he says.

"No . . ." She blinks down to a clipboard and then back to us. "This is Mrs. Thomas. Unless there's been some mistake . . . ?"

I realize there are two things I can do here:

1. I could admit that I had to take my sister's honeymoon because she got sick and I am pretending to be married to a guy named Ethan Thomas so we can snag this sweet honeymoon package, or
2. I could lie my face off and tell them that I just got married and—silly me—I'm not used to my new name yet.

In either case, I am a liar. Option one leaves me with my integrity. However, with option two I won't disappoint my new boss (especially given that half my interview was focused on building a workforce with "a strong moral compass" and people who "put honesty and integrity above everything else"), and won't end up sleeping on the beach, hungry *and* unemployed, with only a giant spa and hotel bill to use as shelter.

I know there's an obvious right choice here, but I do not make it.

"Oh yeah. Just got married."

Oh God. Why? Why does my mouth do this? That was honestly the *worst* choice. Because now, when we return home, I'm going to have to pretend to be married whenever I run into Mr. Hamilton—which could be daily—or fess up to getting fake divorced immediately after the fake wedding.

Gah.

His smile is so big it lifts the mustache. The therapist is relieved the weird moment of tension is gone and excuses herself with a smile. Still beaming, Mr. Hamilton reaches out, shaking my hand. "Well, now, that is some wonderful news. Where was the wedding?"

At least here I can be truthful: "At the Hilton, downtown St. Paul."

"My gosh," he says, shaking his head, "just starting out. What a blessing." He leans in and winks. "My Molly and I are here celebrating our thirtieth anniversary, can you believe it?"

I make my eyes round, like it's just *wild* that this white-haired man has been married for so long, and fumble through some noises about that being *amazing* and *exciting* and *you must just be . . . so happy*.

And then he takes out a metaphorical anvil and

knocks me into the floor: "Why don't you two join us for dinner?"

Me and Ethan, sitting beside each other at a table, having to . . . touch, and smile, and pretend to love each other? I stifle a chortle.

"Oh, we couldn't impose. You two probably never get away together."

"Of course we do! The kids are out of the house—it's just us two all the time. Come on. It's our last night, and I'm sure she's sick of me, to be honest!" He lets out a hearty laugh. "It wouldn't be any imposition at all."

If there's a way out of this situation, I'm not coming up with it fast enough. I think I have to bite the bullet.

Smiling—and hoping I look far less terrified than I feel—I give in. I need this job, and am dying to land in Mr. Hamilton's good graces. I'm going to have to ask Ethan for a huge favor. I'm going to owe him so big, it makes me want to hurl.

"Sure, Mr. Hamilton. Ethan and I would love that."

He reaches out and squeezes my shoulder. "Call me Charlie."

THE HALLWAY WEAVES AND ELONGATES in front of me. I wish it weren't just an illusion borne from dread, and that it really were five miles to our suite. But it isn't, and sooner than I'd like, I'm back at the room, half praying that Ethan is out doing something amazing until tomorrow, and half praying that he's here so we can make it to dinner with the Hamiltons.

As soon as I walk in, I see him sitting on the balcony. Why is he in Maui, hanging out in the hotel room? Although, now that I think about it, it sounds lovely. I grow instinctively itchy at the prospect of sharing the homebody gene with him.

At least he's changed into shorts and a T-shirt, and has his bare feet propped up on the ledge. The wind blows his dark hair all over his head, but I imagine him squinting judgmentally out at the surf, silently telling the waves they could do better.

When I move closer, I see that he's holding a cocktail in a highball glass. His bare arms are tanned and toned; his legs are surprisingly muscular and seem to go on forever. For some reason I expected that, in shorts and a T-shirt, he'd look like a string bean with awkward limbs bending at odd angles. Maybe it's because he's so tall. Or maybe it was just easier to tell myself that only his face could be pretty, and he'd be gnarled and gangly beneath his clothes.

Quite frankly, he's so well-rounded physically, it's a little unfair.

I slide open the door as quietly as I can; he looks pretty

relaxed. I'm sure he's thinking about drowning puppies, but I'm not here to judge. At least not until after he's had dinner with my boss. Then it's on.

I realize I'll need to be charming, so I slap a smile on my face. "Hey there."

He turns, and his blue eyes narrow. "Olivia."

Wow, I am getting sick of his stupid name game. "What're you up to, Elijah?"

"Just enjoying the view."

Well, that's . . . nice. "I didn't know you did that."

He blinks back out to the water. "Did what?"

"Enjoyed things?"

Ethan laughs incredulously, and it occurs to me that I could stand to up my sweet-talking game a bit. "How was the massage?" he asks.

"Great." I search for more words that aren't panicky and groveling. "Super relaxing."

He glances at me again. "This is what *relaxed* looks like on you? Wow." When I don't say anything else, he asks, "What's with you? You're being weirder than usual."

"I've never seen you in shorts before," I admit. His legs, specifically the muscles on them, are a rather interesting development. Quickly, I work to remove the hint of appreciation in my voice. "Awkward."

"I mean, it's not like putting a tray of cleavage on display," he says, waving a casual hand, "but I'm told shorts are still island appropriate."

I'm pretty sure that's another dig on my bridesmaid dress, but I honestly cannot be bothered to chase this one down. "So, funny thing," I say, pulling up a chair beside him and taking a seat. "You know how, at the airport, I was offered the job at Hamilton?"

He nods, already bored.

"Well, guess who's here?" I attempt enthusiasm by way of forced jazz hands. "Mr. Hamilton himself!"

Ethan's head whips my way. And I absolutely get the fear in his eyes: our ability to be completely anonymous has just been hosed. "*Here* here? At the resort?"

"I ran into him in the spa." And I add unnecessarily, "In a robe. He hugged me. It was weird. Anyway, sooooo, he invited us to dinner tonight. With his wife."

He laughs once. "Pass."

I curl my fingers into fists so I don't reach over and slap him. But a punch might leave a mark, so I flatten my hands again and sit on them. "The massage therapist called me Mrs. Thomas. *In front of Mr. Hamilton.*" I pause a beat to see if he gets it. When he doesn't react, I add, "Do you get what I'm telling you? My new boss thinks I got married."

Very slowly, Ethan blinks, and then blinks again. "You could have told him we're just pretending."

"In front of the staff? No way. Plus, he's all about integrity and trust! In the moment, it felt like continuing the lie was the better option, but now we're totally screwed because he thinks *I got married*."

"He thinks that because you literally told him you got married."

"Shut up, Eric, let me think." I lean in, chewing a fingernail, musing. "It could be okay, right? I mean, for all he knows, it'll turn out that you're abusive and I get a quick annulment after this trip. He'll never know I was being dishonest." I sit up, hit with an idea. "Ooh! I could tell him you died!"

Ethan just stares at me.

"We went snorkeling," I say, frowning now. "Sadly, you never came back to the boat."

He blinks.

"What?" I ask. "It's not like you're ever going to see him again after tonight. You don't need him to like you. Or, you know, know you continue to exist."

"You seem pretty sure I'm coming to dinner."

I put on my sweetest expression. I cross my legs and then uncross them. I lean forward, bat my lashes, and smile. "Please, Ethan? I know this is a huge ask."

He leans away. "Do you have something in your eye?"

My shoulders sink, and I groan. I can't believe I'm going to say this. "I'll give up the bedroom if you come tonight and play the part."

He chews his lip, thinking. "So we have to pretend to be married? Like, touching and . . . warm?"

Ethan spits out the word *warm* like most people would say *dismemberment.*

"It would mean everything to me." I think I've got him. I scoot my chair just a little closer. "I promise I'll be the best fake wife you ever had."

He lifts his drink and finishes it. I definitely do not notice how long and defined his throat looks as he swallows. "Fine. I'll go."

I nearly melt in relief. "Thank you so much, oh my God."

"But I get the bedroom."

chapter **six**

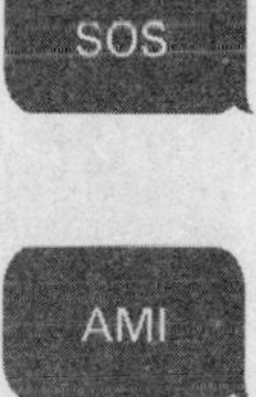

MR. HAMILTON IS HERE AND I TOLD HIM I'M MARRIED AND IDK WHY? NOW I HAVE TO PRETEND TO BE MARRIED TO ETHAN FOR AN ENTIRE DINNER AND I'LL PROBABLY BE FIRED AND HAVE TO SLEEP IN YOUR BATHTUB BECAUSE I'M A TERRIBLE LIAR.

AMI THIS IS A TWIN EMERGENCY

STOP

I don't have any fluids left in my body

I've been with Mom nonstop for over 36 hours

If I don't die from this I might need someone to kill me. Or her.

SLOW DOWN

BUT I'M FREAKING OUT

Your new boss is at the resort? In Maui??

He's here for his anniversary.

Someone called me Mrs. Thomas and I apparently lost my mind.

People are going to be calling you Mrs. Thomas the whole time.

You better get used to it. And calm down. You can do this.

Have we met? I absolutely cannot do this.

Just keep your answers simple.

When you get nervous you look guilty

Omg that's exactly what Ethan said

Who knew Ethan was so smart

Now if you'll excuse me, I have to throw up for the 50th time today

Don't waste my trip

I stare down at my phone, wishing my sister were here. I knew this was all too good to be true. I type out another quick message telling her to call me tonight and let me know how she's feeling, and then I text Diego.

Teach me how to lie

Who is this

GDI DIEGO.

FINE. Who are we lying to?

In Maui???

Please don't ask.

Just tell me how you managed to date those twins w/o either of them finding out.

Teach me, Yoda.

First, only lie when you need to and keep it simple.

You always overexplain and it's secondhand embarrassing.

MOVING ON

Know your story going in

Don't try to make it up on the fly.
God you're so bad at that

Don't fidget and def don't touch your
face. You do that too. Just sit still

Oh, and if you can, touch them.

It creates a sense of intimacy and makes
them want to take their pants off instead of
asking you questions

Ew this is my boss!

I'm just saying it couldn't hurt

You're a scientist. Do some research.

I glance up from my Google search at the sound of a knock.

"Not to be all cliché and husbandy and hassle you about being late"—there's a pause and I can practically see Ethan frowning down at his watch from the other side of the door—"but it's almost six."

"I know." I manage to keep the shouted version of my reply contained to the inside of my head. After Ethan agreed to dinner, I sprinted to the bedroom to try on every article of clothing I brought with me, before texting my sister and Diego in a panic. The room is a disaster, and I'm not sure I'm any more ready to do this now than I was an hour ago. I am a mess.

Ethan's voice carries through the door again, closer this time. "'I know' as in *I'm almost ready*, or 'I know' as in *I know how to tell time, kindly fuck off?*"

Both, if we're being honest. "The first."

Ethan knocks. "Okay if I come in my room?"

My room. I open the door and let him in, feeling delighted by the mess I'm leaving behind me.

Ethan steps in. He's about to meet my boss and spend the next few hours lying his face off, and he's in black jeans and a Surly Brewery shop shirt. He looks like he's going out to dinner at Chili's, not having dinner with the wife's new boss. His calm exterior only amplifies my panic because of course he's not worried; he has nothing to lose. The dread in my stomach blooms. *Ethan* has this, I absolutely do not.

He looks around the room and runs an aggravated hand through his hair. Of course it manages to fall perfectly back into place. "All of this was in one suitcase?"

"I am totally out of my depth here."

"That's been my general impression so far. Be more specific."

I drop onto the bed, kicking aside a hot pink bra and groaning when it snags on the heel of my shoe. "Whenever I tell lies, I get caught. I once told my professor I had to miss class to take care of my sick roommate, and he looked up right as my roommate walked past us in the hallway. He knew her from his Tuesday/Thursday lecture."

"Your mistake was in going to class at all. Just send an email like a normal liar."

"Or there was the one time in high school I had my cousin Miguel call in sick for me and pretend to be my dad, but the office called my mom to confirm because my dad had never called in before."

"Well, that was just poor planning on your part. How is any of this relevant right now?"

"It's relevant because I'm trying to look like a wife, and have been researching how to lie."

Reaching for my leg, Ethan wraps a warm palm around my calf and plucks the bra from my shoe. "Okay. Does a wife have a specific look?"

I snatch the lingerie from where it now dangles on the end of his finger. "I don't know, like Ami?"

His deep laugh echoes through the room. "Yeah, that's not going to happen."

"*Hey.* We're twins."

"This isn't about looks," he says, and the mattress sinks under his weight as he takes a seat at my side. "Ami has this indescribable confidence. It's how she carries herself. Like no matter what happens, she's got her shit together enough for the both of you."

I'm conflicted between being proud of my sister—because, yeah, she does make people feel that way—and vainly curious about what he thinks of me. Vanity and the confrontational side of me that rears its head around Ethan win out. "What impression do I give?"

He looks at my phone, and I'm sure he sees the words *How to lie convincingly* in the search bar. With a laugh, he shakes his head. "Like you should put your head between your legs and pray."

I'm about to push him off the bed when he stands, looks meaningfully down at his watch and then back up at me.

Passive-aggressive hint noted. Standing, I give a final look in the mirror and reach for my purse. "Let's get this over with."

AS WE MAKE OUR WAY to the elevator, I'm reminded of the supreme imbalance of the universe; even in unflattering overhead light, Ethan still manages to look good. Somehow the shadows sharpen his features rather than unattractively exaggerating them. Standing in front of the mirrored doors, I note the result is not the same for me.

As if reading my mind, Ethan bumps his hip into mine. "Stop it. You look fine."

Fine, I think. *Like a woman who loves her cheese curds. Like a woman whose boobs pop out of her bridesmaid dress. Like a woman who deserves your disdain because she isn't perfect.*

"I can hear you thinking about that one word and reading more into it than I intended. You look great." Once inside, he presses the button for the lobby and adds, "You always do."

These three final words bound around my cranium before they absorb. I always look great? To who? Ethan?

The floors count down and it feels like the elevator is holding its breath right along with me. I meet the eyes of my reflection in the mirrored doors and glance over at Ethan.

You always do.

Color blooms high on his cheekbones, and he looks like he'd be happy if the cables snapped and death swallowed us whole.

I clear my throat. "In a 1990 study, researchers showed that it's easier to catch someone in a lie the first time they tell it. We should figure out what we're going to say."

"You needed Google to tell you that?"

"I do better when I'm prepared. You know, practice makes perfect."

"Right." He pauses, thinking. "We met through friends—technically not a lie, so it will be harder for you to screw it up—and got married last week. I am the luckiest man alive, *et cetera, et cetera.*"

I nod in agreement. "Met through friends, dated for a while and oh my God, I was so surprised when you begged me to marry you."

Ethan's lip curls. "I got down on one knee while we were camping at Moose Lake. Proposed with a Ring Pop."

"Details are good! We smelled like campfire the entire next day," I say, "but didn't care because we were so happy and having lots of celebratory tent sex."

The elevator falls deathly silent. I look over in a strange combination of horror and joy that I've managed to render him speechless with the prospect of sex with me. Finally, he mumbles, "Right. We can probably leave out that detail for your boss."

"And remember," I say, loving his discomfort, "I didn't mention you, or being engaged, at the interview, so we need to look a little windswept by it all."

The elevator dings, and the doors open into the lobby. "I don't think we'll have any trouble pulling that off."

"And be charming," I say. "But not like, *likable* charming. Passably charming. They shouldn't leave wanting to spend any actual time with you. Because you're probably going to die or turn out to be terrible in the end." I catch his small, irritated scowl as he heads into the lobby and can't help but throw in a little dig. "Basically, just be yourself."

"Man, I am going to sleep so well tonight." He stretches, like he's prepping to starfish on the enormous bed. "FYI, watch the left side of the sofa. I was reading there earlier today and noticed there's a spring that digs a little."

Soft music echoes through the lobby as we make our way to the exit. The restaurant is just off the beach; it's convenient because when all this blows up in my face, it will only be a short walk to drown myself in the ocean.

Ethan opens the door to the expansive courtyard and motions for me to lead the way down a lighted path. "What is this company again?" he asks.

"Hamilton Biosciences. They're one of the most well-known contract biologics companies in the country, and on the discovery side, they have a new flu vaccine. From all of the papers I've read, it sounds groundbreaking. I really wanted this job, so maybe mention how happy we are that I was hired, and that it's all I've talked about since."

"We're supposed to be on our honeymoon, and you want me to say you've talked nonstop about their flu vaccine?"

"Yes. I do."

"What's your job again? Janitor?"

Ah. There it is. "I'm a medical-science liaison, Eragon. Basically I talk to physicians about our products from a more technical standpoint than does the sales force." I glance over at him as we walk. He looks like he's trying to cram for a test. "He and his wife are here for their thirtieth anniversary. If we're lucky, we can just ask them a bunch of stuff about themselves and not have to talk about us at all."

"For someone who claims to be unlucky, you're putting an awful lot of faith into your lucky streak." He does a small double take when he registers that this has hit me like a truth slap. We stop in front of a shimmering fountain, and Ethan pulls a penny—but not *that* penny—from his pocket and tosses it inside, "Seriously, calm down. We'll be fine."

I try. We follow the path to a Polynesian-style thatched-roof building and step up to the hostess stand. "I believe the reservation is under Hamilton," Ethan says.

Dressed in all white save for a large gardenia pinned in her hair, the hostess scans a screen in front of her and looks up with a bright smile. "Right this way."

I move to step around the podium, and that's when it happens. Ethan moves into my side, his palm pressed against the small of my back, and just like that, our carefully preserved bubble of personal space is gone.

He looks down at me with a sweet smile and soft, adoring blue eyes and motions for me to lead the way with the hand not currently straying south. The transformation is . . . amazing. Debilitating. My stomach is in knots, my heart is lodged in my windpipe, and there's something very *aware* happening along every inch of my skin.

The restaurant is on stilts above a lagoon, and our table is near a railing that overlooks the water. The interior is elegant but cozy, with leaded glass candle holders and wicker lanterns that make the space glow.

Mr. Hamilton stands when he sees us; the fluffy white robe has been mercifully replaced with a floral-print shirt. The giant mustache is as robust as ever.

"There they are!" he crows, nodding to me and reaching out to shake Ethan's hand. "Honey, this is Olive, the new team member I told you about, and her husband . . ."

"Ethan," he supplies, and his dazzling smile punches me right in the vagina. "Ethan Thomas."

"Good to meet you, Ethan. This is my wife, Molly." Charles Hamilton motions to the brunette at his side, rosy cheeks and a deep dimple making her seem too young for a woman who's celebrating three decades of marriage.

We all shake hands and Ethan holds out my chair. I smile and sit as carefully as I can. The rational part of my brain knows he won't do it, but the lizard brain expects Ethan to pull it out from under me.

"Thank you so much for inviting us," Ethan says, megawatt smile in place. He drapes an easy arm across the back of my chair, leaning in. "Olive is so excited to be working with you. It's like she can't shut up about it."

I laugh a *Ha-ha-ha oh, that rascal* laugh and carefully step on his foot beneath the table.

"I'm just glad she hadn't been snatched up yet," Mr. Hamilton says. "We're lucky to have her. And what a surprise to find out that you two just got married!"

"It happened sort of fast," I say and lean into Ethan, trying to look natural.

"Snuck right up on us. Like an ambush!" He grunts when my heel digs farther into the top of his foot. "And what about you two? I hear congratulations are in order? Thirty years is just amazing."

Molly beams up at her husband. "Thirty wonderful years, but even so there are moments I can't believe we haven't killed each other yet."

Ethan laughs quietly, giving me an adoring look. "Aw, hon, can you imagine thirty years of this?"

"Sure can't!" I say, and everyone laughs, thinking of course I'm joking. I reach up to brush my hair away from my forehead before remembering I'm not supposed to fidget. Then I fold my arms across my chest and recall the internet saying not to do that either.

God damn it.

"When Charlie told me that he ran into you," Molly says, "well, I just couldn't believe it. And on your honeymoon!"

I clap lamely. "Yay! It's so—fun."

The waitress appears, and Ethan pretends to lean in and kiss my neck. His breath is hot behind my ear. "Holy shit," he whispers. "*Relax*."

Straightening again, he smiles up to the waitress as she reads off the specials. After a few questions, we order a bottle of pinot noir for the table, and our dinners.

Any hope I had of navigating the conversation away from us is shot down as soon as the waitress leaves. "So how did you two meet?" Molly asks.

A pause. *Keep it simple, Olive.* "A friend introduced us." I'm met with polite smiles as Molly and Charlie wait for the actual story part of the story. I shift in my seat, recross my legs. "And, um, he asked me out . . ."

"We had mutual friends who had just started dating," Ethan interjects, and their attention—thankfully—drifts over to him. "They planned a little party hoping everyone would get to know each other. I noticed her right away."

Molly's hands flutter around her collarbones. "Love at first sight."

"Something like that." The corner of his mouth twitches upward. "She was wearing a T-shirt that said *Particle Collisions Give Me a Hadron*, and I thought any woman who understands a physics pun is someone I need to know."

Mr. Hamilton barks out a laugh and hits the table. Frankly, I can barely keep my jaw from hitting the floor. The story Ethan is telling isn't the real first time we met, but maybe the third or fourth—in fact, it was the night I decided I was not going to put in a single bit of effort with him because every time I tried to be friendly, he'd weasel away and go into another room. And here he is, rattling off what I was wearing. I can barely recall what I wore yesterday, never mind what someone else wore two and a half years ago.

"And I guess the rest is history?" Mr. Hamilton says.

"Sort of. We didn't really get along at first." Ethan's eyes make an adoring circuit of my face. "But here we are." He blinks back to the Hamiltons. "What about you two?"

Charlie and Molly tell us about how they met at a singles dance through neighboring churches, and when Charlie didn't ask her to dance, she walked right up to him and did it herself. I do my best to pay attention, I really do, but it's nearly impossible with Ethan so close. His arm is still draped across my chair and if I lean back just enough, his fingers brush the curve of my shoulder, the back of my neck. It feels like tiny licks of fire each time he makes contact.

I definitely do not lean back more than twice.

Once our entrées arrive, we dig in. With the wine flowing and Ethan charming the pants off of everyone, it turns into not just a tolerable meal but a delightful one. I can't decide if I want to thank him or strangle him.

"Did you know when Olive was a kid, she got stuck in one of those claw arcade machines?" Ethan says, retelling my least favorite—but, I'll admit, funniest—story. "You can look it up on YouTube and watch the extraction. It's comedy gold."

Molly and Charlie look horrified for Little Olive, but I can guarantee they are going to watch the shit out of it later.

"How did you find out about that?" I ask him, genuinely curious. I certainly never told him, but I also can't imagine him engaging in a conversation about me with anyone else, or—even more unbelievable—*Googling* me. The idea actually makes me have to push a laugh back down my throat.

Ethan reaches for my hand, twisting his fingers with mine. They're warm, strong, and hold me tight. I hate how great it feels. "Your sister told me," he says. "I believe her exact words were, 'Worst prize ever.' "

The entire table bursts into hysterics. Mr. Hamilton is laughing so hard his face is a shocking shade of red, made worse by the silvery contrast of his giant mustache.

"Remind me to thank her when we get home," I say, pulling my hand away and draining the last of my wine.

Still laughing, Molly carefully dabs at her eyes with a napkin. "How many brothers and sisters do you have, Olive?"

I take Ethan's earlier advice and keep it simple. "Just the one."

"She's a twin, actually," Ethan volunteers.

Molly is intrigued. "Are you identical?"

"We are."

"They look *exactly* alike," Ethan tells her, "but their personalities are polar opposites. Like night and day. One has it all together, and the other is my wife."

Charlie and Molly lose it again, and I reach for Ethan's

hand, giving him a sweet *Aw, I love you, ya goof* smile while I attempt to break his fingers in my fist. He coughs, eyes watering.

Molly misinterprets his glassed-over expression and looks at us fondly. "Oh, this has been the most fun. Such a lovely way to end this trip."

Quite clearly, she could not be more taken with my fake husband and leans forward, dimple in full force. "Ethan, did Olive mention that we have a spouses group at Hamilton?"

Spouses group? Continued contact?

"She sure didn't," he says.

She's already rubbing her hands together. "We get together once a month. It's mostly wives who manage to make it, but Ethan, you are just darling. I can already tell everyone is going to *love* you."

"We're a very close-knit group," Mr. Hamilton says. "And more than coworkers, we like to think of everyone as family. You two are going to fit right in. Olive, Ethan, I'm just so thrilled to welcome you both to Hamilton."

"I CAN'T BELIEVE YOU TOLD the claw story," I say as we walk along the outdoor path, headed back to the room. "You know they're going to Google it, which means Mr. Hamilton will see me in my underwear."

Thankfully, the personal space bubble is back. Being around an Ethan I don't want to punch is disorienting enough. Being around an affectionate, charming Ethan is like suddenly being able to walk on the ceiling.

That said, dinner was an undeniable success, and as happy as I am that I didn't blow it and still have a job, I'm irritated that Ethan is consistently so great at everything. I have no idea how he does it; he's charm-free 99 percent of the time, but then, boom, he turns into Mr. Congeniality.

"It's a funny story, Olive," he says, walking faster and getting a few paces ahead of me. "Should I have told them about the time you gifted me that Last Will and Testament software at the family Christmas party? I mean, honestly—"

"I was only looking out for your loved ones."

"—I was making *conversation—*" Ethan stops so suddenly that I collide with the brick wall of his back.

I catch my balance, horrified that I've just smashed my entire face into the splendor of his trapezius. "Are you having a stroke?"

He presses his hand to his forehead, head turning so he can frantically scope out the path behind us, back the way we came. "This can't be happening."

I move to follow his gaze, but he jerks me behind an enormous potted palm, where we huddle close.

"*Ethan?*" a voice calls, followed by the click of high

heels on the stone path. She follows up with a breathy "I *swear* I just saw Ethan!"

He turns his face to me. "Big favor: I need you to go along with me." We're pressed so close I can feel his breath on my lips. I smell the chocolate he had for dessert, and a piney hint of his deodorant.

I try to hate it.

"You need my help?" I ask, and if it sounds a little breathy I'm sure it's because I ate too much at dinner and am a little winded from the walk.

"Yes."

My smile literally unfurls. Suddenly, I am the Grinch wearing a Santa hat. "It's gonna cost you."

He looks pissed for about two seconds before panic wipes it away. "The room is yours."

The footsteps get closer, and then a blond head is invading my space. "Oh my God. It *is* you!" she says, bypassing me completely to wrap Ethan in a hug.

"Sophie?" he says, feigning surprise. "I . . . what are you doing here?"

Detangling from the embrace, Ethan glances over at me, eyes wide.

She turns to beckon to the man standing just off to the side, and I take the opportunity to mouth—because oh my God—*This is Simba?!*

He nods, clearly miserable.

Holy awkward! This is way worse than running into your new boss while naked under a robe!

"Billy," Sophie says proudly, pulling the guy forward, and I gape because he looks exactly like Norman Reedus, but somehow greasier. "This is Ethan. The guy I told you about. Ethan, this is Billy. My fiancé."

Even in the dark I see the way Ethan pales. "Fiancé," he repeats. The word lands with a heavy thud, and it's infinitely more awkward with Ethan described only as *the guy I told you about.* Weren't Ethan and Sophie together for a couple of *years*?

It doesn't take a genius to put the pieces together: Ethan's reaction at seeing her across the path, the way he shut down when I asked about a girlfriend on the plane. A fresh breakup, and she's already engaged? *Ouch.*

But it's as if someone has pushed a button somewhere on his back, because robot Ethan is back and suddenly in motion, stepping forward to offer Billy a confident hand. "Nice to meet you."

Moving to his side, I loop a casual arm through his. "Hi. I'm Olive."

"Right, sorry," he says. "Olive, this is Sophie Sharp. Sophie, this is Olive Torres." He pauses and everything goes tight between us in anticipation of what comes next. I have the sense of being on the back of a motorcycle, staring over the lip of the canyon, not knowing if he's going to rev the throttle and send us over the edge. He does: "My wife."

Sophie's nostrils flare and for a fraction of a second, she looks positively homicidal. But then the look is gone, and she gives him an easy smile. "Wow! Wife! Amazing!"

The problem with lying about relationships is that humans are fickle, fickle creatures. For all I know Sophie could be the one who ended things, but seeing that Ethan is no longer on the market will make him seem forbidden—and therefore more alluring. I have no idea what happened to end their relationship—nor do I know if he even wants her back—but if he does, I wonder if he realizes the irony that being married has just made it more likely she'll want him back, too.

She glances at me and then him. "When did this happen?" I'm sure we can all hear how it's an effort for her to keep her voice from being razor sharp, which just makes it that much more uncomfortable (and awesome).

"Yesterday!" I wiggle my ring finger, and the plain gold band winks in the torchlight.

She looks back at him. "I can't believe I didn't hear anything!"

"I mean," Ethan says, laughing sharply, "we haven't exactly spoken, Soph."

And *oh*. Tension. This is so, so awkward (and juicy). My curiosity is officially piqued.

She gives a coy little pout. "Still! You didn't tell me. Wow. Ethan—*married*."

It's impossible to miss the way his mouth hardens, his jaw flexes. "Yeah," he says. "It happened pretty fast."

"Feels like only moments ago we decided to really do this!" I agree with a hearty smile up at him.

He presses a hard, fast kiss to my cheek, and I force myself not to jerk away like I've been slapped with a dead lizard.

"And you're engaged," he says, giving the world's stiffest thumbs-up. "Look at us . . . moving on."

Sophie is small, thin, and wearing a pretty silk tank top, skinny jeans, and sky-high heels. Her tan comes from a bottle, and I'm guessing her hair color does, too, but that's really all I can find wrong with her. I try to imagine her in twenty years—vaguely leathery, long red nails curled around a Diet Coke can—but for now she's still beautiful in a semi-unattainable way that makes me feel dumpy in comparison. It's easy to imagine her and Ethan side by side on a Christmas card, wrapped in J.Crew cardigans and leaning against their broad stone fireplace.

"Maybe we can go to dinner or something," she says, and it's so half-hearted that I actually bark out a laugh before Ethan reaches for my hand and squeezes it.

"Yes," I say, trying to cover. "Dinner. We have it every day."

Ethan looks down at me, and I realize he's not glaring; he's fighting a laugh.

Billy pipes up with a subject change, similarly cool on the dinner idea. "How long are you here?"

I absolutely cannot stomach another fake dinner, so I go for broke. When Ethan answers "Ten days," I wrap my arms around his waist and gaze up at him with what I hope is a sexy frown.

"Actually, pumpkin, I'd feel terrible if we planned something and didn't make it. You know we barely made it out of the room today." I walk some flirty fingers up his chest, toying with the buttons on the front of his shirt. Wow, it is a veritable wall of muscle under there. "I already shared you tonight. I can't make any promises for tomorrow."

Ethan raises a single brow, and I'm wondering if the tension in his expression is because he cannot fathom having sex with me once, let alone continually for an entire afternoon. Pulling himself out of the mental hellscape, he presses a swift kiss to the tip of my nose. "You have a point."

He turns to Sophie. "Maybe we can play it by ear?"

"Absolutely. You still have my number?"

"I'd imagine so," he says with a bemused nod.

Sophie takes a couple of steps backward, and her gold heels click like kitten claws on the sidewalk. "Okay, well . . . congrats, and I hope we see you again!"

With a tug she pulls Billy, and they continue their way down the path.

"It was nice meeting you," I call out before turning back to Ethan. "I might make a terrible wife one day, but at least we know now that I can fake it."

"I guess everyone needs a goal."

Pulling my hands off his body, I shake them out at my sides. "God, why did you kiss my nose? We did not discuss that."

"I must have thought you were okay with it once you started feeling me up."

I scoff at that, setting off again at an acceptable distance behind them toward the hotel. "I got us out of another dinner. If it weren't for me you'd spend tomorrow night across from Malibu Barbie and Daryl Dixon. You're welcome."

"Your boss leaves and now my ex-girlfriend is here?" Ethan takes out his frustration in a series of long strides I have to jog to keep up with. "Have we earned a spot in the eighth circle of hell? Now we have to keep this stupid act up the entire time."

"I have to admit to feeling partly responsible here. If something is going well and I'm around, *look out*. Win a free trip? Boss shows up. Boss goes home? Accomplice's ex-girlfriend appears out of nowhere."

He pulls open the door, and I am met with a blast of refrigerated air and the soothing gurgle-bubble of the lobby fountain.

"I'm a black cat," I remind him. "A broken mirror."

"Don't be ludicrous." He pulls out another penny—still not *that* one—and flicks it off his thumb into the splashing water. "Luck doesn't work that way."

"Please explain to me how luck *really* works, Ethan," I drawl, my attention pointedly following the trajectory of the coin.

He ignores this.

"Anyway," I say, "this resort is huge. It's like, forty acres and has *nine* swimming pools. I bet we don't even see Simba and Daryl again."

Ethan lets a reluctant half smile slip free. "You're right."

"Of course I am. But I'm also exhausted." I walk across the lobby and press the button to call the elevator. "I say we turn in and start fresh in the morning."

The doors open, and we step inside, side by side but so far apart.

I press the button for the top floor. "And thanks to Miss Sophie I have a giant bed waiting for me."

His expression reflected in the glass doors is a lot less smug than it was a few hours ago.

chapter **seven**

Once we're back in the room, it feels about half as big as it did when we arrived, and I'm sure that is entirely due to the fact that clothing will be coming off soon as we get ready for bed. I am not ready.

Ethan tosses his wallet and key card onto the counter. I swear the sound of the items landing on the marble is like a cymbal crash.

"What?" he says in response to my dramatic startle.

"Nothing. Just." I point to his stuff. "*Jeez.*"

He stares at me for a lingering beat before seeming to decide whatever I'm going on about isn't worth it, and turns to toe his shoes off near the door. I walk across the room, and my feet on the carpet sound like boots crunching through knee-high grass. Is this a joke? Is every sound amplified in here?

What if I have to go to the bathroom? Do I turn on the shower to muffle the sounds? What if he farts in his sleep, and I can hear it?

What if I do?

Oh God.

It's like a death march, following him down the short hallway to the bedroom. Once there, Ethan wordlessly moves to one dresser and I move to the other. It's the quiet routine of a comfortable married couple, made *super weird* by the knowledge that we're both ready to crawl out of our skins from the tension.

The massive bed looms like the Grim Reaper between us.

"I don't know if you've noticed, but there's only one shower," he says.

"I did, yeah."

While the second bathroom is simple, with a toilet and small sink, the master bathroom is palatial. The shower is as big as my kitchen back in Minneapolis, and the bathtub should come with a diving board.

I dig through my drawer, praying that, in the mad dash packing post-weddingpocalypse, I remembered pajamas. I really didn't realize until now how much time I spend in nothing but my underwear at home.

"Do you usually do it at night?" he asks.

I spin around. "Uh, pardon?"

Ethan sighs the deep, weary sigh of a long-suffering ghoul. "Shower, Oscar."

"Oh." I press my pajamas to my chest. "Yes. I shower at night."

"Would you like to go first?"

"Since I have the bedroom," I say, "why don't you go first?" Lest this sound too generous, I add, "Then you can get out of my space."

"Such a caretaker, you."

He steps around me to the bathroom, closing the door behind him with a solid *click*. Even with the bedroom's balcony doors shut, I can hear the sound of the tide coming in, the waves crashing against the shore. But it's not so loud that I don't also hear the rustle of fabric as Ethan undresses and drops his clothes onto the bathroom floor, his footsteps as he walks barefoot across the tile, or the soft groan he makes when he moves under the warm spray of water.

Flustered, I jog immediately to the balcony door and step outside until he's finished. Honestly, I'd only want to listen to *that* if he was drowning in there.

I'M SURE ETHAN WOULD LOVE to hear it was a long night for me and I barely slept, but my bed is fucking amazing. Sorry about the couch, dude.

In fact, I'm so rested and rejuvenated that I wake up convinced this running-into-people-from-our-real-life thing isn't a catastrophe. It's fine! We're fine. Sophie and Billy don't want to see us any more than we want to see them and are probably staying all the way on the other side of the resort anyway. And the Hamiltons are checking out today. We are in the clear.

As luck would have it, we run into the Hamiltons on our way to breakfast. Apparently the friendship was deeply solidified last night: they give us each a tight embrace . . . as well as their personal cell numbers.

"I was serious about that spouses club," Molly tells Ethan conspiratorially. "We have fun, if you know what I mean." She winks. "Give us a call when you're home."

They turn back to the reception desk, and we wave as we weave through the crowd toward the restaurant. Ethan leans down, muttering in a shaky voice, "I really don't know what she means by *fun*."

"Could be innocent, like a bunch of wives drinking merlot and complaining about their husbands," I tell him. "*Or* it could be *Fried Green Tomatoes* complicated."

"'*Fried Green Tomatoes* complicated'?"

I nod somberly. "A group of women looking at their labia with hand mirrors."

Ethan looks like he is literally fighting the urge to sprint down the curved driveway and into the ocean. "I think you're enjoying this too much."

"God, I am the worst, right? Enjoying Maui?"

We come to a stop in front of the hostess stand, give our room number, and follow the woman to a small booth toward the back, near the buffet.

I laugh. "A buffet, honey! Your fave."

Once we're seated, Ethan—running on slightly less sleep than I am—glares at the menu, clearly working to burn a hole in it. I wander over to the buffet and fill my plate with giant hunks of tropical fruit and all manner of grilled meats. When I return, Ethan has apparently ordered à la carte and is cradling a large cup of black coffee in his enormous hands. He doesn't even acknowledge my return.

"Hi."

He grunts.

"All that food up there, and you ordered something off the menu?"

Sighing, he says, "I don't like buffets, Olive, Jesus Christ. After what we witnessed two days ago, I'd think you'd agree with me."

I take a bite of pineapple and am pleased to see him cringe when I speak with my mouth full: "I just like hassling you."

"I can tell."

God, he is such a grouch in the morning. "Seriously, though, you think I'm enjoying this vacation *too much*? Do you even hear yourself?"

He puts the mug down carefully, like it's taking every ounce of control he has to not use it for violent means. "We did well last night," he says calmly, "but things just got a whole lot more complicated. My ex-girlfriend—with whom I share a number of mutual friends—thinks we are married. The wife of your new boss wants to have labia-hand-mirror time with me."

"That was just one possibility," I remind him. "Could be that Molly's version of fun is a Tupperware party."

"You don't think this is complicated?"

I shrug at him, turning the blame back where it's deserved. "To be honest, you were the one who had to go and be ridiculously charming last night."

He picks his mug back up and blows across the surface. "Because you *asked* me to be."

"I wanted you to be *sociopath* charming," I say. "*Too* charming, so that afterward people look back and think, 'You know, I didn't get it at the time, but he was always too perfect.' That sort of charming. Not, like, self-deprecating and cute."

Half of Ethan's mouth turns up, and I know what's coming before it launches: "You think I'm cute."

"In a gross way."

This makes him smile wider. "Cute in a gross way. Okay."

The waiter brings his food, and when I look up, I see that Ethan's smile has fallen and he's staring over my shoulder, his face ashen. With a frown, he blinks down to his plate.

"Just remembered that bacon at restaurants is ten thousand times more likely to carry salmonella?" I ask. "Or did you find a hair on your plate and think you're going to come down with lupus?"

"Once more for the people in the back: Being careful about food safety isn't the same as being a hypochondriac or an idiot."

I give him a *Sure thing, Captain* salute, but then it hits me. He's freaking out about something other than his breakfast. I glance around, and my pulse rockets: Sophie and Billy have been seated directly behind me. Ethan has an unobstructed view of his ex and her new fiancé.

For as frequently as I want to open-hand smack Ethan, I can also appreciate how much it would suck to continually run into your ex when they're celebrating their engagement and you're only pretending to be married. I remember running into my ex-boyfriend Arthur the night I defended my dissertation. We were out to celebrate *me*, and my accomplishment, and there he was, the boy who dumped me because he "couldn't be distracted by a relationship." He had his new girlfriend on one arm and the medical journal he'd just been published in in the other hand. My celebratory mood evaporated, and I left my own party about an hour later to go home and binge an entire season of *Buffy*.

A tiny bloom of sympathy unfurls in my chest. "Ethan—"

"Could you *try* chewing with your mouth closed?" he says, and the bloom is annihilated by a nuclear blast.

"For the record, it's very humid here, and I am *congested*." I lean in, hissing, "To think I was starting to feel sorry for you."

"For being cute in a gross way?" he asks, prodding at his plate, glancing over my shoulder again and then quickly zeroing in on my face.

"For the fact that your ex is at the resort with us and sitting right behind me."

"Is she?" He looks up and does a terrible job of being surprised to see her there. "Huh."

I smirk at him, even though he studiously avoids my gaze. With the tiny hint of vulnerability just at the edges of his expression, the bloom of sympathy returns. "What's your favorite breakfast food?"

He pauses with a bite of bacon halfway to his mouth. "What?"

"Come on. Breakfast food. What do you like?"

"Bagels." He takes the bite, chews and swallows, and I realize that's all I'm going to get.

"*Bagels*? For real? Of all the choices in the world, you're telling me your favorite breakfast food is a bagel? You live in the Twin Cities. Can we even get a good bagel there?"

He apparently thinks my question is rhetorical, because he turns back to his meal, completely happy to blink those lashes at me and remain nonverbal. I realize why I hate him—he food- and fat-shamed me, and has always been a monosyllabic prick—but what is his deal with *me*?

I give *friendly* one last try: "Why don't we do something fun today?"

Ethan looks at me like I've just suggested we go on a murder spree. "Together?"

"Yes, together! All of our free activities are for two people," I say, wagging a finger back and forth between us, "and as you just pointed out, we're supposed to be acting *married*."

Ethan has retreated into his neck, shoulders hunched. "Could you maybe not yell that across the restaurant?"

I take a deep breath, counting to five so that I don't reach across the table and poke him in the eye. Leaning in, I say, "Look. We're deep in this lying game together now, so why not make the most of it? That's all I'm trying to do: enjoy what I can."

He stares at me for several quiet beats. "That's awfully upbeat of you."

Pushing back from the table, I stand. "I'm going to go see what we can sign up for tod—"

"She's watching," he cuts in tightly, quickly glancing past me. "Shit."

"What?"

"*Sophie.* She keeps looking over here." In a panic, his eyes meet mine. "Do something."

"Like what?" I ask tightly, starting to panic, too.

"Before you go. I don't know. We're in love, right? Just—" He stands abruptly and reaches for my shoulders, jerking me across the table and planting his mouth stiffly on mine. Our eyes remain open and horrified. My breath is trapped in my chest, and I count out three eternal beats before we burst apart.

He fixes a convincingly loving smile on his face, speaking through his teeth. "I can't believe I just did that."

"I'm going to go gargle bleach now," I tell him.

No doubt it was the worst version of an Ethan Thomas kiss, and it was still . . . not terrible. His mouth was warm, lips smooth and firm. Even when we were staring at each other in horror, he still looked nice that close up. Maybe even nicer than he does from a distance. His eyes are so insanely blue, his lashes are long to the point of absurdity. And he's warm. So war—

My brain is short-circuiting. *Shut up, Olive.*

Oh my God. Pretending we're married means we might have to do that again.

"Great." He stares at me, eyes wide. "Great. See you back in the room in a few."

THE IDEA OF BUILDING A house from the ground up has always terrified me, because I know I'm not a person who cares about details such as doorknobs and drawer pulls and stone pavers. It would be too many choices that I simply don't care about at all.

Looking at the list of activities feels a little like this. We have the option of parasailing, zip-lining, four-wheeling, snorkeling, taking hula kahiko lessons, enjoying a couple's massage, and much, much more. Honestly, I'd be fine with any of them. But Trent, the overeager activities planner, stares at me expectantly, ready to ink "my" name into the schedule wherever I desire.

The issue at hand is really which activity would make Ethan scowl the least?

"A good place to start," Trent says gently, "might be a boat ride? Our boat goes out to the Molokini Crater. It's very calm out there. You'll get lunch and drinks. You could snorkel, or try Snuba—an easy mix of snorkeling and scuba diving—or you could even just stay on the boat if you don't want to get in the water."

An option to sit down and shut up instead of join the fun? Definitely a bonus in the holster when I have Ethan in tow. "Let's do that."

With gusto, Trent enters *Ethan and Ami Thomas* onto the boat manifest and tells me to be back downstairs at ten.

Upstairs, Ethan is already in his board shorts but hasn't yet put on a shirt. A strange, violent reaction worms through me when he turns and I see that he has actual muscles on his muscles. A dark smattering of hair over his broad chest causes my hand to curl into a fist. "How *dare* you."

I know I've said it out loud when Ethan glances at me with a smirk and then tugs his shirt over his head. Immediately, with the abs out of my sight, the fire of hate in my lower belly is extinguished.

"What's the plan?" he asks.

I give myself three silent seconds to linger on the memory of his naked torso before answering, "We're taking a boat to Molokini. Snorkeling, drinks, *et cetera*."

I expect him to roll his eyes or complain, but he surprises me. "Really? Cool."

Warily, I leave this deceptively upbeat version of Satan in the living room to go get my suit on and pack a bag. When I emerge, Ethan valiantly refrains from making a crack about my suit barely containing my boobs or my cover-up being frumpy, and we make our way down to the lobby and follow directions out to a twelve-seater van waiting at the curb.

With one foot propped to climb in, Ethan pulls up short so quickly that I collide with his back. Again.

"Are you having another—?"

Ethan shuts me up with a hand shooting back, gripping my hip. And then I hear it: the high-pitched nails-on-a-chalkboard voice of Sophie.

"Ethan! You and Olive are coming snorkeling?"

"We sure are! What a wild coincidence!" He turns around and murders me with eyeball daggers, before smiling as he faces forward again. "Should we just hop in the back there?"

"Sure, I think those seats are the only open ones." Billy's voice sounds pretty giddy, and when Ethan ducks to climb in, I see why.

There are eight people seated in the van already, and only the very back row is empty. Ethan is so tall he has to practically army crawl to get through the gauntlet of bags and hats and seat belts crisscrossing the path. With slightly more ease, I settle in beside him and glance over. Surprisingly, the fact that he looks absolutely miserable doesn't fill me with abject joy as expected. I feel . . . guilty. I clearly chose poorly.

But this is Olive and Ethan we're talking about; defensiveness is the first reaction out of the gate. This feels like Cheap Airplane Ticket Fiasco, version 2.0. "You could have picked the activity, you know."

He doesn't answer. For someone who was so convincingly newlywed last night to cover for my lie, he sure is surly when we have to do it to cover for his. He must really hate to be indebted to me.

"We can do something else," I tell him. "There's still time to leave."

Again, he says nothing, but then deflates a little beside me when the driver closes the double van doors and gives us all a thumbs-up through the window, indicating we're ready to head out.

Gently, I elbow Ethan. He clearly doesn't get that it's meant as a *Hang in there, tiger!* because he elbows me back. Jerk. I elbow him again, harder now, and he starts to shift to return it again but I evade it, turning to dig my knuckles into his ribs. I did not expect to find Ethan's hysterical tickle spot, and he lets out a deafening, high-pitched shriek that I swear makes me momentarily deaf. It is so startling that the entire van turns to figure out what the hell we're doing in the back seat.

"Sorry," I say to them, and then quieter to him, "That's a sound I haven't heard a man make before."

"Can you not speak to me, please?"

I lean in. "I didn't *know* she was coming."

Ethan slides his gaze to me, clearly unconvinced. "I'm not going to kiss you again, just in case that's what you were thinking this would lead to."

Whowhatnow? The jackass. Gaping at him, I whisper-hiss, "I would honestly rather lick the bottom of my shoe than have your mouth on mine again."

He turns back, looking out the window. The van pulls away from the curb, the driver cues up the mellow island music, and I am ready for a twenty-minute nap when, in front of us, a teenager pulls a bottle of sunscreen out and begins liberally spraying it down one arm and then the other. Ethan and I are immediately lost in a cloud of oily fumes with no window or door.

He and I exchange a look of deep suffering. "Please don't spray that in the van," Ethan says, with a gentle authority that does something weird and wavy to my breathing.

The teen turns, gives us a flat "Oops, sorry," and then tucks the bottle back in her backpack. Beside her, her father is absorbed in a *Popular Science* magazine, completely oblivious.

The fog of sunscreen slowly clears and, aside from the view of Sophie and Billy making out two rows ahead of us, we are able to see out the windows, to the view of the snaking shoreline to our left, the brilliant green mountains to our right. A pulse of fondness fills me.

"Maui is so pretty."

I feel Ethan turn to look down at me, but don't meet his eyes, in case he's confused that my words were delivered without insult to him. His frown could ruin this flash of happiness I'm feeling.

"It is." I don't know why I always expect an argument from him, but it continually surprises me when I get agreement instead. And his voice is so deep; it almost feels like a seduction. Our eyes meet, and then dart apart, but unfortunately our attention lands directly ahead of us, between the heads of the sunscreen teen and her father, where Sophie and Billy are schmoopy-murmuring to each other with their faces only millimeters apart.

"When did you two break up?" I ask quietly.

He looks like he's not going to answer, but then exhales. "About six months ago."

"And she's already engaged?" I let out a soft whistle. "Yeesh."

"I mean, as far as she knows I'm *married*, so I can't be too hurt about it."

"You can be as hurt as you want, but you don't have to *seem* hurt," I say, and when he doesn't answer, I realize I've hit the nail on the head. He's struggling to pretend to be unaffected.

"For what it's worth," I whisper, "Billy looks like a tool. He's the understudy version of Reedus, without any of the scary-sexy charm. This version just looks *oily*."

Ethan grins down at me before seeming to remember that we don't like each other's faces. His smile straightens. "They're just up there making out. There are, like, eight other people in this van. I can see their tongues. It's . . . gross."

"I bet Ethan Thomas has never been inappropriate like that."

"I mean," he says, frowning, "I like to think I can be affectionate, but some things are infinitely better when they happen behind closed doors."

Heat engulfs whatever words remain in my head, and I nod in agreement. The idea of Ethan doing unknown, hot things *behind closed doors* makes everything inside my body turn to goo.

I clear my throat, relieved when I look away, take a deep breath, and the goo dissolves. *Dear Olive Torres: This is Ethan. He is not swoony.*

Ethan leans in a little, catching my eye. "You think you can bring it today?"

"'Bring *it*'?"

"The fake-wife game."

"What's in it for me?" I ask.

"Hm." Ethan taps his chin. "How about I don't tell your boss you're a liar?"

"Okay. Fair." Brainstorming what I can do to help him win the nebulous Best New Partner war I suspect we're fighting with Sophie and Billy, I lean in, meeting him halfway. "I don't want to get your hopes up or anything, but I look really great in this bikini. There's no revenge like being with someone new who has a great rack."

His lip curls. "What an empowering, feminist statement."

"I can appreciate my body in a bikini and still want to set fire to the patriarchy." I look down at my chest. "Who knew what a little meat on my bones would do?"

"Is that what you meant at check-in? About losing your job and baking?"

"Yeah. I'm a stress-baker." I pause. "And eater. I mean, obviously you know that."

He stares at me for a couple of loaded seconds before he says, "You've got a job now. Your baking days can be behind you, if you want." When I look up, he glances quickly away from my boobs. If I didn't definitively know better, I might think he was hoping I'd keep up the baking just a little while longer.

"Yes, I have a job, assuming I can keep it."

"We got through last night, didn't we?" he says. "You'll keep the job."

"And maybe the rack, too."

He reddens a little, and the sign of his discomfort gives me life. But then his eyes do another tiny dip over the front of my cover-up, almost like he can't help himself.

"You had no problem looking in the Skittle dress."

"To be fair, it was a bit like you were wearing a fluorescent light bulb. It drew the eyes."

"After all this, I'm going to have something made for you out of that dress," I promise him. "A tie, maybe. Some sexy briefs."

He chokes a little, shaking his head. After a few beats of silence, he confides, "I had actually just been remembering that Sophie almost got implants when we were together. She always wanted bigger . . ." He mimes cupping boobs.

"You can say it," I tell him.

"Say what?"

"Breasts. Boobs. Jugs. Knockers."

Ethan wipes a hand down his face. "Jesus, Oliver."

I stare at him, daring him to look at me. Finally, he does, and he looks like he wants to crawl out of his skin.

"So she wanted implants," I prompt.

He nods. "I bet she regrets not getting them back when she was enjoying my paychecks."

"Well, there you go. Your fake new wife has great boobs. Be proud."

Hesitating, he says, "But it has to be more than that."

"What do you mean, 'more than that'? I'm not going to wear a thong."

"No, just—" He runs an exasperated hand through his hair. "It's not only about me being with someone hot now."

Wait, what? Hot?

He rolls on like he hasn't said anything completely shocking. "You have to pretend to *like* me, too."

A curl falls over his eye just after he's said this, turning the moment into a Hollywood shot that completely mocks me. A small set of fireworks—only a sparkler, I swear—goes off beneath my breastbone, because he is so goddamn pretty. And seeing him vulnerable, even for a second, is so disorienting it makes me imagine a time when I can look at his face and not hate it.

"I can pretend to like you." I pause, adding out of the self-preservation instinct, "Probably."

Something softens in his demeanor. His hand moves closer, curling around mine, warm and encompassing. My reflex is to jerk away, but he holds me steady, gently, and says, "Good. Because we're going to have to be a lot more convincing on that boat."

chapter **eight**

The boat in question is enormous, with a wide lower deck, a plush indoor area with a bar and grill, and an upper rooftop deck in the full, bright sun. While the rest of the group finds places to stow their bags and get snacks, Ethan and I head straight for the bar, grab drinks, and make our way up the ladder to the empty rooftop. I'm sure the emptiness won't last, but the tiny reprieve from feeling like we're performers onstage is awesome.

It's warm; I take off my cover-up, Ethan takes off his shirt, and then we're both half-naked together, in broad daylight, drowning in silence.

We look at anything but each other. Suddenly I wish we were surrounded by people.

"Nice boat," I say.

"Yeah."

"How's your drink?"

He shrugs. "Cheap liquor. It's fine."

Wind whips my hair into my face, and Ethan holds my vodka tonic while I pull a rubber band out of my bag and tie my hair up. His eyes dart from the horizon to my red bikini and back again.

"I saw that," I say.

He sips his drink. "Saw what?"

"You checked out my chest."

"Of course I did. It's like having two other people up here with us. I don't want to be rude."

As if on cue, a head pops up at the top of the ladder—fucking Reject Daryl Dixon, of course, followed closely by Sophie. I swear I can hear Ethan's soul scream.

They climb onto the deck, holding their own margaritas in plastic cups.

"Hey, guys!" Sophie says, approaching. "Ohmygod. Isn't it *gorge*?"

"*So* gorge," I agree, ignoring Ethan's horrified expression. No way he's judging me any harder than I'm judging myself.

We stand together, the world's unlikeliest foursome, and I attempt to diffuse the uncomfortable tension between us. "So, Billy. Where did you two meet?"

Billy squints up into the sun. "At the grocery store."

"Billy is assistant manager at a Cub Foods in St. Paul,"

Sophie says. "He was stocking school supplies, and I was buying paper plates across the aisle."

I wait, assuming there will be more. There isn't.

The silence stretches on until Ethan comes to the rescue. "The one on Clarence or—?"

"Huh-uh," she hums around her straw, shaking her head as she swallows. "Arcade."

"I don't usually go there," I say. More silence. "I like the one on University."

"Good produce department at that one," Ethan agrees.

Sophie stares at me for a few seconds, and then looks at Ethan. "She looks like Dane's girlfriend."

My stomach drops and inside my cranium, my brain takes the shape of Munch's *The Scream*. Of course Sophie would have met Ami. Individually Ethan and I are above-average intelligent people, so why are we so stupid together?

I send him a barrage of panicked brain waves, but he just nods calmly. "Yeah, they're twins."

Billy lets out an impressed "*Dude*," but Sophie is clearly less excited by the potential for homemade pornos.

"Isn't that sort of weird?" she asks.

I want to shout *YES—VERY—ALL OF THIS IS VERY WEIRD*, but manage to clamp my mouth to my straw and drain about half of my drink. After a long pause of his own, Ethan says, "Not really."

A seagull flies overhead. The boat rocks as we push

through the waves. I reach the bottom of my drink and loudly suck watery air through my straw until Ethan elbows me in the side. This is so painful.

Eventually, Sophie and Billy decide it's time to sit and make their way to a padded bench directly across the deck from where we're standing—close enough that we're very clearly sharing the same general space, but far enough that we no longer have to attempt conversation, or hear whatever disgusting thing Billy is currently whispering in Sophie's ear.

Ethan clamps an arm around my shoulder in a clunky, robotic sign of *We Are Also Affectionate*; again, he was so much smoother last night. With ease, I reach up, sliding my hand around his waist. I'd forgotten he was shirtless, and my palm makes contact with his bare skin. Ethan stiffens a little beside me, so I lean in fully, stroking his hip bone with my thumb.

I'd intended to do it to needle him, but actually . . . it's nice.

His skin is sun-warmed, firm, distracting.

It's like having a single bite of something delicious; I want to go back for more. The point of contact where my thumb touches his hip is suddenly the hottest part of my body.

With a cheesy growl, Billy pulls Sophie onto his lap, and she kicks her feet up, giggly and petite. After a stretch of silence during which I really should have seen it coming, Ethan sits, too, jerking me down onto his thighs. I fall far less gracefully—far less petite—and let out a burp when I land.

"What are you doing?" I ask under my breath.

"God, I don't *know*," he whispers, pained. "Just go with it."

"I can feel your *penis*."

He shifts beneath me. "This was so much easier last night."

"Because you weren't invested!"

"Why is she up here?" he hisses. "There's an entire boat!"

"You guys are so cute over there," Sophie calls, smiling. "So chatty!"

"So chatty," Ethan repeats, smiling through clenched teeth. "Can't get enough of each other."

"Totally," I add, and make it even worse by giving a double thumbs-up.

Sophie and Billy look so natural at this. We, however, do not. It was one thing in the restaurant last night with Mr. Hamilton, where we had our own chairs and some degree of personal space. But here, my sunscreen-slicked legs slide all over Ethan's, and he has to adjust me again. I'm sucking in my stomach and my thighs are shaking from the restraint it's taking to not lean my full weight into him. As if sensing this, he pulls me back into his chest, trying to get me to relax.

"Is this comfortable?" he mumbles.

"No." I am acutely conscious of every doughnut I've ever eaten in my entire life.

"Turn sideways."

"What?"

"Like . . ." He guides both of my legs to the right, helping me curl into his chest. "Better?"

"I mean . . ." Yes. It is better. "Whatever."

He stretches his arms across the deck railing and, gamely, I wrap an arm around his neck, trying to look like someone who enjoys frequent sex with him.

When I glance up, he's just looking up from my chest again.

"Very subtle."

He looks away, blushes, and an electric zap travels down my neck. "They are pretty great, you know," he finally admits.

"I know."

"They do look better in this than in the Skittle dress."

"Your opinion is so important to me." I shift, wondering why I'm so flushed. "And I can feel your penis again."

"Of course you can," he says, with a tiny wink. "It'd be hard not to."

"Is that a size joke, or a boner joke?"

"Uh, definitely a size joke, Orville."

I take a final watery sip of my drink and then exhale directly into his face so that he winces from the fumes of cheap vodka.

Squinting, he says, "You're a real seductress."

"I hear that a lot."

He coughs, and I swear I see Ethan Thomas battling a genuine smile.

And I get it. As much as I hate him . . . I think I'm starting to like *us*.

"Have you ever snorkeled?" I ask.

"Yes."

"Do you like it?"

"Yes."

"Are you usually better at conversations than you are with me?"

"Yes."

We fall back into silence, but we are so close, and across the deck there's only the wet sounds of Sophie and Billy making out. Ethan and I can't *not* talk. "What's your favorite drink?"

He looks at me with pained patience, growling, "Do we have to do this?"

I nod over toward Ethan's ex and her new fiancé, who look like they're only seconds away from dry humping. "Would you rather watch them? Or *we* could make out."

"Caipirinhas," he answers. "You?"

"I'm a margarita girl. But if you like caipirinhas, there's a place a couple miles from my apartment that makes the best ones I've ever had."

"We should go there," he says, and it's clear he's done it without thinking because we both immediately let out the ha-ha-ha of the *Oop, that's not going to happen!* laugh.

"Is it weird that you're not as unpleasant as I initially thought?" he asks.

I use his monosyllabic tactic against him. "Yes."

He rolls his eyes.

Over Ethan's shoulder, the Molokini Crater comes fully into view. It is vibrant green, crescent-shaped, and stunning. Even from here I can see that the clear blue bay is dotted with boats just like ours.

"Look." I nod to the horizon. "We aren't lost at sea."

He lets out a quiet "Wow." And there, for a single breath, we give in to a really lovely moment of enjoying something together. Until Ethan decides to ruin it: "I hope you don't drown out there."

I smile down at him. "If I do, the husband is always a suspect."

"I take back my 'unpleasant' comment."

Another body joins our awkward foursome on the roof: the Snuba instructor, Nick, a sun-streaked blond guy with overtanned skin and bright white teeth, who calls himself an "island boy" but I am fairly sure was born in Idaho or Missouri.

"Who plans to Snuba, and who plans to snorkel?" he asks us.

I toss a hopeful look across the deck to Sophie and Billy—who have mercifully detached their faces from each other—but they both enthusiastically shout, "Snuba!" so I guess we're still stuck with them underwater.

We confirm that we're planning to Snuba, too, and Ethan hauls me up with apparently zero effort, using arms that are remarkably strong. He sets me down an arm's length away in front of him, standing behind me. It's a beat before he seems to remember we should stay in newlywed levels of constant contact, so he folds his arms across my chest, jerking my back against his front. I feel the way we're both already clammy in the heat, and how we immediately suction together.

"Gross," I groan. "You're so sweaty."

His forearm smashes against my boobs.

I step backward, onto his foot. "Oops," I lie, "sorry."

He slides his chest against my back, back and forth, intentionally contaminating me with his man sweat.

He is the worst . . . so why am I fighting the urge to laugh?

Sophie sidles up next to him. "Got your lucky penny?" she asks, and I wish I could explain the tiny jealous monster that rears up inside my chest. She is engaged to someone else. Those little inside jokes and coupley secrets don't belong to her anymore.

Before I can say anything, Ethan slides his arm down, over my chest and across my front so he's pressing a flattened hand to my stomach, holding me tight. "Don't need it anymore. I've got her."

Sophie lets out a highly fake "Aww!" and then looks at me. And wow, it is a loaded, silent exchange. In our heads we are having a dance-off. She is sizing me up, maybe trying to connect the dots from how Ethan went from dating her to marrying me.

I assume that she ended things; otherwise he probably wouldn't care so much about making a show of having a new wife. And I wonder whether the distaste I read on her face is about Ethan moving on so easily or about him moving on with someone who is nothing like her at all.

I lean back against him in an impulsive show of solidarity, and I wonder if he registers that his hips arch subtly against my back in response: an unconscious thrust. Inside my torso, there is an explosion of traitorous butterflies.

A few seconds have passed since he suggested I'm his good luck charm, and it feels too late to say that it's really the opposite—that with my luck, I'll get a sliver on the side of the boat, bleed into the ocean, and attract a school of hungry sharks.

"You all ready to have some fun?" Nick asks, breaking into my frozen silence.

Sophie lets out a sorority girl "Hell yeah!" and high-fives Billy. I expect a forced fist bump from Ethan in response, so am surprised when I feel his lips come in for a soft landing on my cheek.

"Hell yeah!" he whispers into my ear, laughing quietly.

NICK GETS US SUITED UP and fitted with flippers and face masks. The masks only cover our eyes and noses; because we'll be going deeper than with regular snorkeling, we're also given mouthpieces we can breathe through that are attached via a long tube to an oxygen tank on a small raft that we'll pull along the surface above us as we swim. Each tank-raft combination can support two divers, so of course Ethan and I are paired up—which also means we are essentially tethered together.

When we slide into the water and reach for our oxygen nozzles, I can see Ethan investigating the mouthpiece, trying to estimate how many people have slobbered on it and how reliably it's been cleaned between clients. After glancing at me and registering my complete lack of sympathy for his hygiene crisis, he takes a deep breath and shoves it in, giving Nick an ambivalent thumbs-up.

We take hold of the raft that carries our shared oxygen tank. With a final glance at each other over the top, we duck down, disoriented for a beat of breathing through the respirator and seeing through the mask—and, true to habit, we try to swim in opposite directions. Ethan's head pops up above the water's surface again and he jerks his head behind him impatiently, indicating which way he wants to go.

I give in, letting him lead. Underwater, I am immediately consumed with everything around us. The black, yellow, and white kihikihi dart by. Cornet fish slice through our field of vision, sleek and silver. The closer we get to the reef, the more unreal it becomes. With eyes wide behind his mask, Ethan points to a brilliant school of reddish soldierfish as it passes another large mass of exuberant yellow tang. Bubbles erupt from his respirator like confetti.

I don't know how it happens, but one minute I'm struggling to swim faster and the next Ethan's hand is around mine, helping me move toward a small cluster of gray-dotted o'ili. It's so quiet down here; I've honestly never felt this sort of weightless, silent calm, and certainly never in his presence. Soon, Ethan and I are swimming completely in sync, our feet kicking lazily behind us. He points to things he sees; I do the same. There are no words, no verbal jabs. There is no desire to smack him or poke his eyes out—there is only the confusing truth that holding his hand down here isn't just tolerable, it's nice.

BACK NEAR THE BOAT, WE emerge soggy and breathless. Adrenaline dances through me—I want to tell Ethan we should do this every single day of the vacation. But as soon as our masks are pulled up and we are helped from the water, reality returns. Our eyes meet and whatever he was planning to say dies a similar death in his throat.

"That was fun," I say, simply.

"Yeah." He peels off the wetsuit vest, handing it to Nick, and then steps forward when he sees I'm struggling with my zipper. I'm shaking because it's chilly, so I let him unzip me, and work very hard to not notice how big his hands are and how capably he works the stuck zipper free.

"Thanks." I bend, rummaging in my bag for my dry clothes. I am not charmed by him. I am not. "Where should I change?"

Nick winces. "We only have one bathroom, and it tends to get pretty crowded when we start to turn back and everyone's cocktails are hitting their bladder. I'd suggest heading down there soon—but you two are welcome to go in together."

"To . . . gether?" I ask. I look down toward the narrow steps to the bathroom and notice that people are already starting to gather their things to go use it themselves.

"Nothing you haven't seen before!" Ethan says with a wicked grin.

I send a militia of harmful thoughts at him.

He soon regrets being so cavalier. The bathroom is the size of a broom closet. A very small broom closet with a very slippery floor. We crowd into the soggy space, clutching our clothes to our chest. Down here, it feels like the boat is in the middle of a storm; we are victims of every tiny lurch and lean.

"You first," he says.

"Why me first? *You* go first."

"We can both change and get this over with," he says. "You face the door, I'll face the wall."

I hear the wet splat of his board shorts just as I'm working my bikini bottom down my shivering legs, and am highly aware that Ethan's butt is probably only inches away from mine. I experience a moment of pure terror when I imagine how mortifying it would be for our cold, wet butt cheeks to touch.

A little panicky, I scramble for my towel and slip, my right foot coming out from under me in a shallow pool of water near the sink. My foot hooks on something, Ethan shouts in surprise, and I realize that *something* was Ethan's shin. After his hand slaps loudly against the wall, he loses his balance, too.

My back hits the floor, and with a splat, Ethan lands on top of me. If there's pain, I am too distracted by the chaos to register it, and there is a horrified beat of silence where we both realize what's happened: we are completely naked, wet, and clammy, and a tangle of naked arms and legs and *parts* in the most mortifying game of Twister anyone has ever experienced.

"Oh my God, get off me!" I shriek.

"What the fuck, Olive? You knocked me over!"

He attempts to stand, but the floor is slippery and in motion, which means he keeps falling back down on me as he scrambles to find footing. Once we're up, it's clear we both want to die of mortification. We give up on the facing the door or facing the wall in favor of speed; there is no way for us to do this without flashes of butt and boobs and all manner of dangly things, but at this point, we don't care.

Ethan scrambles to pull up a clean pair of shorts, but it takes me about four times as long to stutter-pull my clothing up over my wet body. Thankfully, he's dressed relatively quickly and turns away, pressing his forehead against the wall, eyes closed as I wrestle with my bra and shirt.

"I want you to know," I tell him as I tug it down my torso, "and I'm sure you hear this a lot, but that was by far the worst sexual experience of my life."

"I feel like we should have used protection."

I turn to confirm what I've heard in his voice—repressed laughter again—and catch him smiling, still facing the wall.

"You can turn around now," I say. "I'm decent."

"Are you ever really, though?" he asks, turning and *blushing* and grinning at me. It's a lot to take in.

I wait for the annoyed reaction, but it doesn't arrive. Instead, I realize with surprise that seeing his real smile aimed my way feels like getting a paycheck. "You make a good point."

He seems equally surprised that I haven't snarked back at him, and reaches past me to unlock the door. "I'm feeling queasy. Let's get out of here."

We emerge, red faced for reasons that are immediately misinterpreted, and Ethan gets a high-five from a couple of men we've never met. He follows me to the bar, where I order a margarita and he orders a ginger drink to help his stomach.

One glance at him tells me that he wasn't kidding about feeling queasy—he looks green. We find seats inside, out of the sun but near a window, and he leans forward, pressing his head to the pane, trying to breathe.

I blame this moment right here, because it creates a tiny fracture in his role as nemesis. A true nemesis doesn't show weakness, and for sure, when I reach out to rub his back, a true nemesis wouldn't lean into it, moaning in quiet relief. He wouldn't shift so that I could reach him more easily, and he certainly wouldn't scoot down the bench and rest his head in my lap, staring up at me in gratitude when I gently rake my fingers through his hair, soothing.

Ethan and I are starting to build more of these good moments than bad; it sends the balance swinging into an unfamiliar direction.

And I think I really like it.

Which makes me incredibly uneasy.

"I still hate you," I tell him, pushing a dark curl of hair off his forehead.

He nods. "I know you do."

chapter **nine**

Once we're back on solid ground, most of his color returns, but rather than push our luck—or risk having to dine with Sophie and Billy—we decide to turn in early and order room service.

Although he takes his dinner in the living room, and I take mine in the bedroom, it occurs to me somewhere between my first bite of ravioli and my fourth episode of *GLOW* that I could have sent Ethan back to the hotel and gone out myself. I could have done a hundred different things without even leaving the hotel grounds, and yet here I am, back in the room at night because Ethan had a rough day. At least now I'm only a room away if he needs someone.

Needs someone . . . like *me*? I want to point at and tease myself and this new tenderness for thinking Ethan would seek *me* out as a source of comfort at any time other than when we're trapped on a boat. He wouldn't, and that's not what we're here for anyway!

But as soon as I start shadowboxing myself into a mental froth about needing to enjoy my vacation and not slide into liking this guy who has only been quasi-friendly to me in paradise but never in real life—I remember what it felt like underwater at the crater, how his front felt all along my back up on the deck of the boat, how it felt to run my fingers through his hair. My heartbeat goes all haywire thinking about how his breathing started to sync with the pace of my nails scratching lightly over his scalp.

And then I burst out laughing remembering our naked Twister in the Bathroom of Doom.

"Are you laughing about the bathroom?" he calls from the other room.

"I will be laughing about the bathroom until the end of time."

"Same."

I find myself smiling in the direction of the living room, and realize that staying firmly on Team I Hate Ethan Thomas is going to be more work than it may be worth.

MORNING COMES TO THE ISLAND in a slow, blurry brightening of the sky. Yesterday morning, the cool overnight humidity was gradually burned off by sunshine, but not today. Today, it rains.

It's chilly as I shuffle out of the bedroom in search of coffee. The suite is still pretty dark, but Ethan is awake. He's stretched along the full length of the sofa bed with a thick book open in front of him. He wisely leaves me alone until the caffeine has had time to work its way into my system.

Eventually, I make my way into the living room. "What are your plans today?" I'm still in my pajamas but feeling much more human.

"You're looking at it." He closes the book, resting it on his chest. The image is immediately filed in my brain-cyclopedia as an Ethan Posture, and subcategorized as Surprisingly Hot. "But preferably at the pool with an alcoholic beverage in my hand."

In unison, we frown at the window. Fat drops shake the palm fronds outside, and rain runs softly down the balcony door.

"I wanted to paddleboard . . ." I wilt.

He picks the book back up. "Doesn't look like that'll happen."

My knee-jerk instinct is to glare at him, but he's not even looking at me anymore. I grab the hotel guidebook from the TV stand. There has to be something I can do in the rain; Ethan and I are capable of spending time together *outside*, but there would be bloodshed if we both hung around in this suite all day.

I pull the phone closer and open the directory in front of me. Ethan moves to my side and reads the list of activities over my shoulder. His presence is already—suddenly—like an enormous cast of heat moving around the room and now he's standing shoulder to shoulder with me. My voice grows wavery as I read down the list.

"Zip-lining . . . helicopter . . . hike . . . submarine . . . kayaking . . . off-roading . . . bike ride . . ."

He stops me before I can get to the next one. "Ooh. Paintball."

I look at him blankly. Paintball always struck me as something that gun-obsessed, testosterone-fueled frat boys did. Ethan doesn't really seem the type. "You've played paintball?"

"No," he says, "but it looks fun. How hard can it be?"

"That feels like a dangerous taunt to the universe, Ethan."

"The universe doesn't care about my paintball game, *Olive*."

"My dad gave me a flare gun once when I took a road trip in college with a boyfriend. It went off in the trunk and set our luggage on fire while we were swimming in a river. We had to go to a local Walmart to buy clothes—keep in mind, all we had were our wet bathing suits—and it was this tiny town, like seriously just populated by the creepy people from *Deliverance.* I have never felt more like someone's future dinner than I did walking through the aisles trying to find new underwear."

He studies me for several long seconds. "You have a lot of stories like this, don't you?"

"You have no idea." I glance at the window again. "But seriously. If it's been raining all night, won't it be all muddy?"

He leans against the counter. "So you'd only want to be covered in paint, but definitely not mud?"

"I think the goal is to *not* get covered in paint."

"You are incapable of not arguing with me," he says, "and it is so aggravating."

"Weren't *you* just arguing with me about being covered in paint but not mud?"

He growls, but I see him fighting a smile.

I point across the room. "Why don't you go over to the minibar and work out that aggravation?"

Ethan leans back in, closer than before. He smells unbelievably good, and it is unbelievably annoying. "Let's do paintball today."

Turning the page, I shake my head. "Hard nope."

"Come on," he wheedles. "You can pick what we do after."

"Why do you even want to hang out with me? We don't like each other."

He grins. "You are clearly not thinking about this strategically. You'll get to shoot me with paint pellets."

A video game montage scrolls through my head: my gun spitting out a stream of Skittle-green paintballs, green splatters landing in bursts all across the front of Ethan's vest. And finally, the kill shot—a giant green splat right over his groin. "You know what? I'll go ahead and make us some reservations."

THE HOTEL ARRANGES A BUS to take us to the paintball field. We stop in front of an industrial building fronted by a parking lot on one side, with forest all around. It isn't outright raining—more like a steady, misty drizzle—and oh yeah, it's *muddy*.

Inside, the office is small and smells like—you guessed it—dirt and paint. A big and tall white dude in a hybrid floral/camouflage Hawaiian shirt with a name tag that reads HOGG stands behind the counter to welcome us. He and Ethan discuss the various options for play, but I'm barely listening. Above the counter the walls are covered with helmets and body armor, goggles and gloves. A poster hangs next to another door and reads: STAY CALM AND RELOAD. There are also guns, lots of them.

It's probably a bad time to realize I've never held a gun before, let alone shot one.

Hogg moves to a back room and Ethan turns to me, pointing to a wall with a list of names and rankings—players who have won some sort of paintball war. "This seems pretty intense."

I point to the other side of the room, and a sign that says WARNING: MY BALLS MIGHT HIT YOU IN THE FACE. "The word I think Hogg was going for is 'classy.'" I pick up an empty paintball gun made to resemble a rifle. "Do you remember that scene in *9 to 5* where Jane Fonda is dressed in safari gear and goes through the office looking for Mr. Hart?"

"No," Ethan says, tilting his head up at the gear on the walls, sweetly oblivious. "Why?"

I grin when he looks down at me. "No reason." Pointing to the wall, I ask, "Have you ever shot a gun before?"

Minnesota has some pretty avid sport hunters and who knows? Maybe Ethan is one of them.

He nods and then falls silent while my brain goes down a crazy tunnel, imagining the tragedy of a zebra head mounted on his living room wall. Or a lion. Oh my God, what if he's one of those horrible people who goes to Africa and hunts rhinos?

My fury at this version of Ethan Thomas starts to return

in its full, heated glory, but then he adds, "Just at the shooting range with Dane a couple times, though. It's more his thing than mine." He does a double take when he sees my face. "What?"

I pull in a hulking lungful of air, realizing I just did what I always seem to do, which is to immediately dive into the worst-case scenario. "Before you clarified that, I had an image of you in a safari hat with your foot propped up on a dead giraffe."

"Stop that," he says. "Gross."

I shrug, wincing. "It's just how I'm built."

"Just get to know me, then. Give me the benefit of the doubt."

He says these words calmly, almost offhand, and then frowns down at a belt buckle on the counter that reads, *The first rule of gun safety: Don't piss me off.*

But I'm still reeling in the deep enormity of his insight—and how exposed I suddenly feel—when Hogg returns, thick arms loaded with gear. He hands us each a pair of camouflage coveralls and gloves, a helmet, and a set of goggles. The gun is plastic and very lightweight, with a long barrel and a plastic hopper affixed to the top where the paintballs are stored. But everything else is heavy. I try to imagine running in this and can't.

Ethan inspects his gear and leans over the counter. "Do you have any, uh, protection?"

"Protection?"

The tops of Ethan's ears turn red, and I know in that moment that he is a mind reader and saw my imaginary green paint splats all over his junk. He stares at Hogg meaningfully, but Hogg just shakes his head with a laugh.

"Don't worry about it, big fella. You're gonna be just fine."

I pat his shoulder. "Yeah, big fella. I've got your back."

THE GAME TAKES PLACE ON five acres of dense forest. Dozens of wooden shelters lead off into the tree line, bundles of logs are scattered for cover, and a few bridges stretch overhead, spanning the length between trees. We're instructed to gather, along with other players, beneath a large metal overhang. The rain is more mist than droplets now, but there's a damp chill in the air and I feel my shoulders inch up toward my ears beneath my baggy coveralls.

Ethan glances down at me, and from behind his goggles his eyes crinkle in mirth. He's barely stopped laughing since I stepped out of the changing stall.

"You look like a cartoon," he says.

"I mean, it's super flattering on you, too," I shoot back. But as far as comebacks go, it's pretty limp given that Ethan actually does look pretty great in the camo paintball get-up.

He has this sexy-soldier thing happening that I did not expect to be into, but apparently I am.

"Elmer Fudd," he adds. "Hunting wabbits."

"Would you shut up?"

"You're like a pathetic Private Benjamin."

"Private Benjamin is already pretty pathetic."

Ethan is gleeful. "I know!"

Blessed be: our instructor, Bob, approaches. He is short but solid and paces in front of our group like a general readying his troops. One immediately gets the sense that Bob wanted to be a cop but it didn't work out.

He tells us we'll be playing a version called *death match*. It sounds both great and terrible: our group of about twenty is split up into two teams, and we essentially just run around shooting each other until everyone on one team is eliminated.

"Each player has five lives," he says, eyeing each of us shrewdly as he passes. "Once you're hit you'll lock your weapon, attach the barrel cover, and return to camp." He points to a small building wrapped in protective fencing; a scribbled sign reading BASE CAMP hangs overhead. "You'll stay there until your wait time is up, then return to the game."

Ethan leans in, his words warm against my ear. "No hard feelings when I take you out immediately, right?"

I look up at him. His hair is damp from the humidity,

and he's biting back a grin. He's literally biting his lip, and for a breathy moment I want to reach out and tug it free.

But I'm mostly glad he doesn't assume that we're going to be working together today.

"Don't threaten me with a good time," I say.

"There are some hard and fast rules," Bob continues. "Safety first. If you think it's dumb, don't do it. Goggles on, always. Anytime your gun is not in use, you are to keep it locked and the barrel covered. That includes if you've been hit and are exiting the field."

Someone claps just behind me and I look over my shoulder. A tall, heavyset bald man is nodding along with the instructor and practically vibrating with energy. He's also shirtless, which seems . . . *odd*, and wearing a utility belt with canisters of extra paint and supplies. I share a quizzical look with Ethan.

"You've played before?" Ethan surmises.

"As often as I can," the man says. "Clancy." He reaches out, shaking Ethan's hand.

"Ethan." He points to me, and I wave. "Her name's Skittle."

"Actually," I say, glaring up at him, "it's—"

"You must be pretty good then," Ethan says to Clancy.

Clancy folds hairy arms across his chest. "I've hit prestige in *Call of Duty* about twelve times, so I'll let you be the judge."

I can't resist. "If you don't mind my asking, why aren't you wearing a shirt? Won't it hurt to be hit?"

"The pain is part of the experience," Clancy explains. Ethan nods like this makes a hell of a lot of sense, but I know him well enough by now to see the amusement in his eyes.

"Any tips for newbies?" I ask.

Clancy is clearly delighted to have been asked. "Use the trees—they're better than flat surfaces because you can move around them, real slinky. For lookout, always bend at the waist." He illustrates for us, popping up and down a few times. "Keeps the rest of your body protected. Don't, and you'll know what it feels like to take a power ball to your biscuits at two hundred and seventy feet per second." He blinks over to me. "No offense, Skittle."

I wave him off. "No one likes being hit in the biscuits."

He nods, continuing. "Most important, never, *ever* go prone. Hit the ground, and you're a dead man."

People around us clap as Bob finishes and begins to divide us up into two teams. Ethan and I deflate a little when we both end up on Team Thunder. This means, sadly, I will not be hunting him through the forest. His dismay deepens when he sees the opposing team: a small handful of adults and a group of seven fourteen-year-old boys here for a birthday party.

"Hold up," Ethan says, motioning in their direction. "We can't shoot at a bunch of *kids*."

One with braces and a backward cap steps forward. "Who're you calling a kid? You scared, Grandpa?"

Ethan grins easily. "If your mom drove you here, you're a kid."

His friends snicker in the background, egging him on. "Actually, *your* mom drove me here. Took my dick in the back seat."

At this, Ethan lets out a bursting laugh. "Yeah, that sounds exactly like something Barb Thomas would do." He turns away.

"Look at him hiding like a little bitch," the kid says.

Bob steps in and levels a glare at the teen. "Watch your mouth." He turns to Ethan. "Save it for the field."

"I think Bob just gave me permission to take out that little asshole," Ethan says in wonder, lowering his goggles.

"Ethan, he's scrawny."

"Means I won't waste much ammo on him."

I put a hand on his arm. "You may be taking this a little too seriously."

He grins over at me and winks so I can see he's just having fun. Something flutters alive in my rib cage. Playful Ethan is the newest evolution in my traveling partner, and I am completely here for it.

• • •

"I FEEL LIKE I SHOULD have paid closer attention to the rules." Ethan is panting at my side, mud-streaked and splattered with purple paint. We both are. Spoiler alert: paintball fucking hurts. "Is there a time limit for this game?" He pulls out his phone and starts Googling, groaning when the service is spotty.

I roll my head back against the wooden shelter and squint up into the sky. Our team's original plan was to divide up and hide near the bunkers, assigning a few defenders to stay in the neutral territory and cover advancing attackers. I'm not really sure where that plan went wrong, but at some point there was an ill-advised ambush and there are only four of us remaining. Everyone on the opposing team—including all the teenage shit-talkers—is still in.

Now Ethan and I are trapped behind a dilapidated wall, being hunted from all sides by children who are way more cutthroat than we expected. "Are they still out there?" I ask.

Ethan stretches to see over the barricade and immediately drops back down again. "Yeah."

"How many?"

"I only saw two. I don't think they know where we are."

He crawls to look out the other side and quickly gives up. "One of them is pretty far away, the other is just hanging out on the bridge. I say we wait. Someone will come by and draw his attention sooner or later, and we can run for that stand of trees over there."

A few seconds pass, filled with the sound of distant screams and the occasional eruption of paintballs. This is about as far from the real world as I can imagine. I can't believe I'm enjoying myself.

"Maybe we should try to outrun them," I say. I don't relish the thought of taking more paintballs to the ass, but it's cold and damp where we're hunkered, and my thighs are starting to do the shaky cramp dance. "We might be able to get away. You're surprisingly not terrible at this."

He glances at me and then squints back out to the woods. "You have the agility of a boulder. We should probably stay put."

I reach out and kick him, tickled when he grunts in feigned pain.

Because we're just squatting here, hiding from a group of aggressive pubescent boys, I'm tempted to strike up conversation, but hesitate, immediately second-guessing myself. Do I *want* to get to know Ethan? I used to think I already knew the most important thing about him—that he's a judgmental dude who has a thing against curvy women eating high-calorie State Fair food. But I've also learned that:

1. He does something math-y for work.
2. To my knowledge, he's had one girlfriend in the time since I first met him two and a half years ago.
3. He is very good at frowning (but also great at smiling).
4. He insists he doesn't mind sharing food; he just does not eat at buffets.
5. He often takes his younger brother on expensive, adventurous trips.

The rest of the list slides into my thoughts, uninvited.

6. He's actually hilarious.
7. He gets seasick.
8. He seems to be made of muscle; must confirm somehow that there are actual organs inside his torso.
9. He's competitive but not in a scary way.
10. He can be exceedingly charming if bribed with a comfortable mattress.
11. He thinks I *always look great.*
12. He remembered my shirt from the third time we met.
13. From what I can tell, he has a nice penis in those pants.

Why am I thinking about Ethan's penis? Super gross.

Obviously, I came here with what I thought was a pretty clear picture of who he was, but I have to admit that version seems to be crumbling.

"Well, since we've got some time to kill," I say, and move from more of a squat to a sit, "can I ask you a totally personal and invasive question?"

He rubs at the spot on his leg. "If it means you won't kick me again, yes."

"What happened between you and Sophie? Also, how did you two happen in the first place? She is very . . . hmm, *90210*. And you seem more . . . hmm, *Big Bang Theory*."

Ethan closes his eyes and then leans to look outside the barricade. "Maybe we should just run for it—"

I pull him back. "We have one more life each, and I'm using you as a human shield if we leave. Talk."

He takes a deep breath and blows his cheeks out as he exhales. "We were together for about two years," he says. "I was living in Chicago at the time, if you remember, and went to the Twin Cities to visit Dane. I stopped by his office and she worked in the same building. I saw her in the parking lot. She'd dropped a box full of papers, and I helped her pick them up."

"That sounds like an incredibly clichéd beginning to a movie."

To my surprise, he laughs at this.

"And you moved there?" I ask. "Just like that."

"It wasn't 'just like that.'" He reaches to wipe some mud from his face, and I like the gesture, the way I can tell it comes from vulnerability during this conversation more than vanity. In a weird burst of awareness, I register this is the first time I'm really *talking* to Ethan. "It was after a few months, and I'd had a standing job offer in the Cities for a while. Once I was back in Minneapolis, we decided, you know, why not? It made sense to move in together."

I pull my jaw closed once I register that it's been hanging open. "*Wow.* It takes me a few months to decide if I like a new shampoo enough to stick with it."

Ethan laughs, but it's not a particularly happy sound and makes something squeeze inside my chest.

"What happened?" I ask.

"She didn't cheat or anything that I know of. We got an apartment in Loring Park, and things were good. *Really* good." He meets my eyes for a brief pulse, almost like he's not sure I'll believe him. "I was going to propose on the Fourth of July."

I lift a brow in question at the specific date, and he reaches up to scratch his neck, embarrassed. "I thought it might be cool to do it while the fireworks were going off."

"Ah, a grand gesture. I'm not sure I would have pegged you as the type."

He laugh-groans. "I got that far, if that's what you're wondering. A friend was having a barbecue, and we went over to his place, hung out for a while, then I took her up to the roof and proposed. She cried and we hugged, but it registered later that she never actually said yes. Afterward we went back inside and started to help him clean up. Sophie said she wasn't feeling great and would meet me at home. When I got there, she was gone."

"Wait, you mean like *gone* gone?"

He nods. "Yep. All her stuff was gone. She'd packed up and left me a note on a dry-erase board in our kitchen."

My brows come together. "A *dry-erase board*?"

" 'I don't think we should get married. Sorry.' That's what she said. *Sorry.* Like she was telling me she splattered tomato sauce on my favorite shirt. You know I cleaned that board a hundred times and those damn words never went away? And I don't mean that in a metaphorical sense. She used a Sharpie, not a dry-erase marker, and it literally stained the words into the board."

"Oof. That's awful. You know you can actually get rid of permanent marker if you go over the words with a dry-erase one. Not that that's particularly helpful now . . ."

He blinks at me. "I'll remember that for next time."

"I can't believe you grand-gestured, and she dry-erase-boarded you. God, no offense, but Sophie is a giant dick."

This time when he laughs, it's louder, lighter, and the smile reaches his eyes. "None taken. It was a dick thing to do, even if I'm glad she did it. I thought we were happy, but the truth is, our relationship lived on the surface. I don't think it would have worked much longer." He pauses. "I just wanted to be settled, maybe. I think I grand-gestured for the wrong person. I realize I need someone I can talk to, and she doesn't really like to go too deep."

This doesn't entirely mesh with my image of him as a jet-setting daredevil, but then again, neither did the vision of him on the plane, clutching the armrests. Now I have new Ethan Facts to add to the list.

14. Doesn't know how to Google cleaning tips.
15. He's introspective.
16. As much as he would probably deny it now, he's a romantic.

I wonder whether there are two very different sides of Ethan, or I've just never looked much deeper than what Dane and Ami have told me about him all this time.

Remembering the way he froze when he saw Sophie on our way back to the hotel, I ask, "Had you seen each other since then? Before—"

"Before dinner with Charlie and Molly? Nope. She still lives in Minneapolis. I know that. But I never saw her around. I definitely didn't know she was engaged."

"How do you feel about it?"

He taps his finger on the edge of a stick and stares off

into the distance. "I'm not sure. You know what I realized on the boat? We broke up in July. She said they met while he was stocking school supplies. That's August? Maybe September? She waited a month. I was such a mess after—like big time. I think a part of me thought we might actually get back together until I saw her at the hotel, and it all hit me at once that I was being totally delusional."

"I'm sorry," I say, simply.

He nods, smiling at the ground. "Thanks. It sucked, but I'm better now."

Better now doesn't necessarily mean *over her*, but I'm kept from asking for clarification when shots ring through the air, too close for comfort. We both jump, and Ethan pushes himself up to peek over the edge while I stumble to stand next to him. "What's happening?"

"I'm not sure . . ." He moves from one side of the enclosure to the other, watching, his finger resting on the trigger.

I clutch my own gun to my side, and my heart is pounding in my ears. It's just a game, and I could technically surrender at any time, but my body doesn't seem to know that it isn't real.

"How many shots do you have left?" he asks.

I was a little trigger-happy at the start of the game, firing off in random bursts without really focusing on aim. My gun feels light. "Not many." I peek inside the hopper, where four yellow balls roll around in the plastic canister. "Four."

Ethan opens up his own hopper and drops two more into my gun. Footsteps pound on the dirt. It's Clancy, still shirtless and nothing more than a pasty, skin-colored blur. He fires off a shot and ducks behind a tree. "Run!" he shouts.

Ethan reaches for my sleeve, tugging me away from the wall and pointing toward the woods. "Go!"

I break into a sprint, feet pounding against the wet ground. I'm not sure if he's behind me but I race for the next tree and duck behind it. Ethan slides to a stop across the clearing and looks back. A single player is just wandering around.

"It's that big, mouthy kid," he whispers, grinning. "Look at him all alone."

I peer into the woods around us, uneasy. "Maybe he's waiting for someone."

"Or maybe he's lost. Kids are dumb."

"My ten-year-old cousin built a robot cat out of some gum, a couple of screws, and a Coke can," I tell him. "Kids these days are way smarter than we were. Let's *go.*"

Ethan shakes his head. "Let's take him out first. He only has one life left."

"*We* only have one life left."

"It's a game, the object is to win."

"We have to sit down the entire drive back. My bruised ass doesn't care if we win."

"Let's give it two minutes. If we can't get a shot, we'll run."

I reluctantly agree and Ethan motions for us to cut through the trees and surprise him on the other side. I follow closely, watching the woods and keeping my steps quiet. But Ethan is right, there's nobody else around.

When we reach the edge of the small clearing, the kid is still there, just hanging out, poking at sticks with his gun. Ethan leans in, his mouth next to my ear. "He's got a fucking headphone in. How cocky do you have to be to listen to music in the middle of a war zone?"

I pull back to see his face. "You're really enjoying this, aren't you?"

His smile is wide. "Oh, yeah."

Ethan lifts his gun, silently creeping forward with me at his side.

We're two steps into the clearing when the kid looks up with a sneer, lips curled around a set of heavy braces. He raises his middle finger, and only then do I realize it's a trap. We don't turn in time to see his buddy come from behind us, but the next thing I know, my entire ass is purple.

"I CAN'T BELIEVE HE FLIPPED us off before his buddy shot us," Ethan growls. "Smug little shit."

We're in the relaxation room of the hotel spa, waiting to be called back, and dressed in matching white robes. We are both so sore we didn't even balk when we remembered what the *couple* part of a couple's massage entails: being naked and oiled up in the same room together.

The door opens and a smiling dark-haired woman walks in. We follow her down a long, dimly lit hall to an even darker room. A sunken hot tub bubbles in the center; steam rises invitingly.

Ethan and I make eye contact and then immediately look away. I clutch at my robe, aware that I'm not wearing anything underneath. I thought we'd head straight for the massage tables, enduring only a few quick moments of awkward maneuvering while we slipped under our respective sheets.

"I thought we were just scheduled for massages?" I say.

"Your package comes with time in the whirlpool for a presoak, and then your therapists will meet you." Her voice is feathery and calm. "Is there anything else I can get you, Mr. and Mrs. Thomas?"

Instinct has me opening my mouth to correct her, but Ethan swoops in.

"I think we're good," he says, and smiles his megawatt smile. "Thank you."

"Enjoy." She bows, and then quietly closes the door behind her.

The hot tub gurgles between us.

His smile slips away and he looks up at me, grim. "I'm not wearing anything under here," Gesturing to the ties of his robe, he adds, "I assume you're equally—"

"Yep."

He considers the steaming water, and his longing is nearly palpable. "Look," he says, at length. "Do what you've got to do, but I can hardly walk. I'm getting in."

The words are barely out before he tugs at the tie and I get a flash of bare chest. Turning abruptly, I'm suddenly very interested in the table of snacks and bottled waters against the wall. There's some shuffling and the sound of fabric falling to the ground before he moans, deep and low, "Holy shiiiiiiit." The sound is like a tuning fork, and a shiver rockets through my body. "Olivier, you have to get in."

I pick up a little cup of dried fruit, take a nibble. "I'm good."

"We're both adults here, and you can't even see anything. Look."

I turn and reluctantly glance over my shoulder. He's right, the bubbling water reaches just below his shoulders, but it's still a problem. Who knew I had such a thing for collarbones? His mouth tugs up into a smile and he leans back, stretching his arms across the sides and sighing dramatically. "God, this feels amazing."

Every one of my bruises and sore muscles practically

whimpers in reply. The steam is like a set of fingers luring me in. Bubbles, jets, and the subtle scent of lavender everywhere.

Naked collarbones.

"*Fine*," I say, "but close your eyes." He does, but I bet he can still peek. "And cover them, too." He cups his palm across his eyes, grinning. "With *both* hands."

Once he's sufficiently blinded, I wrestle out of my robe. "When I signed up for this honeymoon, I had no idea it would involve so much nudity."

Ethan laughs from behind his hands, and I dip my foot into the water. Warmth engulfs me—it's almost too hot—and I hiss as I sink deeper into the water. It feels unreal, the heat and bubbles all along my skin.

I let out a shaky breath. "Oh *God*, this feels so good."

His back straightens.

"You can look. I'm decent," I say.

He lowers his hands, expression wary. "That's debatable."

Jets pulse against my shoulders and the bottoms of my feet. My head lolls to the side. "This feels so good, I don't even care what you say."

"Well then, I wish I had the energy to say something really bright."

I snort out a laugh. I feel drunk. "I am so glad I'm allergic to shellfish."

Ethan sinks lower into the water. "I know we're paying the price, but did you have fun today?"

Maybe it's the fact that the hot water has left me more Jell-O than sore muscles and bruises, but I actually did. "Even considering I had to throw away my favorite tennis shoes and can barely sit? Yeah, I did. You?"

"I did. Actually, aside from the whole Sophie thing, this vacation hasn't been completely terrible."

I peek at him through one eye. "Whoa, easy on the flattery."

"You know what I mean. I thought I'd hang by myself at the pool, eat too much, and head home with a tan. I thought I'd *tolerate* you."

"I feel like I should be offended by that, but . . . same, really."

"Which is why it's so crazy to be *here.*" Ethan motions around us before stretching to reach a pair of bottled waters on the ledge of the tub. My eyes follow the movement, the way the muscles of his back bunch and then lengthen, the way droplets of water roll off his skin. So much skin. "God, your sister would freak if she could see us now."

I blink back to attention, reaching for the bottle he hands me. "My sister?"

"Yeah."

"My sister thinks you're cool."

"She . . . really?"

"Yeah. She hates all the trips you and Dane go on, but she doesn't get my Ethan hate."

"Huh," he says, considering this.

"But don't worry, I'm not going to tell her I've enjoyed small snippets of your company. A smug Ami is the worst Ami."

"You don't think she'll be able to tell? Don't you guys have some kind of twin telepathy or something?"

I laugh as I twist open my water. "Sorry to disappoint you, but no."

"What's it like having a twin?"

"What's it's like *not* having a twin?" I reply, and he laughs.

"Touché."

Ethan must be warm because he slides back a little before moving to a different bench inside the hot tub, one that's a little higher and leaves more skin exposed to the air.

The problem, you see, is that it also leaves more skin exposed to me.

A lot more.

I see shoulders, collarbones, chest . . . and when he reaches up to push his hair off his forehead, I'm shown several inches of abs below his nipples.

"Have you guys always been so . . ." He trails off, waving a lazy hand like I know what he's asking.

And I do. "Different? Yeah. According to my mom,

since we were babies. Which is good, because trying to keep up with Ami would have driven me insane by now."

"She's definitely a lot. Is it weird now that she's married?"

"It's been different since she met Dane, but that was bound to happen, you know? Ami's life is plugging along like it's supposed to. I'm the one who stalled out somewhere."

"But that's all about to change. That's got to be exciting."

"It is." It's strange to be talking about this stuff with Ethan, but his questions seem genuine, his interest sincere. He makes me want to talk, to ask questions. "You know, I don't think I know what you do for a living. Something with math? You showed up to Ami's birthday party in a suit and tie, but I just assumed you'd evicted some orphans or put small mom-and-pop shops out of business."

Ethan rolls his eyes. "I'm a digital identification planner for a research company."

"That sounds made up. Like in *Father of the Bride* when she tells Steve Martin that her fiancé is an independent communications consultant, and he says that's code for 'unemployed.' "

He laughs over the top of his water bottle. "We can't all have jobs as self-explanatory as 'drug dealer.' "

"Har, har."

"Specifically," he says, "I specialize in budgetary analysis and breakdown, but in simple terms I tell my company how much each of our clients should spend on digital advertising."

"Is that fancy for 'Boost this Facebook post! Put that much on Twitter!'?"

"Yes, Olive," he says dryly. "That's often what it is. Mostly, you're right, it's a lot of math."

I scrunch up my face. "Hard pass."

He lets loose a shy smile that rattles my bones. "Honestly? I've always loved geeking out about numbers and data, but this is next level."

"And you seriously dig it?"

He shrugs, lifting a distractingly muscular shoulder. "I always wanted a job where I could just play around with numbers all day, looking at them in different ways, try to crack algorithms and anticipate patterns—this job lets me do all of that. I know it sounds super geeky, but I genuinely enjoy it."

Huh. My job has always just been a job. I love talking science, but I don't always love the sales aspect of the position. Basically, I tolerate it because it's what I've been trained to do and I'm good at it. But Ethan talking about his job is surprisingly hot. Or maybe it's just the water, which continues to bubble between us. The heat is making me drowsy, slightly light-headed.

Careful to keep the boobage below the surface, I reach for a towel. “I feel like I’m melting,” I say.

Ethan hums in agreement. “I’ll get out first and let the therapists know we’re ready.”

“Sounds good.”

He uses his finger to indicate that I should turn around. “Not that we haven’t seen everything already,” he says. I hear him drying off, and the image of it does weird, electric things to my body. “The Bathroom of Doom sort of took care of that.”

“I feel like I should apologize,” I say. “You did throw up directly afterward.”

He laughs quietly, under his breath. “As if *that* would be my reaction to seeing you naked, Olive.”

The door opens and closes again. When I turn to ask him what he meant, he’s gone.

ETHAN DOESN’T COME BACK TO get me, and as soon as Diana, our new massage therapist, leads me down to the couples’ massage room, I see why. He seems to be frozen in horror, staring at the massage table.

“What’s with you?” I ask out of the corner of my mouth as Diana walks across the room to dim the lights.

“Do you see two tables in here?” he whispers back.

I look back and don't get what he's saying until— Oh. "Wait," I say, looking up at him. "I thought we were each getting a massage?"

Diana smiles calmly. "You will, of course. But since I'll be teaching you, and you'll be practicing on each other, we can only do one at a time."

My head whips up to Ethan, and we share the exact same thought, I know it: *Oh, hell no.*

Diana mistakes our terror for something else, because she laughs lightly, saying, "Don't worry. Many couples are nervous when they come in, but I'll show you some different techniques and then leave you to practice them, so you don't feel like you're being graded or supervised."

Is this a brothel? I want to ask, but of course don't. Barely. Ethan stares bleakly at the table again.

"Now," Diana says, walking around the table to lift the sheet for one of us to climb under, "which of you would like to learn first, and which wants to receive the massage?"

Ethan's answering silence has to mean that he's doing the same mental calculation I am: *Do we have to stay?*

Particularly given his exit line about reacting to seeing me naked, I have no idea how this question shakes down in Ethan's brain, but given my newfound fascination with his collarbones, chest hair, and abdominals, I'm actually tempted to go through with it. And I'm wondering whether it would be easier to receive a massage first so I don't have to touch him and pretend to be unaffected. That said, one look at his enormous, strong hands and I'm not sure having those fingers oil-slicked and rubbing all over my naked back would be that much easier.

"I'll learn first," I say, just as Ethan says, "I'll massage her first."

Our wide eyes meet.

"No," I say, "you can climb in. I'll, um, do the rubbing."

He laughs uncomfortably. "Seriously, it's cool. I'll massage first."

"I'm going to grab some towels," Diana says gently, "and give you time to decide."

Once she's gone, I turn to him. "Get in the sheets, Elmo."

"I'd really rather do the . . ." He mimes squeezing, like he's going to honk my boobs.

"I don't think there will be any of *that*."

"No, I just mean—" He growls, wiping a hand down his face. "Just get on the table. I'll turn around so you can slip in. Naked, or whatever."

It's dim in here, but I can tell he's blushing. "Are you—oh, my God, Ethan, are you worried about getting a boner on the table?"

He lifts his chin, swallowing. It's a good five seconds before he answers. "Actually, yeah."

And with that one single word, my heart gives an aching

jab against my breastbone. His response was so honest and real that my throat becomes tight at the thought of teasing him.

"Oh," I say, and lick my lips. My mouth is suddenly so dry. I look over at the table and feel my skin grow a little clammy. "Okay. I'll get in the sheets. Just—I mean, just don't make fun of my body."

He goes totally silent, totally still, before whispering an impassioned "I would *never* do that."

"I mean, sure," I say, feeling acutely the way my voice comes out a little strangled, "except when you *have*."

He opens his mouth to reply, brow furrowed in deep concern, but Diana returns with her stack of towels. Ethan huffs out an incredulous breath through his nose, and even when I look away, I can tell he's trying to get my eyes back on his face. I've always appreciated my body—I even sort of like my new curves—but I don't want to be in a position where I feel like anyone has to touch me and doesn't want to.

Then again, if I don't trust him and don't want him touching me, I could just tell Diana we aren't up for this today.

So why don't I?

Is the truth that I really, *really* want Ethan's hands on me?

And if he doesn't want to, he can tell her himself, right?

I look at him, searching for any sign that he's uncomfortable, but his sweet blush is gone, and instead he wears a look of heated determination. Our eyes meet for one . . . two . . . three seconds, and then his gaze drops to my lips, to my neck, and down the entire length of my body. His brow quirks, lips part a little, and I catch how his breathing picks up. When he meets my eyes again, I hear what he's trying to tell me: *I like what I see.*

Flushed, I fumble with the tie of my robe; we're supposed to be married, which means we're supposed to know what the other looks like naked, and although we definitely got flashes in the bathroom on the boat, I'm not sure I'm ready for Ethan to get such a lingering, steady look when I drop the robe and hop up on the table. Thankfully, as Diana holds the sheet up and turns her face away to give me privacy, Ethan also makes a show of fiddling with his robe tie. Quickly, I drop my robe and scurry into the warm, soft cocoon.

"We'll start with you facedown," she says in a gentle, soothing voice. "Ethan, come stand on this side of the table."

I roll onto my stomach as gracefully as I can, fitting my head into the foam face rest. I am shaking, excited, nervous, and so warm all over that the pleasure of the heated blankets has quickly worn off and I want to kick them to the floor.

Diana is talking softly to Ethan, about how to fold back

the sheet, laughing about how if we do this at home there's no need for the same kind of modesty. He laughs, too; charming, breezy Ethan is back, and I admit it is easier like this, staring at the floor instead of making eye contact with the man I still hate but also suddenly want to fuck into a coma.

I hear a pump, then the wet sound of oil on hands, Diana's quiet "About this much," and then, "I start here."

Her hands come over my shoulders, kneading gently at first and then with pressure. She talks through what she's doing, explaining how to move away from the point of muscle insertion, spanning the length and shape of the muscle. She explains where to apply pressure, where to avoid tender places. I'm starting to unwind, to fall deeper into the mattress, and then she gives a gentle prompt: "Now you try."

More oil. A shifting of bodies beside the table, and a deep, shaking breath.

And then the heat of Ethan's hands comes over my back, following the path of Diana's, and I am melting, biting my lips to keep a moan inside. His hands are huge, stronger even than hers—a professional—and when he reaches up with a gentle finger to sweep a strand of my hair off my neck, it feels like a kiss.

"This okay?" he asks quietly.

I swallow before speaking. "Yeah . . . It's good."

I feel the way he pauses, and then works lower at her encouragement, shifting the sheet away to expose my lower back. Even with the awareness that Diana is standing beside him, I don't think I've ever been this warm or this turned on. His hands stroke my skin, fingers kneading, slick and warm.

"Now," Diana says, "when you get to the backside, remember: push together, don't spread."

I cough out an incredulous laugh into the face cradle, grabbing a fistful of the sheets. Beside me, with his hands hovering just above my tailbone, Ethan laughs under his breath. "Um. Noted."

Carefully, she shows him how to discreetly fold the sheet and expose only my leg and one butt cheek. I've had massages before, so of course I've had my butt massaged by professionals . . . but I have never felt more exposed in my life than I do right now.

Strangely, I don't hate it.

More oil, more slick sounds of hands rubbing together, and then those enormous hands come down, pressing into the muscle the way Diana instructs. Behind my closed lids, my eyes roll back in pleasure. Who knew a butt massage could be so awesome? It's so good, in fact, that I forget to be self-conscious, and instead let out a near-moan, "Who knew you were so good at this?"

Ethan's laugh is a deep, rumbling sound that sends vibrations through me.

"Oh, I'm sure you knew whether he was good with his

hands," Diana says playfully, and it's on the tip of my tongue to tell her to scram and leave us to our brothel room in peace.

He makes his way down my legs, to my feet. I'm ticklish, and it's sweet the way he's careful, but steadies me, wordlessly reassuring me that I can trust him. He works his way back up, and then down each arm, massaging my palms, and to the end of each fingertip before he slides them carefully back under the blankets.

"Great job, Ethan," Diana says. "You still with us, Ami?"

I moan.

"Think you could massage him now?" Diana says with laughter in her voice.

I moan again, longer. I'm not sure I can move yet. And if I did, it would be to roll over and pull Ethan under the blankets with me. The heavy ache low in my belly isn't going to go away on its own.

"That's usually the way this goes," she says.

"Totally fine with me," Ethan says, and it could be my mushy brain, but his voice sounds deeper, slower, like thick, warm honey. Like maybe he's a little turned on, too.

"The best thing about this," Diana says, "is that now you can teach her, too." I feel bodies shift behind me, and she sounds farther away, close to the door when she says, "I'll leave you two to swap if you like, or you can feel free to head back to the spa for another warm soak."

I sense when she's gone, but the silence somehow feels fuller.

After a few long beats, Ethan carefully asks, "You okay?"

Somehow, I manage a slurred "*Ohmygod.*"

"Is that a good 'oh my God' or a bad 'oh my God'?"

"Good."

He laughs, and it's that same maddening, amazing sound again. "Excellent."

"Don't get smug."

I sense him coming nearer, and feel his breath on my neck. "Oh, Olivia. I just had my hands all over you, and you're so relaxed you can barely speak." He steps away, and then his voice comes from a distance, like he's walked to the door: "You'd better believe I will be smug as hell."

chapter **ten**

I wake up and immediately groan in pain; despite the wonder-massage, I am so sore from being pelleted in the woods that I can barely pull the covers back. When I look, my arms are dotted with bruises so colorful, for a second I second-guess whether I showered yesterday after paintball. There is a deep purple one on my hip the size of an apricot, a few on my thighs, and an enormous one on my shoulder that looks like a rare geode.

I check my phone, opening the newest message from Ami.

Checking in for a body count.

We remain alive against all odds.

How are you feeling?

Same.

Not ready to venture out into the world just yet, but alive.

And The Husband?

Oh he went out.

Yeah. He's feeling better and was a little restless.

But you're still sick.

Why isn't he taking care of you?

He's been in this house for days.

He needed some guy time.

I glare at my phone, knowing I have no reply that isn't going to end in us arguing. "Maybe he ran out of beard wax," I mumble, just as I hear Ethan shuffling down the hall toward the bathroom.

"I can barely move," he says through the bedroom door.

"I'm polka-dotted." I whimper down at my arms. "I look like something from *Fraggle Rock*."

A knock sounds. "Are you decent?"

"Am I ever?"

He cracks the door open, leaning in a few inches. "I can't be social today. Whatever we do, please let it be just the two of us."

And then he ducks back out, leaving the door open and me alone with my brain while I try to process this. Again: When did the default plan become that we spend this entire vacation together? And when did the idea of that not send us both into a wavy bout of nausea? And when did I start falling asleep thinking about Ethan's hands on my back, my legs, and *between* my legs?

The toilet flushes, the water runs, and I hear the sound of him brushing his teeth. I am tripping—I am used to the rhythm of his tooth brushing, am no longer shocked by the sight of his live-wire hair in the morning. I'm no longer horrified at the notion of spending the day just the two of us. In fact, my mind spins with the options.

Ethan emerges from the hallway bathroom and does a double take when he looks into the bedroom at me.

"What's with you?"

I look down to understand his meaning. I'm sitting ramrod straight, with my sleep mask on my forehead, the blankets clutched to my chest, eyes wide.

Honesty has always seemed to work best for us: "I'm freaking out a little that you suggested we spend the day together, just us, and it doesn't make me want to rappel down the balcony."

Ethan laughs. "I promise to be as irritating as possible." And then he turns, shuffling back to the living room, calling out, "And as smug, too."

With this reminder of yesterday, my stomach twists and my lady parts wake up. Enough of that. Pushing up, I follow him out, no longer caring that he's going to see me in my skimpy pajamas, or that he's in boxers and a threadbare

T-shirt. After our encounter in the bathroom on the boat, the hot tub, and his hands all over my oiled-up skin yesterday, no secrets remain.

"We could hang at the pool?" I suggest.

"People."

"Beach?"

"Also people."

I look out the window, thinking. "We could rent a car and drive along the coast?"

"Now you're talking." He tucks his hands behind his head, and his biceps pop distractingly. I roll my eyes—at myself, obviously, for even noticing—and because he's Ethan and nothing gets past him, he cheekily does it again.

"What are you looking at?" He starts to alternate between his two arms, speaking in a staccato rhythm to match the bicep flexes. "It—looks—like—Olive—likes—muscles."

"You're reminding me so much of Dane right now," I say, fighting a laugh, but there's no need because the laugh dies in my throat at the way Ethan's entire demeanor changes.

He drops his arms and leans forward, resting his elbows on his thighs. "Well, okay then."

"Is that an insult?" I ask.

He shakes his head, and then seems to chew on his answer for a while. Long enough for me to get bored and go into the kitchen to brew some coffee.

Finally, he says, "I get the sense that you don't like Dane very much."

Oh, this is some thin ice. "I like him fine," I hedge, and then grin. "I like him more than I like you."

It's a weird silence that follows. Weird, because we both know I'm full of shit. Ethan's frown slowly turns into a grin. "Liar."

"Okay, I admit you're not Satan anymore, but you're definitely one of his henchmen. I mean," I say, bringing two mugs into the living room and setting his on the coffee table, "I always thought Dane was sort of fratty and, like, a Budweiser-in-a-beer-cozy type, but what confused me is how you could be *worse* when you look so much more put-together."

"What do you mean by 'worse'?"

"Come on," I say, "you know. Like how you're always pulling him off to these crazy trips as soon as Ami has something nice planned. Valentine's Day away in Vegas. Their anniversary last year, you took him to Nicaragua to go *surfing*. You and Dane went skiing in Aspen on her—well, *our*—thirty-first birthday. I ended up eating Ami's free birthday dessert at Olive Garden because she was too drunk to hold a fork."

Ethan stares at me, confused.

"What?" I ask.

He shakes his head, still staring. Finally, he says, "*I* didn't plan those trips."

"What?"

Laughing without humor, he runs a hand through his hair. The bicep pops again. I ignore it. "Dane plans all of the trips. I actually got in trouble with Sophie for going along for the Vegas one on Valentine's Day. But I had no idea he was missing events. I just assumed he needed brother time."

A few seconds of silence in which I rewire my memory of all of these things, because I can tell he's sincere. I specifically remember being there when Dane told Ami about the Nicaragua trip, how he was going to have to miss the anniversary of their first date, and she looked devastated. He said, "Ethan—the dumbass—got nonrefundable tickets. I can't say no, babe."

I'm about to tell Ethan this when he speaks first. "I'm sure he didn't realize that he was canceling plans she'd made. He wouldn't do that. God, he would feel awful."

Of course he would see it this way. If the roles were reversed, I would do or say anything to defend my sister. Taking a mental step back, I have to admit that now is not the time to hash this out, and we are not the people to do it. This is between Ami and Dane, not Ethan and me.

Ethan and I are in a good spot; let's not ruin it, shall we?

"I'm sure you're right," I say, and he looks up at me gratefully, and maybe with a bit more clarity, too. All this time I thought he was behind those trips—he gets that now. Not only isn't he the judgmental asshole I thought he was, he's also not the terrible influence that resulted in my sister's hurt feelings. It's a lot to process.

"Come on," I tell him. "Let's get dressed and get ourselves a car."

ETHAN'S HAND COMES OVER MINE as we leave the hotel. "In case we run into Sophie," he explains.

"Sure." I sound exactly like the eager nerd in a teen movie agreeing with something too readily, but whatever. Holding Ethan's hand is weird but not entirely unpleasant. In fact, it's nice enough that I feel a little guilty. We haven't seen her and Billy since snorkeling, so all this performative affection is probably unnecessary. But why take chances, am I right?

Besides, I have become a big fan of those hands.

We rent a lime-green Mustang convertible because we are idiot tourists. I'm sure Ethan expects an argument about who should drive, but I gleefully toss him the keys. Who doesn't want to be chauffeured around Maui?

Once we're on the northwestern coast, Ethan opens the

speed as much as he can—people just don't drive fast on the island. He puts on a Muse playlist, and I veto it and put on the Shins. He grumbles, and at a stoplight, chooses the Editors.

"I'm not in the mood for this," I say.

"I'm driving."

"I don't care."

With a laugh, he gestures for me to pick something. I put on Death Cab and he grins over at me—it brightens the sun. With their chill sound blowing in the air around us, I close my eyes, face to the wind, my loose braid trailing behind me.

For the first time in days, I am completely, no-hesitation, no-doubting-it *happy.*

"I am the smartest woman alive for suggesting this," I say.

"I'd like to argue for the sake of arguing," he says, "but I can't."

He smiles over at me, and my heart does an uneasy somersault beneath my breastbone because I realize I'm wrong: for the first time in *months*—maybe years—I'm happy. And with Ethan, of all people.

Being an expert at self-sabotage, I revert back to old habits. "That must be hard for you."

Ethan laughs. "It *is* fun to argue with you."

It's not a jab, I realize—it's a compliment.

"Stop that."

He glances at me and back to the road. "Stop what?"

"Being *nice*." And God, when he looks at me again to see whether I'm joking, I can't help grinning. Ethan Thomas is doing something weird to my emotions.

"I did promise to be irritating and smug, didn't I?"

"You did," I agree, "so get to it."

"You know, for someone who hates me, you sure moaned a lot when I touched you," he says.

"Shut up."

He grins over at me and then back at the road. " 'Press together. Don't spread.' "

"Will you. Shut up."

He laughs this wide-open laugh; it's a sound I've never heard, and it's an Ethan I've never seen: head tilted back, eyes crinkled in joy. He looks as happy as I feel.

And miraculously, we spend hours together without arguing once. My mom texts a few times, Ami, too, but I ignore them both. I'm honestly having one of the best days I can remember. *Real life can wait.*

We explore the rugged shoreline, find several breathtaking blowholes, and stop to eat roadside tacos near a coral-strewn bay of crystalline aquamarine water. I have nearly forty pictures of Ethan on my phone now—and sadly none of them can be used as blackmail, because he looks great in every single one.

He reaches over, pointing to my phone screen when I scroll to a photo of him. He's grinning so wide I could count his teeth, and the wind is whipping hard enough to press his shirt tight to his chest. Behind him, the Nakalele blowhole majestically erupts nearly a hundred feet into the air. "You should frame that one for your new office," he says.

I look over my shoulder at him, unsure whether he's kidding. An inspection of his expression doesn't clear things up for me.

"Yeah, I don't think so." I tilt my head. "It's oddly obscene."

"It was windy!" he protests, clearly thinking I'm referring to the fact that every contour of his chest is visible beneath the blue T-shirt.

Which—yes, but: "I was talking about the enormous ejaculation behind you."

Ethan goes quiet, and I glance up at him again, shocked that he hasn't immediately run with this one. He looks like he's biting his tongue. I register I've veered away from insult territory and sprinted headlong into sexual-speak territory. I think he's gauging whether I intended to be flirty.

And then he seems to decide that I hadn't—which is true, but now that I'm thinking about it, maybe I should have been—and bends to take the last bite of his taco. I exhale, swiping to the next photo: a picture he took of me standing in front of the famous heart-shaped rock. Ethan looks over my shoulder again, and I feel us both go still.

Admittedly, it's a great picture of me. My hair is up, but blown loose from the braid. My smile is enormous; I don't look like the pessimist I am. I look entirely smitten with the day. And hell, with the wind plastering my shirt to my torso, the twins look amazing.

"Send me that one, okay?" he says quietly.

"Sure." I airdrop it to him, and hear the small *ding* when his phone receives it. "Don't make me regret that."

"I need an accurate image for my voodoo doll."

"Well, as long as *that's* your intention."

"As opposed to?" He leans into the naughty tone, and won't let up on the eye contact, which suddenly screams *spank bank*.

My stomach rolls again. A masturbation insinuation. Suggestive humor. This feels like free-falling without a parachute.

"What are we doing tonight?" he asks, blinking away and immediately clearing the mood.

"Do we really want to push it?" I ask. "We've been together for . . ." I pick up his arm and glance at his watch. "Like eighty years straight. There are bruises, but no bloodshed yet. I say we quit while we're ahead."

"What does that entail?"

"I get the bedroom and Netflix, you wander the island to check on your hidden horcruxes."

"You know in order to create a horcrux you have to have murdered someone, right?"

I stare up at him, hating the tiny fluttering that gets going in my chest because he knows the *Harry Potter* reference. I knew he was a book lover, but to be the same kind of book lover I am? It makes my insides melt. "You just made my joke very dark, Ethan."

He balls up his taco wrapper and leans back on his hands. "You know what I want to do?"

"Oh—I know this one. You want to have dinner at a buffet."

"I want to get drunk. We're on an island, on a fake honeymoon, and it's fucking *gorgeous* out. I know you like your cocktails, Octavia Torres, and I haven't seen you as much as tipsy once. Doesn't the idea of a few drinks sound fun?"

I hesitate. "It sounds dangerous."

This makes him laugh. "Dangerous, like we'd end up either naked or dead?"

It feels like being punched, hearing him say this, because that is exactly what I meant, and the idea of ending up dead doesn't scare me nearly as much as does the alternative.

ABOUT HALFWAY BACK TO THE hotel, we pull into the dusty lot of Cheeseburger Maui—which boasts $1.99 Mai Tai

Wednesdays. This is thrilling as it is Wednesday and I am broke.

Ethan unfolds from the front seat, stretching distractingly. I definitely do not grab an eyeful of happy trail. But if I did, I would notice how soft it looks against his hard, flat—

"Ready?" he asks, and my attention rockets to his face.

"Ready," I say in my best aggressive robot voice. Definitely not caught swooning. I hold out my hand, beckoning, and for a hilarious beat, Ethan clearly thinks I want to hold his hand. He stares at it, bewildered.

"Keys," I remind him. "If you're getting drunk, I'm driving."

After he sees the logic here, he tosses them over to me, and given that I am the least athletic person alive, I manage to nearly catch them but ultimately slap them into a pile of gravel near the tire.

Ethan laughs as I jog to retrieve them, and when I pass as he holds the bar door open for me, my elbow slips and digs into his stomach. Oops.

He barely winces. "That all you got?"

"God, I hate you."

His voice is a growl behind me: "No, you don't."

The inside of the restaurant is over-the-top and kitschy and so positively magical that I pull up short. Ethan collides with my back, nearly sending me sprawling. "What the hell, Olive?"

"Look at this place," I tell him. There is a life-size shark coming out of the wall, a pirate complete with pirate ship mural in the corner, a crab wearing a life preserver suspended in a net overhead.

Ethan whistles in response. "It's something else."

"We're having such a good day not murdering each other that I'm going to be polite and suggest that we can go somewhere a little more hifalutin' if you'd prefer, but I don't see a buffet anywhere, so . . ."

"Stop acting like I'm such a snob. I like this place." He sits down and picks up a sticky menu, perusing it.

A waiter in a Cheeseburger Maui T-shirt stops at our table and fills our water glasses. "You guys want food, or just drinks?"

I can tell Ethan is about to say *just drinks*, but I jump in first. "If we're in this for the long haul, you're going to need food."

"I just had tacos," he argues.

"You're like six foot four and weigh two hundred pounds. I've seen you eat, and those tacos aren't going to sustain you for long."

The waiter *mm-hmms* appreciatively beside me, and I look up at him. "We'll check out the menu."

We order drinks, and then Ethan leans his elbows on the table, studying me. "Are you having fun?"

I pretend to focus on the menu and not the curl of

unease I feel at the sincere tenor to his words. "Shh. I'm reading."

"Come on. Can't we have a conversation?"

I put on my best confused face. "A what?"

"The exchange of words. Without banter." He exhales patiently. "I'll ask you something. You'll answer, then ask me something."

Groaning, I say, "Fine."

Ethan stares at me.

"God, *what*?" I ask. "Ask me a question, then!"

"I asked you whether you're having fun. *That* was my question."

I take a sip of my water, roll my neck, and give him what he wants. "Fine. Yes. I'm having fun."

He continues to watch me, expectantly.

"Are *you* having fun?" I ask obediently.

"I am," he answers easily, leaning back in his chair. "I expected this to be a hellmouth on a tropical island, and am pleasantly surprised that I only feel like poisoning your meals about half the time."

"Progress." I lift my water glass and clink his.

"So when was your last boyfriend?" he asks, and I nearly choke on a piece of ice.

"Wowza, that escalated quickly."

He laughs and gives a wince I find so adorable I want to spill his water into his lap. "I didn't mean that to be creepy.

We were just talking about Sophie yesterday, and I realize I didn't ask anything about you."

"That's okay," I assure him with a casual wave. "I'm fine not talking about my dating life."

"Yeah, but I want to know. We're sort of friends now, right?" Blue eyes twinkle when he smiles, the dimple makes an appearance, and I look away, noticing that others are noticing his smile, too. "I mean, I did rub your butt yesterday."

"Stop reminding me."

"Come on. You liked it."

I did. I really did. Taking a deep breath, I tell him, "My last boyfriend was a guy named Carl, and—"

"I'm sorry. *Carl*?"

"Look, they can't all be sexy Sophie names," I say, and immediately regret it because it makes him frown, even when the waiter places a giant, alcohol-soaked, fruit-filled drink in front of him. "So, his name was Carl, and he worked at 3M, and—God, it's so dumb."

"What's dumb?"

"I broke up with him because when the whole thing with 3M and the water pollution went down, he defended the company and I just could not handle it. It felt so corporate and gross."

Ethan shrugs. "That sounds like a pretty reasonable reason to break up to me."

I meet his high-five without thinking, and then mentally log how awesome it is that he chose that moment to high-five me. "Anyway, so that was . . . a while ago, and here we are." He's already put away about half of his mai tai, so I turn it back to him. "Has there been anyone since Sophie?"

"A couple Tinder dates." He drains the rest of his drink, and then notices my expression. "It's not that bad."

"I guess not. In my head, I just picture every dude on Tinder is expecting it to just be sex."

He laughs. "A lot probably are. Probably a lot of women are, too. I'm certainly not expecting sex on the first date."

"Or, what? The fifth?" I say, gesturing to the table, and then clap my mouth shut because *HELLO, THIS IS NOT A DATE.*

Thankfully, my idiocy coincides with the waiter coming by to take another drink order, so by the time Ethan turns back to me, he's ready to move on.

And as it turns out, Ethan is a really cute, happy drunk. His cheeks turn pink, he's got a permagrin, and even when we return to the topic of Sophie, he's still giggling.

"She wasn't very nice to me," he says, and then laughs. "And I'm sure it made it worse that I stayed. Nothing is harder in a relationship than not respecting the person you're with." He leans his chin heavily into his hand. "I didn't like myself with her. I was willing to try to be the guy she wanted rather than who I really am."

"Examples, please."

He laughs. “Okay, here’s one that might give you a sense of it: we had a couple’s photo shoot.”

“White shirts and denim with a fence backdrop?” I ask, wincing.

He laughs harder. “No, she wore white, I wore black. In front of an artfully dilapidated barn.” We both groan. “More importantly, though, we never fought. She hated fighting, so it was like we couldn’t even disagree.”

“Sounds just like me and you,” I say sarcastically, giving him a grin.

He laughs, and his smile lingers as he looks at me. “Yeah.” After a pause that seems to hang, heavy and expectant, he inhales deeply and says, “I’ve never been like that before.”

God, I relate to this more than I can say. “Honestly, I get that.”

“Do you?”

“Before Carl—” I say, and he snickers again at the name, “I dated this guy, Frank—”

“*Frank*?”

“We’d met at wor—”

But Ethan will not be deterred. “I know your problem, Odessa.”

“What’s my problem, Ezra?”

“You’re only dating guys who were born in the 1940s.”

Ignoring him, I press on. “Anyway, I’d met Frank at

work. Things were going well, we had a good, sexy vibe *ifyouknowwhatImean*," I say, and I expect Ethan to laugh at this, but he doesn't. "Anyway, he saw me freaking out about a presentation one day—I was nervous because I didn't feel I'd had enough time with the material to get comfortable—and I swear, seeing me like that totally turned him off. We stayed together another few months, but it wasn't the same." I shrug. "Maybe it was all in my head, but, yeah. That insecurity just made it worse."

"Where did you meet Frank again?"

"Butake." As soon as I say it, I realize it was a setup.

"Bukkake!" he sings, and I push his water toward him.

"It's *Butake*, you dumbass, why do you always do that?"

"Because it's *funny*. Didn't they run the company name through some test audiences or—or—what's it called?"

"Focus groups?"

He snaps his fingers together. "*That*. Like, Urban Dictionary is *right there*! It's like naming a kid Richard." He leans in, whispering like he's imparting some great wisdom. "He's gonna be called Dick. It's just a matter of time."

I register that I'm staring at him with overt fondness when he reaches forward, touching a careful fingertip to my chin.

"You're looking at me like you like me," he says.

"It's the mai tai goggles you're wearing. I hate you as much as ever."

Ethan lifts a skeptical brow. "Really?"

"Yep." *Nope.*

He exhales a little growl and polishes off his sixth mai tai. "I thought I rubbed your butt pretty well, well enough to at least be shifted up into the *strongly dislike* category." The waiter, Dan, returns, grinning down at sweet, pliable Ethan. "One more?"

"No more," I quickly answer, and Ethan protests with a drunken *Psssshhhhhh*. Dan waggles his eyebrows at me, like I might have a great time with this one tonight.

Look, Dan, I'm just hoping I can get him to the car.

I can, in fact, but it takes both me and Dan to keep him on task. Drunk Ethan is not only happy, he is exceedingly friendly, and by the time the three of us get out the door, he's received a phone number from a cute redhead at the bar, bought a drink for a man wearing a Vikings T-shirt, and high-fived about forty strangers.

He babbles sweetly on the drive home—about his childhood dog, Lucy; about how much he loves to kayak in the Boundary Waters and hasn't been in too long; and about whether I've ever had dill pickle popcorn (the answer is hell yes)—and by the time we get back to the hotel, he's still drunk off his ass, but slightly more collected. We make it through the lobby with only a few more stops so Ethan can make new friends with strangers.

He stops to give a hug to one of the valet attendants

who helped us check in. I give an apologetic smile over Ethan's shoulder and check his name tag: Chris.

"Looks like the honeymooners are having a good time," Chris says.

"Maybe too good." I lean toward escape—I mean, the path to the elevator. "Just taking this one upstairs."

Ethan lifts a finger and beckons Chris closer. "Do you want to know a secret?"

Uhhhh . . .

Amused, Chris leans in. "Sure?"

"I *like* her."

"I would hope so," Chris whispers back. "She's your wife."

And boom goes my heart. *He's drunk*, I tell myself. *This isn't a* thing *he's saying, just drunk words.*

Safely in the suite, I can't help but let Ethan collapse on the enormous bed for the night. He's going to be rocking a pretty serious headache in the morning.

"God, I'm so tired," he moans.

"Rough day of sightseeing and drinking?"

He laughs, one hand reaching up and coming in for a heavy landing on my forearm. "That isn't what I mean."

His hair has fallen over one eye, and I'm so tempted to move it aside. For comfort, of course.

I reach out, carefully sweeping the hair across his forehead, and he looks up at me with such intensity that I freeze with my fingers near his temple.

"What do you mean, then?" I ask quietly.

He doesn't break eye contact. Not even for a breath. "It's so exhausting pretending to hate you."

This pulls me up short, and—even though I know it now, the truth of it still blows through me—I ask, "So you *don't* hate me?"

"Nope." He shakes his head dramatically. "Never did."

Never? "You sure seemed to."

"You were so mean."

"*I* was mean?" I ask, confused. I scrabble back through the mental history, trying now to see it from his perspective. *Was I mean?*

"I don't know what I did." He frowns. "But it didn't matter anyway, because Dane told me not to."

I am so lost. "He told you not to what?"

His words are a quiet slur: "He said, 'Hell no.' "

I'm starting to understand what he's telling me, but I repeat it again anyway: "Hell no to *what*?"

Ethan looks up at me, gaze swimming, and reaches up to cup the back of my neck. His fingers play with my braid for a contemplative beat, and then he pulls me down with a surprisingly careful hand. I don't even resist; it's almost as if, in hindsight, I've known this moment was coming forever.

My heart vaults into my throat as we move together; a few short, exploratory kisses followed by the unbinding relief of something deeper, with tiny sounds of surprise and hunger coming from both of us. He tastes like cheap alcohol and contradictions, but it is still hands-down the best kiss of my life.

Pulling back, he blinks up at me, saying, "That."

I'll need to see if there is a doctor in the hotel tomorrow. Something is definitely wrong with my heart: it's pounding too hard, so tight.

Ethan's eyes roll closed, and he pulls me down beside him on the bed, curling his long body around mine. I can't move, can barely think. His breathing evens out, and he succumbs to a drunken slumber. Mine follows much later, under the perfect, heavy weight of his arm.

chapter **eleven**

I open the door to our suite as quietly as I can. Ethan wasn't awake yet when I finally gave up on waiting for him and went to get something to eat, but he is now. He's sitting on the couch in nothing but boxers. There's so much tan skin to take in—it sends my pulse skyrocketing. We'll have to talk about what happened last night—the kissing, and the fact that we slept together all night, curled in a matching set of parentheses—but it would probably be much easier if we could just skip the awkward talk and go straight to the making out again.

"Hey," I say quietly.

"Hey." His hair is a mess, his eyes are closed, and he's leaning back as if he's just focusing on breathing or planning to start a petition to ban all sales of $1.99 mai tais.

"How's the head?" I ask.

He answers with a gravelly groan.

"I brought you some fruit and an egg sandwich." I hold out a to-go carton of some mango and berries and a wrapped package with the sandwich, and he looks at both of them like they're filled with buffet seafood.

"You went downstairs to eat?" he asks. The follow-up *Without me?* is clearly implied.

His tone is dickish, but I forgive him. No one likes a pounding head.

Setting the food down on the table, I head into the kitchen to get him some coffee. "Yeah, I waited for you until about nine thirty, but my stomach was digesting itself."

"Did Sophie see you there alone?"

This feels like being jerked to a standstill. I turn to look at him over my shoulder. "Um, what?"

"I just don't want her to think that there's trouble in our marriage."

We spent all afternoon talking about how he's better off without Sophie, he kissed me last night, and this morning he's worried about what she thinks. Awesome. "You mean our *fake* marriage?" I say.

He rubs a hand across his forehead. "Yeah. Exactly." Dropping his hand, he looks up at me. "So?"

My jaw tightens, and I feel the storm build in my chest. This is good. Anger is good. I can do angry at Ethan. It's so much easier than feeling the tickling edges of smitten. "No,

Ethan, your ex-girlfriend was not at breakfast. Neither was her fiancé, or any of the new friends you made in the lobby last night."

"The what?" he asks.

"Never mind." Obviously he doesn't remember. Excellent. We can pretend the rest didn't happen, either.

"Are you in a bad mood?" he asks, and a dry, sardonic laugh bursts out of me.

"Am *I* in a bad mood? Is that a serious question?"

"You seem upset or something."

"*I* seem—?" I take a deep breath, pulling myself to my full height. Do I seem upset? He kissed me last night, said sweet things implying that maybe he'd wanted to do that for a while, and then passed out. Now he's grilling me about who might have seen me getting food alone in the hotel. I don't think my reaction is overblown.

"I'm great."

He mumbles something and then reaches for the fruit, opening the lid and peering in. "Was this from the—"

"No, Ethan, it's not from the buffet. I ordered a freshly made fruit plate. I brought it up to spare us the twelve-dollar room service delivery charge." My palm is itchy to smack him for the first time in two days, and it feels glorious.

He grunts out a "Thanks," and then picks up a piece of mango with his fingers. He stares at it, and then bursts out laughing.

"What's so funny?" I ask.

"Just remembering that girlfriend of Dane's who had a mango tattoo on her ass."

"What?"

He chews, and swallows before speaking. "Trinity. The one he was dating like two years ago?"

I frown; discomfort worms through me. "Couldn't have been two years ago. He was with Ami three and a half years ago."

He waves this away. "Yeah, but I mean before he and Ami were exclusive."

At these words, I drop the sugar spoon I'm holding and it clatters dissonantly on the counter. Ami met Dane at a bar, and by her account, they went home that night, had sex, and never looked back. As far as I know, there was never a time they *weren't* exclusive.

"How long was it again that they were seeing other people?" I ask, with as much control as possible.

Ethan pops a blackberry into his mouth. He's not looking at my face now, which is probably good, because I'm sure I look like I'm ready to do a murder. "Like the first couple years they were together, right?"

Bending, I pinch the bridge of my nose, trying to channel Professional Olive, who can keep her cool even when being challenged by condescending physicians. "Right.

Right." I can either freak out, or milk this moment for information. "They met at that bar but it wasn't until . . . when did they decide to be exclusive again?"

Ethan looks up at me, catching something in my tone. "Um . . ."

"Was it right before they got engaged?" I don't know what I'll do with myself if he agrees with this shot in the dark, but it suddenly makes sense that Dane would refuse to commit until he was impulsively ready to enter holy matrimony.

My brain is nothing but fantasies of fire and brimstone.

Ethan nods slowly, and his eyes scan my face like he's trying to read my mood, and can't. "Remember? He ended it with the other women right around the time Ami had her appendix out, and then he proposed?"

I slam my hand down on the counter. "*Are you fucking kidding me?*"

Ethan bolts to stand, pointing a finger at me. "You played me! Don't even pretend like Ami didn't know all this!"

"Ami *never* thought they were seeing other people, Ethan!"

"Then she lied to you, because Dane tells her everything!"

I am already shaking my head, and I really want to hurt

Dane but Ethan is closer and it'll be a fantastic rehearsal. "You're telling me that Dane was sleeping around for the first *two years* they were together, and he let you think Ami was okay with it? She started cutting out wedding dresses she liked in magazines after a few months of dating him. She treated her wedding like a game show challenge to win as much as she could—and it *consumed* her. She has an apron specifically for baking cupcakes, for crying out loud, and has *already picked out names for their future children*. Does Ami seem like the kind of chill gal who would be *fine* with an open relationship?"

"I . . ." He seems less certain now. "Maybe I'm wrong . . ."

"I need to call her." I turn to head to the bedroom to find my phone.

"Don't!" he shouts. "Look, if that's what he told me, then I'm telling you this in confidence."

"You have *got* to be joking. There is no way I'm not talking to my sister about this."

"Jesus Christ, Dane was right."

I go very still. "What is *that* supposed to mean?"

He laughs, but it's not a happy sound.

"Seriously, Ethan? What does that mean?"

He looks up at me, and with a pang I miss the sweet adoration in his expression last night, because the anger here is painful.

"Tell me," I say, more quietly now.

"He told me not to bother with you. That you're angry all the time."

I feel this like a punch to my sternum.

"Can you believe I wanted to ask you out?" he says, and laughs humorlessly.

"What are you even talking about?" I ask. "When?"

"When we first met." He bends, resting his elbows on his thighs. His long form curls up into an exhausted C, and he rakes a fantastic hand through his mess of hair. "That first time at the fair. I told him how pretty I thought you were. He thought that was weird—that it was weird for me to be attracted to you. Like, it meant I was into his girlfriend or something because you were twins. He told me not to bother anyway, that you were sort of bitter and cynical."

"Dane told you I was bitter? Bitter about *what*?" I am flabbergasted.

"I mean, I didn't know at the time, but it seemed to mesh with how you acted. You clearly didn't like me from the get-go."

"I only didn't like you because you were such an asshole when we met. You looked at me eating cheese curds like I was the most repulsive woman you'd ever seen."

He looks up at me, eyes narrowed in confusion. "What are you talking about?"

"Everything seemed fine," I say. "While everyone was deciding what we wanted to go see first, I went to get some cheese curds. I came back and you looked at them, looked at me in complete revulsion, and then walked away to check out the beer competition. From that point on, you've always acted so disgusted around me, and food."

Ethan shakes his head, eyes closed like he has to clear away this alternate reality. "I remember meeting you, being told I couldn't ask you out, and then going to do our own thing for the afternoon. I have *no* recollection of the rest."

"Well, I sure do."

"That certainly explains what you said two days ago," he says, "about not making fun of your body during the massage. Certainly explains why you were always so dismissive to me afterward."

"Excuse me? I was the dismissive one? Are you for real right now?"

"You acted like you wanted nothing to do with me after that day!" he seethes. "I was probably just trying to get my head on straight about being attracted to you, and of course you interpret it as something about your body and cheese curds? Jesus, Olive, that is so like you, to focus on the negative in every interaction."

Blood pulses in my ears. I don't even know how to process what I'm hearing, or the undeniable ache it shoves through me that I think he might be right. Defensiveness pushes aside introspection: "Well, who needs to see the upside of things when you've got your brother telling you that I'm a shrew and to stay away from me anyway?"

He throws up his hands. "I didn't see anything that contradicted what he'd said!"

I take a deep breath. "Does it occur to you that your attitude can foster how people react to *you*? That you hurt my feelings by reacting that way, whether you meant to or not?" I am mortified when I feel my throat grow tight with tears.

"Olive, I don't know how to say it more plainly: I was *into* you," he growls. "You're hot. And I was probably trying to hide it. I'm sorry for that *totally unintentional* reaction, I really am, but every indication I had—from you or Dane—was that you thought I was a waste of space."

"I didn't at first," I say, leaving the rest unsaid.

He clearly reads the *I do now* in my expression, though, and the line of his mouth hardens. "Good," he says, voice hoarse. "Then the feeling is conveniently mutual."

"What a fucking relief." I stare at him for two rapid breaths, just long enough to imprint his face in the space marked *DICKHEAD* in my braincyclopedia. And then I turn, storm back to the bedroom, and slam the door.

I fall back onto the bed, reeling. Part of me almost wants to get up and make a list of everything that just happened so I can process it in some sort of organized way. Like, not only was Dane sleeping around for the first two years of his relationship with my sister, but he told Ethan not to bother with me.

Because Ethan wanted to ask me out.

I don't even know what to do with this information because it is so at odds with my mental history of him. Until the past couple of days, there has never been a hint of Ethan wanting anything to do with me—not even a flash of softness or warmth. Is he making that up?

I mean, why would he do that?

So does that mean he's right about me? Did I misinterpret everything in that first interaction, and carry it with me for the past two and a half years? Was a single ambiguous look from Ethan enough to send me into this place of no return, where I decide we're bitter enemies? Am I really that angry?

I feel my breath grow tight as the rest of it nudges back into my thoughts: Is it even possible that Ami knew about Dane seeing other people? She knew I was lukewarm on him from the get-go—so I have to give some space to the possibility that they had their own arrangement, and she didn't tell me because she knew I would worry or protest out of protectiveness. Frankly, it's hard for me to even imagine Ami and Dane in an open relationship, but whether or not it's true, I can't exactly call her from Maui and ask. That is not a phone call conversation; that's an in-person conversation, with wine, and snacks, and a careful lead-in.

I pick up a pillow and scream into it. And when I pull it away, I hear a quiet knock at the bedroom door.

"Go away."

"Olive," he says, sounding much calmer. "Don't call Ami."

"I'm not calling Ami, just—seriously—go away."

The hallway falls silent, and a few seconds later, I hear the heavy click of the suite door closing.

WHEN I WAKE UP, IT'S midday, and the sun pours brightly across the bed, bathing me in a hot rectangle of light. I roll away from it, straight into a pillow that smells like Ethan.

That's right. He slept in this bed with me last night. He is everywhere in this room—in the neat row of shirts hanging in the closet, the shoes lined up by the dresser. His watch, his wallet, his keys; even his phone is sitting there. Even the sound of the ocean is tainted with the memory of him, of his head in my lap on the boat, struggling to overcome seasickness.

For a dark flash I derive some joy out of the image of Ethan sitting miserably by the pool, surrounded by people he'd love to befriend when tipsy, but whom he wants to generally avoid when sober. But the joy falls away when I remember everything about our fight: the reality that I've spent the past two and a half years hating him for a reaction he had that wasn't at all what I thought it was, and the reality that the Ami/Dane aspect isn't going to be resolved for a few more days, at least.

Which leaves only one thing for me to chew on, and that's Ethan admitting that he wanted to ask me out.

It's genuinely a rewrite of my internal history, and it takes a lot of mental maneuvering. Of course I found Ethan attractive when I first met him, but personality is everything, and his left a giant gaping hole in the column of positive attributes. Until this trip, that is, when he was not only the best sparring partner but also entirely adorable on several occasions . . . and frequently shirtless.

Groan. I stand up, walking to the door and peeking out. No sign of Ethan in the living room. Darting into the bathroom, I close the door and turn on the faucet, splashing water on my face. I stare at myself in the mirror, thinking.

Ethan wanted to ask me out.

Because Ethan *liked* me.

Dane told him I was always angry.

I proved Dane right that very first day.

My eyes widen as an additional possibility occurs to me: *What if Dane didn't want me to date his brother?* What if he didn't want me in his business, knowing that he was the one planning all these trips, that he was seeing other women, and God knows what else?

He's used Ethan as a scapegoat, as a shield—what if he used the convenience of my grouchy reputation to create a buffer zone? What a dick!

Bursting out of the bathroom, I turn to the left to begin my Ethan Search and run directly into his brick-wall chest. The *oof* that erupts from me is cartoon-level comical. He makes it worse by catching me easily and holding me at a distance, looking down warily. I have the absurd image of Ethan holding me back with an outstretched hand on my forehead while I try to take swings at him with ineffectually short arms.

Stepping back, I ask, "Where were you?"

"Pool," he says, "I was coming to grab my phone and wallet."

"Where are you going?"

He lifts a shoulder. "Not sure."

He's guarded again. Of course he's guarded. He admitted he was attracted to me, and up until this trip I'd only ever been rude to him. Then I stormed out of the room after implying he's still a waste of my time.

I don't even know where to start. I realize, of the two of us, I have the most to say right now. I want to start with an apology, but it's like pushing water through a brick—the words just won't come.

I start with something else: "I'm not trying to do that thing I do, where I look for the worst possible explanation for things, but . . . do you think Dane was trying to keep us apart?"

Ethan immediately scowls. "I don't want to talk about Dane *or* Ami right now. We can't get into it with them while we're here and they're there."

"I know, okay, I'm sorry." I look up at him for a beat and catch just a flicker of emotion behind his eyes. It's enough to give me the bravery to push on. "But should we talk about us?"

"What *us*?"

"The *us* that is having this conversation?" I whisper, eyes wide with meaning. "The *us* that is on this vacation together, having a fight, having . . . feelings."

His eyes narrow. "I don't think *us* is a very good idea, Olive."

This denial is good; it's familiar disagreement. It bolsters my resolve. "Why? Because we argue?"

"That's a pretty mild term for what we do."

"I *like* that we argue," I tell him, willing the sticky, tender words out. "Your ex-girlfriend never even wanted to disagree. My parents won't get a divorce but don't speak to each other. And—I know you don't want to talk about it, but—I feel like my sister is in a marriage where"—I hedge, so we don't just go down that road all over again and I end up angry—"she doesn't actually know her husband all that well. But it's always been safe for *us* to say exactly what we're thinking with each other. It's one of my favorite things about being with you. Do you have that with everyone?" I ask, and when he doesn't immediately answer, I tell him, "I know you don't."

His brows pull down, and I can tell he's turning this around in his mind. He may be mad at me, but at least he's listening.

I chew my lip, looking up at him. Time for a different tack. "You said I'm hot."

Ethan Thomas rolls his eyes at me. "You know you are."

I take a deep breath, holding it. Even if nothing happens once we get back home—and it might be smarter for both of us if we keep our distance, because who knows what nuclear fallout there will be when I finally talk to Ami—I sincerely doubt we'll be able to keep our hands to ourselves for the next five days.

At least I know I won't. My anger toward Ethan has melted into a fondness and attraction so acute it's hard to not throw my arms around him in this hallway, right now, even when he's wearing his surly face—furrowed brows, mouth a hard line—and his hands are curled into defensive balls at his side. Maybe every time I wanted to smack him in the past, I really just wanted to press my face onto his.

I narrow my eyes back at him. I am not afraid of relying on cheap seduction.

I reach for his hand, and the movement *accidentally* presses my boobs together.

He notices. His nostrils flare, and his eyes move higher on my face, as if he's trying to keep them from sinking. Ethan Thomas is definitely a boob man.

I bite my lip, saw my teeth back and forth. In response, he licks his own lips, and swallows, holding steady. I'm going to need to work for this.

I take a step closer, reach out, and rest my other hand on his stomach. Holy lord it is firm and warm, and spasms slightly beneath my fingertips. My voice shakes, but I sense I'm getting to him, and it gives me the confidence to press on. "Do you remember kissing me last night?"

He blinks to the side, exhaling slowly, like he's busted. "Yes."

"But do you *remember* it?" I ask, taking another step closer so that we're nearly chest to chest.

He hesitates, and then looks back at me, brows drawn. "What do you mean?"

"Do you remember the kiss itself?" My fingers scratch lightly at his stomach, down to the hem of his shirt, and I slip my thumb under, stroking. "Or do you just remember that it happened?"

Ethan licks his lips again, and fire erupts in my belly. "Yes."

"Was it good?"

I can tell his breathing is accelerated now as well. In front of me, his chest rises and falls rapidly. I, too, feel like I can barely get enough oxygen. "Yeah."

"Did you forget your words, Elvis?"

"It was good," he manages, and rolls his eyes but I can see him fighting a smile, too.

"Good how?"

His jaw ticks, like he wants to argue with me about why I'm asking him this when I was obviously there, too, but the heat in his eyes tells me he's just as turned on as I am, and is willing to play along. "It was the kind of kiss that feels like fucking."

All the air is sucked out of my lungs, and I'm left staring up at him, speechless. I was expecting him to say something safe, not something that would send my libido spiraling out of any controlled orbit.

Running both hands up his chest, I relish the exhaled little grunt he can't seem to keep contained. I have to rise on my toes to reach him, but I don't mind the way he's making me work for it. With his gaze locked on mine, he doesn't bend until I'm right there, at the limit of where I can reach.

But then he gives in to it entirely: with a soft moan of relief, his eyes fall closed, his arms come around my waist, and Ethan covers my mouth with his. If last night's kiss felt like a drunken impulse, this one feels like a complete unburdening. He takes my mouth slowly, and then with more vigor until his deep groan vibrates all the way to the marrow of my bones.

It's heaven to dig my hands into the silk of his hair, to feel the way he lifts me up from the floor so that I'm at his level, high enough for me to wrap my legs around his waist. His kiss makes me come undone; I can't be embarrassed that I fall so quickly into wild hunger because he's right there with me, nearly frantic.

I speak the single word into his mouth: "Bedroom."

He carries me down the hall, maneuvering me easily through the doorway, toward the bed. I want to eat his soft little grunts, the bursting exhales he gives when I tug on his hair or lick at his lip or move my mouth to his jaw, his neck, his ear.

I pull him over me when he lowers me to the mattress, taking his shirt off before his chest even touches mine. All that smooth, warm tanned skin under my hands makes me crazed, like I'm feverish. *Next time*, I think. *Next time I'll undress him slowly and enjoy every inch revealed, but right now I just need to feel his weight over me.*

His mouth makes its way down my body; hands already familiar with my legs now explore my breasts, my stomach, the delicate skin beside my hip bones, and lower. I want to take a picture of him like this: his soft hair brushing against my stomach as he makes his way down, his eyes closed in pleasure.

"I think this is the longest we've gone without arguing," he murmurs.

"What if all of this was just a ruse to get a great blackmail photo?" I am breathless as he kisses a string of heat across my navel.

"I've always wanted someone who appreciates the long con." He bares his teeth, biting the sensitive juncture of hip and thigh.

I start to laugh but then a kiss is pressed between my legs, where I am overheated and aching, and Ethan reaches up, resting a palm over my heart to feel it hammering. With focus and quiet, encouraging sounds, he makes me fall apart so thoroughly I am a demolished, giggling mess in his arms afterward.

"You okay there, Olivia?" he asks, sucking gently at my neck.

"Ask later. Nonverbal now."

His growl tells me he's happy with this answer; hungry fingers slide up over my stomach, my breasts, my shoulders.

I manage to pull myself together, too tempted by his collarbones and chest hair and abdomen to let a walloping orgasm keep me from exploring. With his lips parted and fingers loosely tangled in my hair, Ethan watches me move down his body, kissing him, tasting him until he stops me with tense, dark eyes.

Reaching down, he pulls me back up and rolls over onto

me in an impressive display of agility. I feel the air sweetly pressed out of my lungs, the smooth slide of his body over mine.

"This okay?" he asks.

I'd argue with him about the word *okay* when things are very clearly *sublime*, but now is not the time to nitpick. "Yeah. Yes. Perfect."

"You want to?" Ethan sucks at my shoulder, sliding his warm palm up and over my hip, to my waist, my ribs, and back down again.

"Yeah." I gulp down an enormous breath of air. "Do you?"

He nods against me, and then laughs quietly, coming up for a kiss. "I really, really do."

My body screams *yes* just as my mind screams *birth control.*

"Wait. Condoms," I groan into his mouth.

"I've got some." He jumps up, and I'm distracted enough by the view of him crossing the room that it takes me a second to realize what he's said.

"Who were you planning on having sex with on this trip?" I ask him, fake scowling over from the bed. "And in which bed?"

He tears open the box and glances at me. "I don't know. Better to be prepared, right?"

At this, I push up on an elbow. "Were you thinking you'd have sex with *me*?"

Ethan laughs, ripping the foil open with his teeth. "Definitely not you."

"Rude."

He makes his way back over to me, treating me to a very lovely view. "I think it would have been delusional for me to think I could ever get this lucky."

Does he know he's chosen the perfect words to complete this mad seduction? I can hardly argue; being with him right now represents the most astonishing luck I've ever had, too. And when he climbs over me, pressing his mouth to mine and running a hand down my thigh to cup my knee and pull it up over his hip, arguing is suddenly the last thing on my mind.

chapter **twelve**

Ethan looks at me, smiles, and then turns his head down and pokes at his lunch. It's an ironically bashful expression for the hot, objectifying pervert who, barely a half hour ago, watched me with the intensity of a predator while I got dressed. When I asked him what he was doing, he said, "Just having a moment."

"What kind of moment were you having?" I ask now, and Ethan looks back up.

"Moment—what?"

I realize I'm digging for a compliment. He was watching me get dressed with a thirst I didn't see in his eyes even on mai tai night. But I guess I'm still in that weird fugue where I don't actually believe that we're getting along swimmingly, let alone having fun being naked together.

"In the room," I say. " 'Having a moment.' "

"Oh," he says, and winces. "Yeah. About that. Was just freaking out a little over having sex with you."

I bark out a laugh. I *think* he's joking. "Thank you for being so consistently on-brand."

"No, but really," he amends with a smile, "I was enjoying watching. I liked seeing you put your clothes back on."

"One would think the undressing part would be the highlight."

"It was. Believe me." He takes a bite, chewing and swallowing while studying me, and something in his expression takes me back an hour, to when he kept whispering, *It's good, so good,* in my ear before I fell to pieces beneath him. "But afterward, seeing you put yourself back together was . . ." He glances over my shoulder, searching for the right word, and I'm guessing it's going to be a great one—*sexy*, or *seductive*, or perhaps *life-altering*—but then his expression turns sour.

I point my fork at him. "*That* is not a good face for this conversation."

"Sophie," he says, both in explanation and greeting as she steps up to the table, cocktail in one hand and Billy's arm in the other.

Of course. I mean, of *course* she approaches us right now, wearing a bikini under a tiny, sheer cover-up, looking like she just walked off the set of a *Sports Illustrated* photo shoot. Meanwhile, my hair is twisted up in a haystack on my head, I have zero makeup on, and am sex-sweaty, wearing running shorts and a T-shirt featuring smiling ketchup and mustard bottles dancing together.

"Hey guys!" Her voice is so high-pitched it's like having someone blow a whistle next to my head.

I study Ethan from across the table, eternally curious how that relationship worked once upon a time: Ethan with his deep, warm-honey voice; Sophie with her cartoon mouse voice. Ethan with his watchful gaze; Sophie with her eyes that bounce all over a room, searching for the next interesting thing. He's also so much bigger than she is. For a second I imagine him carrying her around the Twin Cities in a BabyBjörn, and have to swallow back a giant cackle.

We let out a flaccid "Hey," in unison.

"Catching a late lunch?" she asks.

"Yeah," he says, and then puts on a plastic expression of marital happiness. If *I* recognize how forced it is, Sophie—his live-in girlfriend of nearly two years—has got to see through it, too. "Spent the day in."

"In *bed*," I add, too loudly.

Ethan looks at me like I am eternally hopeless. He exhales through his nose in a long, patient stream. For once, I'm not even lying and I still sound like a maniac.

"That was our day yesterday." Sophie's eyes slide to Billy. "Fun, right?"

This entire thing is so weird. Who talks to each other like this?

Billy nods, but isn't looking at us—who can blame him? He doesn't want to hang out with us any more than we want them here. But his reaction is clearly not enough for her because a cloudy frown sweeps across her face. She glances at Ethan, hungrily, and then away again, like the loneliest woman on the planet. I wonder how he'd feel if he looked up and noticed it—the flat-out yearning in her expression, the *Did I make a mistake?* expression—but he's back to obliviously poking at his noodles.

"So," she says, staring directly at Ethan. It looks like she's sending him messages with the power of her mind.

They are not penetrating.

Finally, he glances up with a forced blank expression. "Hm?"

"Maybe we can get drinks later. Talk?" She's clearly asking him, singular, not us, plural. And I assume Billy is also not included in the invitation.

I want to ask her, *Now you want to talk? You didn't when he was yours!*

But I refrain. An awkward weight descends, and I look up at Billy to see whether he feels it, too, but he's pulled his phone out of his pocket and is scrolling through Instagram.

"I'm not . . ." Ethan looks over at me, brows drawn. "I mean, maybe?"

I give him an *Are you fucking serious?* face, but he misses it.

"Text me?" she asks softly.

He lets out a garbled sound of agreement, and I want to snap a picture of her expression and his to show him later and make him explain what the hell is happening. Does Sophie regret breaking up with Ethan? Or is it only bothering her because he's "married" and not pining over her anymore?

This dynamic is fascinating . . . and just so, *so* weird. There's no other way to explain it.

I let myself imagine this bubbly person in front of me leaving a note that says simply, *I don't think we should get married. Sorry.*

And, in fact, I can totally see it. She's candy-sweet at the surface and probably terrible at communicating negative emotions. Meanwhile, I'm like a sour patch kid on the surface, but will happily detail all the ways I think the world is going to hell.

After lingering for a few more stilted beats, Sophie tugs at Billy's arm, and they make their way toward the exit. Ethan lets out a long breath aimed at his plate.

"Seriously, why do they insist on socializing with us?" I ask.

He takes his grumpy feelings out on a piece of chicken, harshly stabbing it. "No idea."

"I think drinks tonight would be a bad idea."

He nods but doesn't say anything.

I turn to watch Sophie's high and firm retreating backside, then look back to Ethan. "You okay?"

I mean, we had sex like an hour ago. Even with his ubiquitous ex wandering around the hotel, the correct answer here is *Yes*, right?

Ethan nods and gives me what I've come to know is a fake smile. "I'm fine."

"Good, because I was about to flip the table over the way she was staring at you with sad dog eyes."

He lifts his head. "She what?"

I don't like how immediately this perked him up. I want to be honest with him, but my words come out forced. "Just—she seemed to want to make eye contact with you."

"I mean, we *made* eye contact. She asked to meet us for drinks . . ."

"Yeah, no. She wanted to meet *you* for drinks."

Ethan very deliberately tries to look cool about this and does a very bad job at it. He's fighting a gloating smile.

And I get it. Who hasn't wanted to wave their shiny new relationship in the face of the person who dumped them? Even the best among us aren't above that kind of pettiness. And yet, heat rushes to my face. I'm not just wary in this moment, I'm humiliated. A very obvious vacation screw. At the very least, dude, put away your boner for your ex for a good six hours after having sex with someone else.

I stop myself.

This is exactly what I do. I assume the worst. Needing a break, I stand and drop my napkin on the table. "I'm going to head up and shower. Think I want to do some shopping around the hotel shops for souvenirs."

He stands, too, more out of surprise than courtesy, I think. "Okay. I could—"

"No, it's okay. I'll catch up with you later."

He doesn't say anything else, and when I look back near the exit, his expression is hidden from me: he's back in his seat, staring down at his meal.

RETAIL THERAPY IS REAL AND glorious. I'm able to noodle around the hotel shops and find a few thank-you gifts for Ami, some souvenirs for my parents, and I even buy a T-shirt for Dane. He may be a jerkface, but he did miss his honeymoon.

Although I can lose myself in the mental blankness of perusing overpriced island tchotchkes, in the background, the low hum of irritation with Ethan remains, and is accompanied by the throbbing baseline of stress over whether we made a terrible mistake by sleeping together. It's possible we did, and if so, we've just made the remaining five days here exponentially more awkward than they would be if we still hated each other.

This day has been emotionally draining: waking up with the memory of a kiss, a fight with Ethan, the realization about Dane, reconciliation and sex, and then the predictable daily Sophie run-in that wedged a whole boatload of uncertainty between us. This day has lasted four years.

My first go-to whenever I'm upset has always been my sister. I pull out my phone and focus on the swaying palm trees overhead in its reflection. I want to ask if she's okay. I want to ask if Dane is around, to see what he's been doing, and with who. I really want her advice about Ethan, but know that I can't get into any of that without explaining all the details that led up to it first.

I can't do that over the phone. I certainly can't do it over text with her. So, needing some anchor to home, I text Diego instead.

What's the latest in the frozen tundra?

I had a date last night.

Oooh, was it good?

Well, he reached forward to retrieve a piece of food from my teeth without warning.

So . . . no, then?

I'm guessing you and Ethan haven't murdered each other yet?

Close, but no.

Now is definitely not the time to break the news that Ethan and I did The Deed, and Diego is definitely not the one to tell—I'll lose all aspects of message control.

Well I'm sure you're managing to somehow suffer through a dream vacation.

Exactly, it's amazing. Even I can't complain. How is Ami?

Emaciated, bored, married to a bro.

And Mom/Dad?

Rumor has it your dad brought her flowers and she pulled off every petal and used them to spell PUTA in the snow.

Wow. That's. Wow.

So, all is the same here.

I sigh. That's exactly what I worried about.

OK. I'll see you in a few days.

Miss you, mami.

Miss you, too.

I return to the room with my bags, expecting—maybe hoping—that Ethan is out so that I can use the calm of my post-shopping brain to figure out how I'm going to handle him.

But of course he's there, showered, dressed, and sitting on the balcony with a book. He hears me come in, and stands, stepping inside.

"Hey."

Just a glance at him and I'm remembering what happened only a few hours ago, and how he looked down at me, his movements slowing just before he came, eyes heavy, mouth slack with pleasure. I drop the bags onto a chair in the living room and busy myself by digging through them to pretend to look for something.

"Hey," I say, faux-distracted.

"Did you want to grab dinner?" he asks.

My stomach rumbles but I lie: "Um . . . not super hungry."

"Oh. I was just waiting to see—" He cuts the words short, rubbing his chin with mild aggravation.

My response to this is completely unrelated, but it's what my brain decides to throw out into the room: "I thought you might be having drinks with Sophie."

He has the nerve to look confused. "I . . . no?"

"You could have gone to dinner without me, you know." I don't have anything to do with my hands, so I aggressively roll my plastic shopping bag closed and shove it deeper on the chair. "We don't have to eat every meal together."

"What if I *wanted* to go with you?" he asks, studying me, clearly vexed. "Would that break your new, confusing rules?"

I bark out a laugh. "Rules? What are rules?"

"What are you talking about?"

"You sleep with me and then have an emotional brain fart with me in front of your ex. I would say that's breaking a pretty big rule."

He frowns immediately. "Wait. This is about *Sophie*? Is this another cheese curd misreading of the situation?"

"No, Ethan, it isn't. I don't give a crap about Sophie. This is about *me*. You were more focused on her reaction to you than you were on what *I* was feeling in the moment. I don't often put myself in situations where I'm a rebound or a distraction, and so you can probably understand that it was awkward for me to see her, too. But you had zero awareness of it. And obviously that's to be expected if you don't have feelings for me, but . . ." I trail off lamely. "Anyway. It's not about Sophie."

Ethan pauses, mouth open like he wants to speak but isn't sure what to say. Finally, he manages, "What makes you think I don't have feelings for you?"

It's my turn to hesitate. "You didn't say you did."

"I didn't say I didn't, either."

I am tempted to continue this ridiculousness just to be a brat, but someone has to be an adult here. "Please don't pretend you don't understand why I'm pissed."

"Olive, we've barely had a conversation since we had sex. What do you have to be pissed about?"

"You were totally freaking out at lunch!"

"You're freaking out now!"

I realize that he's not denying anything I've said. "Of course I'm going to be annoyed watching you quietly soak up Sophie's jealousy after you just had sex with me."

"'Quietly soak up—'?" He stops, shaking his head. Ethan holds up his hands in a request for a temporary cease-fire. "Can we just get dinner? I am starving and have no idea what's going on here."

PERHAPS UNSURPRISINGLY, DINNER IS TENSE and silent. Ethan orders a salad, I order a salad—clearly we do not want to have to wait long for our food to arrive. We both avoid alcohol, too, but I could honestly use a few margaritas.

Once the waitress leaves, I pull out my phone and pretend to be incredibly busy, but really I'm just playing poker.

Obviously, I was right: the sex was a huge mistake, and now we have five days left together. Should I suck it up, pull out the credit card, and get a room for myself? It would be a huge expense, but it might allow the vacation to continue to be . . . fun. I could do all the activities left on my bucket list, and even if it's 30 percent as fun as doing it with Ethan, it's still 100 percent more fun than I'd be having at home. But the idea that I may be done with the particular brand of Ethan-hassling fun I've been enjoying so far is a bummer.

"Olive."

I look up in surprise when he says it, but he doesn't immediately continue. "Yeah?"

He opens his napkin, sets it on his lap, and leans on his forearms, meeting my eyes directly. "I'm sorry."

I can't tell if it's an apology for lunch, for the sex, or for about a hundred other things he could probably stand to apologize for. "About . . . ?"

"About lunch," he says gently. "I should have focused only on you." He pauses and runs a finger over a dark brow. "I wasn't at all interested in having drinks with Sophie. If I was withdrawn, it was because I was hungry and tired of running into her."

"Oh." Everything in my head seems to come to a standstill, words momentarily on hiatus. That was so much easier than getting a new hotel room. "Okay."

He smiles. "I don't want things to be weird with us."

Frowning, I ask, "Wait. Are you apologizing so you can have sex with me again?"

Ethan looks like he can't decide if he wants to laugh or

throw his fork at me. "I think I'm apologizing because my emotions tell me I need to?"

"You have emotions besides irritation?"

Now he laughs. "I don't think I registered that I seemed to be quietly enjoying her jealousy. I won't lie and say that it doesn't bring me some pleasure that she's jealous, but that's independent of how I feel about you. I didn't mean to seem preoccupied with Sophie after we'd just been together."

Wow. Did some woman text him that apology? That was fantastic.

"She texted me earlier, and I replied," he says, and turns his phone around so I can read it. The text says simply, *Gonna pass on drinks. Have a nice trip*. "Before you got back to the room. Look at the time stamp," he says, and points, grinning. "You can't even say that I did it because you were mad, because I had no idea you were mad. Finally, my cluelessness comes in handy."

Our waitress slides our salads down in front of us, and now that things are better between us, I regret not getting a burger. Forking a piece of lettuce, I say, "Okay, cool."

"'Okay, cool,'" he repeats slowly. "That's it?"

I look up at him. "I mean it: that was an impressive apology. We can go back to being rude to each other for fun now."

"What if I feel like being nice to each other for fun now?" he asks, and then flags down the waitress.

I narrow my eyes at him. "I'm trying to imagine 'nice' on you."

"You were pretty nice on me earlier," he says in a quiet growl.

At the side of the table, a throat clears. We both look up to see that the waitress has returned.

"Oh. Hi. That was timely." I wave to her, and Ethan laughs.

"Can we get a bottle of the Bergström Cumberland pinot?" he asks her.

She leaves and he shakes his head at me.

"You're going to loosen me up with alcohol now?" I ask, grinning. "That's one of my favorite wines."

"I know." He reaches across the table, taking my hand, and my insides turn warm and wavy. "And no, I'm going to loosen you up by refusing to fight with you."

"You won't be able to resist."

Bending, he kisses my knuckles. "Wanna bet?"

chapter **thirteen**

As Ethan chatters easily throughout his meal and into dessert, I stare at him, working to not let my jaw fall open too frequently: I don't think I've seen him smile this much, ever.

Part of me wants to pull my phone back out and take a picture; it's the same part of me that wants to catalog every one of his features: the dramatic brows and lashes; the contrast of his bright eyes; the straight Roman line of his nose; his full, intelligent mouth. I get the sense that we're living on a cloud; no matter what I tell my head and my heart, I worry I'm in for a rough crash landing when we fly home to Minnesota in a matter of days. As much as I fight the thought, it keeps returning, uninvited: *This can't last. It's too good.*

He drags a strawberry through a drizzle of chocolate syrup beside the cheesecake we're sharing, and holds the fork aloft. "I was thinking we could do Haleakalā at sunrise tomorrow."

"What's that?" I steal the fork and eat the perfect bite he's crafted. He doesn't even scowl—he *smiles*—and I try to not let this throw me. Ethan Thomas is totally fine with me eating off his fork. Olive Torres from two weeks ago is floored.

"It's the highest point on the island," he explains. "According to Carly at the front desk it's the best view around, but we have to get there pretty early."

"Carly at the front desk, eh?"

He laughs. "I had to find someone to talk to while you were off shopping all afternoon."

Only a week ago I would have made a cutting sarcastic remark in response to this, but my brain is full of nothing but heart-eyes and the urge to kiss him.

So I reach across the table for his hand. He takes mine without any hesitation, like it is the most natural thing in the world.

"So I think," I say quietly, "that if we're going to be up for the sunrise, we should probably get to bed soon."

His lips part, eyes drop to my mouth. Ethan Thomas is quick on the uptake: "I think you're right."

ETHAN'S ALARM GOES OFF AT four, and we startle awake, mumble into the darkness, and roll in a naked, sheet-tangled tumble from bed and into our layers of clothing. Although we are on a tropical island, Front Desk Carly told Ethan the predawn temperatures at the peak of the mountain are frequently below freezing.

Despite our best intentions for an early bedtime, the man kept me up for several hours with his hands, and mouth, and a shockingly large vocabulary of dirty words; it feels like a thick sex fog hovers in my brain even when he turns on the lights in the living room. With teeth brushed and kisses given, Ethan brews coffee and I pack a bag with water, fruit, and granola bars.

"Wanna hear my mountain-climbing story?" I ask.

"Is bad luck involved?"

"You know it."

"Let's hear it."

"Summer after sophomore year in college," I begin, "Ami, Jules, Diego, and I took a trip to Yosemite because Jules was on a fitness kick and wanted to climb Half Dome."

"Uh-oh."

"Yes!" I sing. "It's a terrible story. So, Ami and Jules were in great shape, but Diego and I were, let's say, more marathon couch potatoes than runners. Of course, the hike itself is insane and I thought I was going to die at least fifty times—which has nothing to do with luck, just laziness—but then we start the final vertical ascent up the subdome. No one told me to watch out where I put my hands. I reached into a crevice to get a grip and grabbed a rattlesnake."

"What!"

"Yeah, bit by a fucking rattlesnake, and fell like fifteen feet."

Ethan gapes at me. "What did you do?"

"Well, Diego wasn't going to climb that last stretch, so he was there standing over me, acting like his plan was to pee on my hand. Thankfully the ranger came over and had some antivenin, and it was okay."

"See?" Ethan says. "*That's* lucky."

"To be bitten? To *fall*?"

He laughs incredulously. "Lucky that they had the *antivenin*. You didn't die on Half Dome."

I shrug, dropping a couple of bananas in the backpack. "I see what you're saying."

I can feel him still watching me.

"You don't really believe this, though, right?" Off my look, he adds, "That you have some sort of chronically bad luck?"

"Absolutely. I've already shared a couple of winners, but just to keep it recent: I lost my job the day after my roommate moved out. In June, I got some car repairs done *and* a ticket when a hit-and-run shoved my brand-new car into a no-parking zone. And this summer an old woman fell asleep on my shoulder on the bus, and I only realized she was dead, and not actually asleep, after I'd missed my stop."

His eyes go wide.

"I'm kidding about that last one. I don't even take the bus."

Ethan bends, cupping his hands over his knees. "I don't know what I would actually do if someone died on me."

"I think the odds are pretty slim." Even half-asleep, I grin as I pour our coffee into two paper cups and slide one in front of Ethan.

Straightening, he says, "I guess I'm suggesting that you give the idea of luck too much power."

"You mean how positivity breeds positivity? Please don't tell me you think you're the first one to mention this to me. I realize part of it is outlook, but honestly—it's luck, too."

"Okay, but . . . my lucky penny is just a coin. It doesn't have any great power, it's not magic, it's just something I found before a bunch of awesome things happened. So now I associate it with those awesome things." He lifts his chin to me. "I had my penny the night we ran into Sophie. Logically, if everything was about luck, that wouldn't have happened."

"Unless my bad luck countered your good luck."

His arms come around my waist, and he pulls me into the heat of his chest. I'm still so unaccustomed to the ease of his affection that thrill passes in a shiver down my spine.

"You're a menace," he says into the top of my head.

"It's just how I'm built," I tell him. "Ami and I are like photo negatives."

"It's not a bad thing." He tilts my chin, kissing me once, slowly. "We're not supposed to be carbon copies of our siblings . . . even when we are outwardly identical."

I think about all this as we move into the hallway. I've spent my entire life being compared to Ami; it's nice having someone like me for me.

But, of course, this awareness—that he likes me the way I am—trips the following one, and once we're in the elevator and headed to the lobby, the thought bursts out of me, unattended. "I guess I'm a pretty firm one-eighty from Sophie, too."

I immediately want to sift the words out of the air and shove them back into my face.

"I guess, yeah," he says.

I want him to add, "But not in a bad way," again, or even "I'm glad," but he just grins down at me, waiting for me to spew some more nonsense.

I will not indulge him. I bite my lips closed and glare up at him: he knows exactly what he's doing. What a monster.

Ethan continues to smile down at me. "Are you jealous?"

"Should I be?" I ask, and then immediately amend, "I mean, we're just having a vacation fling, aren't we?"

He lets surprise slowly—skeptically—take over his features. "Oh, is that all this is?"

The way this lands feels like a boulder rolling down my spine. We're only a couple of days away from hate and into tenderness—it's way too soon to be talking about this in any serious way.

Or is it? I mean, technically we're in-laws now. It's not like we can leave the island and never see each other again; at some point we're going to have to deal with what we're doing . . . and what the fallout will be.

We step out of the elevator, pass through the lobby, and, in the darkness, get into a cab; I still haven't answered him. This is one I need to sit with for a little bit, and Ethan is apparently fine with that because he doesn't prompt me again.

What's amazing is that even at four thirty in the morning there is traffic headed up through the national park to the crater's peak; there are vans with bicycles, hiking groups, and couples like us—we're a sort of couple—planning to lay down a towel and huddle together in the morning chill.

It takes an hour to get through the traffic and to the top, where we scrabble up a series of rocks to the peak. Even though the sky is still mostly dark, the view is breathtaking. There are clusters of people standing huddled together in the cold or sitting on the ground with blankets, but it's oddly quiet, like everyone is respectful enough to keep their voices down when they're about to witness a 360-degree sunrise.

Ethan spreads out a couple of beach towels we borrowed

from the hotel and beckons me down. He guides me to sit between his long, outstretched legs and pulls me back against his chest. I can't imagine he's very comfortable, but I am in heaven, so I give in to it and just let my guard down for a long, quiet stretch.

I wish I knew what was happening, both between us and inside my heart. It feels like the organ itself has gotten bigger, like it's demanding to be seen and heard, reminding me that I am a warm-blooded female with wants and needs that go beyond the basics. Being with Ethan increasingly feels like spoiling myself with a perfect new pair of shoes or an extravagant dinner out. I just remain unconvinced that I deserve this daily . . . or that it can last.

It's obvious to me that we've both fallen into quiet reflection about *us*, and I'm not at all surprised when he says, "I asked you something earlier."

"I know."

We're just having a vacation fling, aren't we?

Oh, is that all this is?

He goes quiet again; obviously he doesn't have to repeat what he said. But I don't feel entirely sure where my head is on this particular issue. "I'm . . . thinking."

"Think out loud," he says. "With me."

My heart does this tight, twisting maneuver at the way he so easily asks me for what he needs and knows I can give him: transparency.

"We didn't even like each other a week ago," I remind him.

His mouth comes to a gentle landing on the side of my neck. "I think we should chalk all that up to a silly misunderstanding. Would it help if I treated you to cheese curds when we got home?"

"Yes."

"You'd promise to share them with me?" He kisses me again.

"Only if you ask very nicely."

At this point, I can only attribute my own pre-Maui feelings about Ethan to being reactionary and defensive. When someone doesn't like us, it's natural to not like them in return, right? But the memory that Dane told him I was always angry does bring up something Ethan has been hesitant to discuss . . .

I know I tend to be the pessimist to Ami's optimist, but I'm not angry. I'm not sharp. I *am* cautious and wary. The fact that Dane told Ethan that—and that Dane happened to be sleeping with other women when he said it—makes me particularly wary of Dane.

"I don't think we can have this conversation without also exploring the possibility that Dane wanted to keep us away from each other."

I feel the way he stiffens when I say this, but he doesn't move away or let me go. "Why would he do that, though?"

"My theory?" I say. "He let Ami believe he was monogamous, and you knew he wasn't. If you and I started talking, it would eventually slip out that he was seeing other people. Just like it did, here."

Behind me, Ethan shrugs, and I know him well enough now to imagine the expression he's making: unconvinced, but unconcerned. "It probably just felt weird to him," he says. "The idea of his big brother dating his girlfriend's twin sister."

"*If* I agreed to go out with you," I add.

"Are you telling me you wouldn't have?" he counters. "I saw the thirst in your eyes, too, Olivia."

"I mean, you're not horrible to look at."

"Neither are you."

These words are spoken into the sensitive skin behind my ear; the particular Olive-and-Ethan brand of compliment blows through me, soft and seductive. Ethan's reaction to me at the wedding gave no indication he thought anything other than that I was a short green satin troll. "I'm still rewiring that aspect of things."

"I always assumed my attraction was obvious," he says. "I wanted to translate your frowns and find out what your problem with me was and then bend you over the back of my couch."

All of my internal organs turn to goo at his words. I

work to remain upright, letting my head fall back into the crook of his neck.

"You still haven't answered my question," he reminds me quietly.

I bite back a smile at his persistence. "Is this just a fling?"

"Yeah," he says. "I'm fine with a fling, I guess, but I want to know so I can figure out how to handle it once we're home."

"You mean whether or not you'll tell Dane?" I ask carefully.

"I mean whether I'll need some time to get over you."

This corkscrews an ache through my heart. I turn my head so that I can meet his kiss as he bends to deliver it and let the feeling of relief and hunger wash over me. I try to imagine seeing Ethan at Ami and Dane's house, keeping my distance, and not wanting to touch him like this.

I can't. Even in my imagination it's impossible.

"I'm not entirely done with whatever this is," I admit. "Even if it is a fling, it doesn't feel—"

"Don't say it."

"—*flung*." I grin up at him and he groans.

"That was almost as bad as your 'on the cuff' line at the wedding."

"I knew that would hold a special place in your memory."

Ethan bares his teeth on my neck, growling.

"So, I guess what I'm saying is," I begin, and then take a deep breath like I'm about to jump off a cliff into a pool of dark water, "if you wanted to keep seeing each other once we're home, I wouldn't be *totally* opposed."

His mouth moves up my neck, sucking. His hand slides beneath my jacket and shirt, coming to a warm stop over my breastbone. "Yeah?"

"What do *you* think?"

"I think I like it." He kisses along my jaw to my mouth. "I think this means I get to do *this* even after our fake honeymoon is over."

I arch into his palm, urging it over with my own hand until he's cupping my breast. But with a frustrated growl, Ethan pulls his fingers back down to my stomach. "I wish we'd had this conversation back at the room."

"Me too." Because we definitely can't fool around now: the sun isn't visible yet, but it's off the horizon, lighting the sky a million shades of orange, red, purple, and blue.

"Did we just decide something?" he asks.

I squeeze my eyes closed, grinning. "I think so."

"Good. Because I'm sort of crazy about you."

Holding my breath, I quietly admit, "I'm crazy about you, too."

I know, if I turned back to look at his face, he'd be smiling. I feel it in the way the band of his arms tightens around me.

We watch together as the sky continues to transform

every few seconds, an unreal canvas changing constantly in front of us. It makes me feel like a little girl again, and instead of imagining a castle in the sky, I'm living in it; truly the only thing we can see all around us is this dramatic, painted sky.

The gathered audience falls into a unified silence, and my own spell is broken only when the sun is high and bright and the mass of bodies begins to shift in preparation to leave. I don't want to leave. I want to sit right here, leaning against Ethan, for eternity.

"Excuse me," Ethan says to a woman in a passing group. "Would you mind taking a photo of me and my girlfriend?"

Okay . . . maybe it's time to run back to the hotel room.

chapter **fourteen**

"Someone explain to me the physics of my suitcase weighing approximately fifty pounds more when I leave than it did when I arrived," I say. "All I've added to it are a couple of T-shirts and a few small pieces of souvenir jewelry."

Ethan comes over to the side of the bed, pressing a large hand down on my bag and helping me zip it closed, with effort. "I think it's the weight of your questionable decision to buy Dane an *I Got Lei'd in Maui* T-shirt."

"You don't think he'll appreciate my dark humor?" I ask. "I mean, my dilemma really is whether I give it to him before or after we tell him we're sleeping together."

Shrugging, he pulls the suitcase off the bed and looks over at me. "He'll either laugh or give you the pouty silent treatment."

"Frankly, I could deal with either of those options."

I'm shoving things into my carry-on, so it takes me a few seconds to realize that Ethan hasn't immediately shot something back at me.

"I'm kidding, Ethan."

"Are you?"

I've been able to push this out of my thoughts for the majority of this trip, but reality is poking at our blissful vacation bubble much sooner than I'd like. "Is Dane going to become a thing between us?"

Ethan sits on the edge of the mattress and pulls me between his knees. "I said it before . . . It's clear you don't really like him, and he's my brother."

"Ethan, he's fine."

"*Fine*. He's also your brother-in-law."

I step back, frustrated. "My brother-in-law who was essentially cheating on my sister for two years."

Ethan closes his eyes, sighing. "There is *no way*—"

"If he was seeing Trinity with the Mango Butt two years ago, then he was definitely cheating on Ami."

He takes a deep breath and releases it slowly. "You can't just go in like a bull in a china shop and throw all this at Ami as soon as we get home."

"Have some faith in my ability to be subtle," I say, and when he fights a smile, I add, "I did not choose that bridesmaid dress, for the record."

“But you did choose the red bikini.”

“Are you complaining?” I ask, grinning.

“Not at all.” His smile fades. “Look, I know you and Ami and your entire family are close in a way that Dane and I aren’t—sure, we travel together, but we don’t really talk about this kind of stuff. I don’t know if it’s our place to get into this. We don’t even know if it’s true.”

“But for argument’s sake, how would you feel if it was, and he was lying to Ami for years?”

Ethan stands, and I have to tilt my head to look up at him. My first instinct is to think he’s annoyed with me, but he isn’t, I guess: he takes my face in his hands and bends to kiss me. “I’d be disappointed, of course. I just have a really hard time thinking he’d do that.”

As usual, my fuse for the Dane conversation has reached its fiery end. Things are already bittersweet today—I don’t want to leave the hotel, but I’m excited to see where things go between us back home—and bringing in the stress of Ami and Dane isn’t going to make anything easier.

I hook a finger under the waistband of his shorts, feeling the warm skin of his navel, tugging him even closer to me. With a smile of understanding, his mouth comes back over mine, urgent now, like we’ve both just become hyperaware of the brutal end to this fairy tale. The way he’s touching me with such familiarity gives me as strong a rush as the sensation of his kiss. I love how smooth and full his lips feel.

I love how he spreads his hands when he's touching me, like he's trying to feel as much of my skin as he can. We're already dressed and ready to go, but I don't protest for a single second when he roughly pulls my shirt over my head and reaches back to unhook my bra.

We fall back onto the mattress; he's careful to not land directly on top of me, but I've already grown semi-addicted to the sensation of his weight, to the heat and solidity and sheer size of him. The clothes we're planning to wear on the plane land in a pile beside the bed and he comes over me, hovering on straight arms propped near my shoulders. Ethan's gaze roams across every inch of my face.

"Hey, you," I say.

He grins. "Hey."

"Look at this. Somehow we ended up naked again."

A tanned shoulder lifts and drops. "I can see this being a regular problem."

"Problem, perfection. Tomato, tomahto."

His flash of a laughing grin fades quickly, and the way his eyes search my face looks like he's going to say something more. I wonder if he can read my thoughts, how I'm silently begging him to not bring up Dane or everything that could screw this up back home, and thankfully he doesn't. He just carefully lowers over me, groaning quietly when my legs come up along his sides.

He knows what I like already, I think, skirting my hands down his back as he starts to move. *He's been paying attention this entire time, hasn't he? I wish I could go back in time and see him through these new eyes.*

THRIFTY JET SEEMED HORRIFYINGLY LOW-BUDGET on the way here, but on the flight home, the tight quarters are a convenient excuse to wrap my arm around Ethan's and spend several hours huffing the lingering smell of the ocean on his skin. Even he seems calmer on this flight: after being tense and monosyllabic at takeoff, once we're in the air, he wraps a big hand around my thigh and falls asleep resting his cheek against the crown of my head.

If, two weeks ago, someone had shown me a photograph of us right now, I think I might have died of shock.

Would I have believed the look on my face—the giddy, sex-sated grin I can't seem to wipe clean? Would I have trusted the calm, adoring way he watches me? I haven't felt like this before—this type of intense, free-falling happiness that doesn't carry with it any unease or uncertainty about me and Ethan and what we're feeling. I've never adored someone with such heated abandon, and something tells me he hasn't, either.

My uncertainty is all about what waits for us at home—specifically, what sort of rift any drama between Dane and Ami will cause between us all.

So then I have to ask myself: Is it worth saying anything to my sister? Should I let bygones be bygones? Should I take a novel approach and not leap to the worst conclusion but have a little faith instead? I mean, maybe she knows all this already, anyway, and they've worked through it. Maybe finding out that I know Dane wasn't monogamous early on would only embarrass her and make her constantly self-conscious or defensive when I'm around them both.

I look up at Ethan, who's still asleep, and it hits me that just because I think I know what's going on, it doesn't mean I really do. This guy right here is the perfect example. I thought I knew exactly who he was, and I was completely wrong. Is it possible there are sides to my twin I don't know at all, too? I gently shake him awake, and he inhales, stretching, before looking down at me. It's like a punch to the chest how much I like his face.

"Hey," he says, voice gravelly. "What's up? You okay?"

"I like your face," I tell him.

"I'm glad you wanted to tell me that this very moment."

"And," I say, smiling nervously, "I know we don't like this topic, but I wanted to let you know that I've decided to not say anything to Ami about Dane."

Ethan's face relaxes, and he leans forward, kissing my forehead. "Okay, cool."

"Things are going so great for all of us right now—"

"I mean, yes," he cuts in with a laugh, "except for the ciguatera toxin that caused them to miss their honeymoon."

"Except for that." I wave a faux-casual hand. "Anyway, things are going well, and I should just let the past be in the past."

"Totally." He kisses me once and leans back, smiling with his eyes closed.

"I just wanted to let you know."

"I'm glad you did."

"Okay, go back to sleep."

"I will."

THE PLAN: ONCE WE LAND, we'll grab our bags, share a cab back to Minneapolis, and each spend the night at our respective home. We've already agreed the cab will drop me off at my apartment building in Dinkytown—so he can see me get in safely—before taking him to Loring Park. I'm sure it will be weird to sleep alone, but we agreed to meet up for breakfast, at which point I am positive that I will maul him instead of doing what we'd planned to do: figure out how and when to tell Ami and Dane about us.

Everything about this end of the trip stands out for how starkly different it is from the beginning. We aren't uncomfortable. We're holding hands, walking through the airport terminal, bickering lightly about which one of us is going to give in first and show up at the other's doorstep.

He bends at the luggage carousel, planting a kiss on my mouth. "You could just come over now and save yourself the trip later."

"Or *you* could."

"But my bed is really great," he argues. "It's big, firm but not hard . . ."

I immediately see where all our future problems lie: we are both stubborn homebodies. "Yeah, but I want to get in my own bathtub and use every single bath product I own and have missed for these past ten days."

Ethan kisses me again and pulls back to say more, but his eyes flitter over my shoulder and his entire demeanor changes. "Holy shit."

The words sound echoey, from a distance, multiplied. I turn to see what he's gaping at and my stomach absolutely plummets: Ami and Dane are standing only a few yards away, holding a WELCOME HOME FROM OUR HONEYMOON! sign. Now I understand what I've heard; Ami and Ethan spoke the same words, at the same time.

There is a riot in my brain: just my luck. I'm temporarily unable to decide what to process first: the fact that my sister is here, that she saw me kissing Ethan, that Dane saw me kissing Ethan, or the reality that—even eleven days after they were knocked down by a toxin—they both still look positively horrible. I think Ami has lost over ten pounds, and Dane has likely lost more. The gray sheen to Ami's complexion hasn't entirely gone away, and her clothes sag on her frame.

And here we are, tanned, rested, and making out in baggage claim.

"What am I seeing?" Ami says, dropping her half of the sign in shock.

I'm sure I'll examine my reaction later, but given that I can't tell whether she's excited or angry right now, I let go of Ethan's hand and take a step away from him. I wonder how it looks to her: I left for her honeymoon, paid almost nothing, suffered not at all, and came home kissing the man I was supposed to hate—and never once mentioned any of this to her on the phone or in texts. "Nothing, we were just saying goodbye."

"Were you *kissing*?" she asks, brown eyes saucer-wide.

Ethan tosses out a confident "Yes" just as I state an emphatic "*No*."

He looks down at me, smirking at how easily that lie came out of me. I can tell he is more proud of my smoothness than he is annoyed by my answer.

"Okay, yes," I amend. "We were kissing. But we didn't

know you were going to be here. We were going to tell you guys tomorrow."

"Tell us what, exactly?" Ami asks.

Ethan takes this one readily and slides his arm around my shoulder, pulling me close. "That we're together."

For the first time, I get a good look at Dane. He's staring directly at Ethan, his eyes narrowed like he's trying to beam words into his brother's cranium. I try to tamp down my reaction, knowing it's probably just my own read on the situation, but his glare looks a lot like *What did you tell her?*

"It's cool," Ethan says calmly, and my resolution to mind my own beeswax returns, heightened by the potent mix of adrenaline in my blood.

"Everything is *very* cool," I say, too loudly, and give Dane a dramatic, and probably ill-advised, wink. "Super cool."

I am a maniac.

He bursts out laughing and finally breaks the ice, stepping forward to hug me first, and then his brother. Ami continues to stare at me in shock, and then slowly shuffles over. She feels like a skeleton in my arms.

"Dude, are you two really a thing now?" Dane asks his brother.

"We are," Ethan tells him.

"I think I can approve it at this point," Dane says, smiling and nodding at each of us like a benevolent boss.

"Um," I say, "that's . . . good?"

Ami still has not relaxed her expression one bit. "How did this even happen?"

I shrug, wincing. "I hated him until I didn't?"

"That's actually a very accurate synopsis." Ethan slides an arm around my shoulders again.

My sister shakes her head slowly, gaping at the two of us in turn. "I don't know whether to be happy or horrified. Is this the apocalypse? Is that what's happening?"

"We could totally trade twins sometime," Dane says to Ethan, and then erupts into a fratty laugh.

My smile droops. "That would . . ." I shake my head emphatically. "No thank you."

"Oh my God, shut *up*, honey," Ami says, laughing and hitting his shoulder. "You are so gross."

Everyone laughs except me, and I realize it too late, so my *ha-ha-ha* comes out like a pull-string toy.

But I think that's my problem with Dane, in a nutshell: he's gross. And unfortunately, my sister loves him, I've been hooking up with his brother, and not five minutes ago I gave Dane the all-clear wink. I made my decision; I'm pretty sure I'm going to have to put on my big-girl pants and deal.

chapter **fifteen**

I wanted to stay in Maui. I wanted to stay in bed with Ethan for weeks, and listen to the ocean while I fell asleep. But even so, the moment I'm back in my apartment, I want to kiss every piece of my furniture and touch every single thing I've missed for the past ten days. My couch has never looked so inviting. My television is way better than the one we had in the suite. My bed is fluffy and clean, and I can't wait until it's dark enough to justify taking a running leap into my pillows. I am a homebody, through and through, and there's nothing like being home.

This feeling lasts about thirty minutes. Because after I've unpacked, I check my fridge and realize there's nothing in there, so if I want to eat, I have to either order crappy delivery food, or put my pants back on and leave the house.

I sprawl in the middle of the living room on my fluffy

faux-fur rug and groan at the ceiling. If I'd gone to Ethan's, I could have made him go get me food.

The doorbell rings. I ignore it because my family would just waltz right in like they own the place, and nine times out of ten it's my upstairs neighbor Jack, a fiftysomething guy who pays way too close attention to my comings and goings. But then it rings again, which a few seconds later is followed by a knock. Jack never rings twice, and he never knocks.

Standing, I peek through the peephole and see a chiseled jaw, a long, muscular neck. I've missed that neck. Ethan! My heart reacts before my brain does—leaping happily into my throat—and so when I pull the door open with a grin, it takes a beat to remember that I'm not wearing pants.

Ethan smiles at me and then his eyes drop to my lower half and he makes the same seductive expression I know I'm directing at the bag of food he's carrying.

"You missed me," I say, taking the Chinese takeout from his hand.

"You're pantsless."

I smirk at him over my shoulder. "You should probably get used to it. I mostly behaved myself at the hotel, but ninety-nine percent of the time I'm home I'm in my underwear."

He raises a brow and tilts his head toward the hallway

I'm sure he's guessed leads to my bedroom. I get it—in a movie we would be crashing against the wall, passionately pinballing our way down the hall toward the bed because we missed each other so much after an hour apart, but in truth, that airport run-in was stressful as hell, I am starving, and this takeout smells amazing.

"Garlic chicken first, sex second."

I get all fluttery inside—and I am not normally a swooner—when he smiles at the way I'm diving into the food he brought. He kisses my forehead and then turns, easily finding my silverware drawer and grabbing us both some chopsticks. We stand in the kitchen, eating chicken out of the containers. Something inside me uncoils because I was happy to be home, but now I'm giddy. I feel more myself with him than without, and that happened so fast, it's dizzying.

"My fridge was empty," he tells me. "Figured yours was, too, and it was only a matter of time before you came to my door because you were so lonely."

I shove a mouthful of noodles in my mouth and speak around them: "Yeah, that sounds like me."

"So needy," he agrees, laughing.

I watch him tuck into the Mongolian beef and give myself a few quiet seconds to stare at the face I've missed for the past hour. "I like that you just showed up," I tell him.

"Good." He chews and swallows. "I was pretty sure you

would, but there was a twenty percent chance you'd be like, 'Get the hell out of my apartment, I need to do a fancy bath tonight.' "

"Oh, I definitely want a fancy bath."

"But after the food and sex."

I nod. "Right."

"I'll snoop around your apartment while you're doing that. I'm not a bath guy."

This makes me laugh. "Do you think this feels so easy because we hated each other first?" I ask.

He shrugs, digging into the container for a giant piece of beef.

"We're a week in," I say, "and I'm pantsless and eating greasy food in front of you."

"I mean, I saw you in that bridesmaid dress. Everything else is an improvement."

"I take it back," I tell him. "I still hate you."

Ethan comes over, bends, and kisses my nose. "Sure."

The mood shifts. So many times I've gone from uneasy to angry with him, but now it's from happy to heated. He slides the food onto the counter behind me, cupping my face.

When he's only an inch away, I whisper, "I just realized you and I shared a container of food and it didn't gross you out."

He kisses me and then rolls his eyes, moving his mouth

to my cheek, my jaw, my neck. "I told you, I don't mind sharing. It's"—*kiss*—"about"—*kiss*—"buffets. And. I. Was. Right."

"Well, I'm forever grateful that you're such a weirdo."

Ethan nods, kissing my jaw. "That was the best honeymoon I've ever been on."

I pull his mouth back to mine and then hop up on him, relieved that he anticipates he'll need to catch me, and lift my chin toward the bedroom. "That way."

ONCE ETHAN AND I DISCOVER that we live only two miles apart, you'd think we'd find a way to alternate between apartments at night. You'd be wrong. Clearly I am terrible at compromise, because from Wednesday night when we return home, to Monday morning when I begin my new job, Ethan spends every night at my place.

He doesn't leave things here (except a toothbrush), but he does learn that I have to hit my alarm four times before getting out of bed to go to the gym, that I don't use my favorite spoon for anything as menial as stirring coffee, that my family can and will show up at the most inopportune moment, and that I require him to turn on the television or play some music every time I use the restroom.

Because I am a lady, obviously.

But with this familiarity comes the awareness of how fast everything is moving. By the time we're closing in on two weeks together—which in the grand scheme of life is *nothing*—it feels to me like Ethan has been my boyfriend since the moment I met him at the State Fair years ago.

Things are easy, and fun, and effortless. This isn't how new relationships are supposed to be: they are supposed to be stressful, and exhausting, and uncertain.

The morning before I go to work at Hamilton Biosciences for the first time is not the time to be having an existential crisis about moving too fast with my new boyfriend, but my brain didn't get the memo.

In a new suit, cute-but-comfortable heels, and with my hair blow-dried to a silky sheet down my back, I look over at Ethan at my small dining room table. "You haven't said anything about how I look this morning."

"I said it with my eyes when you stepped out of the bedroom, you just weren't looking." He takes a bite of toast and speaks around it. "You look beautiful, and professional, and intelligent." Pausing, to swallow, he adds, "But I also like the island-scrappy version of you."

I scrape some butter across my toast, then set the knife down with a clatter. "Do you think we're moving too fast?"

Ethan sips his coffee, blue eyes now focused on the scrolling news on his phone. He's not even fazed by this question. "Probably."

"Does that worry you?"

"No."

"Not even a little?"

He looks back up at me. "Do you want me to stay at my place tonight?"

"God no," I say, in a complete knee-jerk response. He smiles, smug, and looks back down. "But maybe?" I say. "Should you?"

"I don't think there are rules to this."

I gulp my scalding coffee and then roar in pain. "Ow!" I stare at him, placid as ever, back to being nose-deep in the *Washington Post* mobile app. "Why are you not freaking out a little?"

"Because I'm not starting a new job today and looking for reasons to explain my stress about it." He puts his phone down and folds his arms on the table. "You're going to be great, you know."

I grunt, unconvinced. Ethan is more intuitive than I ever gave him credit for.

"Maybe we should get together with Ami and Dane for drinks later," he suggests. "You know, to process your first day, to make sure everyone is okay with this current situation. I feel like I've been hogging you."

"Stop that."

"Stop what?"

"Being so emotionally balanced!"

He pauses and a slow grin takes over his face. "Okay?"

I grab my coat and purse and make for the door, fighting a grin because I know he's laughing at me behind my back. And I'm totally okay with it.

I AM REMINDED HOW SMALL Hamilton Biosciences actually is when I step into the lobby, where a woman named Pam has been working the desk for thirty-three years. Kasey, the HR representative I interviewed with a couple of months ago, greets me and beckons me to follow. If we turned left, we'd end up in the office suite of the legal team of three. But we take a right down the hall that leads us to the mirror-image suite that houses the HR department of two.

"Research is just across the courtyard," Kasey says, "but all of the medical affairs folks—if you remember!—are upstairs in this building."

"That's right!" I adopt her upbeat tone, following her into her office.

"We'll just have a few forms to get you rolling, and then you can head upstairs to meet with the rest of your team."

My heart takes off at a gallop as the reality of this sets in. I've been in a blissed-out la-la land for the past couple of weeks, but real life is back, front and center. For now, I'll only have one direct report working under me, but from what Kasey and Mr. Hamilton told me when I was here last, there should be lots of opportunities for growth.

"You'll have some manager training," Kasey is saying, rounding her desk, "which I believe is this Thursday. Gives you a little time to get in, get settled."

"Great."

I smooth my hands down my skirt and try to swallow down my nerves while she opens up some files on her computer, while she bends and retrieves a folder from a cabinet near her knee, while she opens it and pulls out some forms. I see my name at the top of all of them. Anxiety slowly gives way to thrill.

I have a job! A job that is solid, and secure, and—let's be honest—will probably be boring sometimes but will pay the bills! It's what I went to school for. It's perfect.

Elation fills my chest, making me feel buoyant.

Kasey organizes a stack of paperwork for me, and I begin signing. It's the usual: I won't sell company secrets, won't commit various forms of harassment, won't use alcohol or drugs on the premises, won't lie, cheat, or steal.

I'm deep into the stack when Mr. Hamilton himself peeks his head into her office. "I see our Olive is back on the continent!"

"Hey, Mr. Hamilton."

He winks, and asks, "How's Ethan doing?"

I glance quickly to Kasey and back. "Um, he's great."

"Olive just got married!" he says. "We ran into each other on her honeymoon in Maui."

Kasey gasps. "Oh, my God! I thought you were with a sick relative! I am so glad I misunderstood!" My stomach seems to melt away; I had completely forgotten about telling Kasey this stupid lie in the airport. She doesn't seem to notice anything off and barrels on: "We should have a party!"

"Oh, no," I say, "please don't." Insert awkward laugh. "We are all partied out."

"But for sure he should join the spouses club!" she says, already nodding vigorously at Mr. Hamilton.

I know Mrs. Hamilton founded the club, but my God, Kasey, take it down a notch or two.

Mr. Hamilton winks at me. "I know Molly put on the hard sell, but it *is* a fun group."

This is going too far already. I'm so bad at lying that I've forgotten lies I've already told. Ethan and I aren't going to be able to keep this up for very long at such a close-knit company. I have a sinking feeling inside, but feel a tiny twinge of relief knowing that I'm going to put this lie to rest at last.

"I'm sure the spouses club is amazing." I pause, and I know I could leave it at that, but I've just signed all these forms and really want to make a fresh start here. "Ethan and I aren't actually married. It's sort of a funny story, Mr. Hamilton, and I hope it's okay if I come by later and tell you about it."

I'd wanted to keep it simple, but I can tell I should have built up my version a little bit. This just sounds . . . bad.

He processes this for a beat before glancing at Kasey, then back to me and saying quietly, "Well, regardless . . . welcome to Hamilton," before ducking out.

I want to drop my head to the desk and then bang it a few (dozen) times. I want to let out a long string of curse words. I want to get up and follow him down the hall. Surely he'll understand the situation once I lay it out for him?

I look back at Kasey, who is regarding me with a mixture of sympathy and confusion. I think she's starting to realize that she didn't really misunderstand what I'd said about a sick relative. She's realizing I lied about that, too.

Not exactly the best way to start day one at a new job.

TWO HOURS LATER, AFTER I sign all the forms, after I meet the group that will be my medical affairs team (and genuinely liking all of them), Mr. Hamilton's assistant, Joyce, calls me down to his office.

"Just a welcome, I assume!" my new manager, Tom, says cheerfully.

But I think I know better.

Mr. Hamilton lets out a low "Come on in" after I knock, and his expectant smile flattens marginally when he sees me. "Olive."

"Hi," I say, and my voice shakes.

He doesn't say anything right away, confirming my assumption that this meeting is a chance for me to explain myself. "Look, Mr. Hamilton"—I don't dare call him Charlie here—"about Maui."

Put on your big girl pants and own it, Olive.

Mr. Hamilton puts his pen down, takes off his glasses, and leans back in his chair. Right now, he looks so different from the man I sat across from at dinner, who howled with laughter every time Ethan teased me. I'm sure he's thinking about that meal, too, and how much Molly loved Ethan, how she invited him into her spouses group, how they were so genuinely happy for us, while we sat there and lied to their faces.

I gesture to the chair, silently asking if I may sit, and he waves me forward, sliding the arm of his glasses between his teeth.

"My twin sister, Ami, was married two weeks ago," I tell him. "She married Ethan's brother, Dane. They hosted a seafood buffet, and the entire wedding party—except for me and Ethan—fell ill with food poisoning. Ciguatera toxin," I add, because he's a scientist and maybe he knows these things.

He seems to, because his bushy eyebrows lift, and he lets out a quiet "Ah."

"My sister, Ami . . . she wins everything. Raffles, sweepstakes," I say, smiling wryly, "even coloring contests."

At this, Mr. Hamilton's mustache twitches under a grin.

"She won the honeymoon, too, but the rules were really strict. It was nontransferable, nonrefundable. The dates were set hard and fast."

"I see."

"So, Ethan and I went in their place." I give him a wobbly smile. "Before that trip, we hated each other. Or, I hated him because I thought he hated me." I wave this off. "Anyway, I am terrible at lying and really hate doing it. I kept almost explaining it to everyone I saw. And when the massage therapist called me Mrs. Thomas, and you asked if I'd gotten married, I panicked because I didn't want to admit that I wasn't Ami." I fidget with a magnetic paperclip holder on his desk, unable to look at him. "But I didn't want to lie to you, either. So, either I lie and tell you I'm committing fraud to steal a vacation, or I lie and tell you I'm married."

"Pretending to be your sister to get a vacation doesn't sound like such a horrible lie, Olive."

"In hindsight—and I mean, *immediate* hindsight—I knew that, too. I don't think the massage therapist would have reported me or anything, but I really didn't want to be sent home. I panicked." I finally look up at him, feeling the apology all the way to my breastbone. "I'm really sorry for lying to you. I admire you immensely, admire the foundation of this company, and have been feeling sick over it for the past couple weeks." Pausing, I say, "For what it's worth—and at the risk of being unprofessional—I think that dinner with you was the reason I fell for Ethan on that trip."

Mr. Hamilton sits forward to rest his elbows on his desk. "Well, I guess I'm reassured that it made you uncomfortable to lie," he says. "And I appreciate your bravery in telling me."

"Of course."

He nods, and smiles, and I exhale for the first time all day, it seems. This has been weighing on me, making my stomach feel wavy for hours.

"The truth is," he says, and slides his glasses back on, looking at me over the rims, "we enjoyed that dinner. Molly really loved your company, adored Ethan."

I smile. "We had a great—"

"But you sat across the table for an entire meal and lied to me."

Dread turns the surface of my skin cold. "I know. I—"

"I don't think you're a bad person, Olive, and honestly—under any other circumstance, I think I'd really like you." He inhales slowly, shaking his head. "But this is a weird situation for me. To think we were together for hours and you were fooling us. That's weird."

And I have no idea what to say. My stomach feels like a concrete block now, sinking inside me.

He slides a folder closer to him and opens it. My HR folder. "You signed a morality clause in the employment contract," he says, looking down at the papers before turning his face back up to me. "And I'm truly sorry, Olive, but given the oddness of this situation and my overall discomfort with dishonesty, I'm going to have to let you go."

I DROP MY HEAD ONTO the bar table and groan. "Is this really happening?"

Ethan rubs my back and wisely stays quiet. There is literally nothing that can turn this day around, not even the best cocktails in the Twin Cities or the best pep talk from a new boyfriend.

"I should go home," I say. "With my luck, the bar will catch fire and fall into a black hole."

"Stop." He pushes the basket of peanuts and my martini closer and smiles. "Stay. It'll make you feel better to see Ami."

He's right. After I left Hamilton with my tail between my legs, half of me wanted to go home and burrow in my bed for a week, and half of me wanted to pull Ethan on one side and Ami on the other and have them hold me up for the rest of the night.

And now that I'm here, I actually *need* to see my sister's indignant rage over my getting fired on my first day—even if it isn't entirely fair, and a large part of me doesn't blame Mr. Hamilton at all. But it will make me feel a million times better.

Straightening beside me, Ethan looks toward the door and I follow his attention. Dane has just arrived, but there's no Ami with him, which is weird since they usually commute together.

"What's up, party people?" he booms across the room. A few heads turn, which is just how Dane likes it.

Ugh. I push down the snarky voice in my head.

Ethan stands to greet him with a bro hug, and I give Dane a limp wave. He flops down onto a barstool, shouts for an IPA, and then turns to us, grinning. "Man, you guys are so tan. I'm trying not to hate you."

Ethan looks down at his arms like they're new. "Huh, yeah, I guess."

"Well, if it makes you feel any better," I say, and then affect a stuffy British accent, "I've been sacked." I'm trying—and failing—to bring some levity to my mood, but Dane misinterprets my meaning and goes in for an immediate high-five.

"*Yeah* you have!" Dane shouts, hand outstretched.

I don't want to leave the poor man hanging, so I tap a

finger to the middle of his palm and shake my head. "Like, fired," I clarify, and Ethan follows it up with a quiet "Not sexy."

Dane's mouth pinches into a weird little butthole and he lets out a sympathetic "Oooh, that sucks."

He's not even doing anything douchey right now, but I swear his perfectly manicured beard and his fake glasses that he doesn't even need and his trendy pink dress shirt just make me want to toss my martini in his face.

But that reaction is just so . . . Olive, isn't it? I'm back in town for only a few days and I'm already in A Mood? Lord.

"I'm so grumpy," I say out loud, and Dane laughs like *I know, right?* but Ethan leans in.

"To be fair, you did just lose your job," he says quietly, and I smile grimly at him. "Of course you're grumpy."

Dane stares at us. "It's gonna be hard to get used to seeing you guys together."

"I bet," I say with semi-intentional meaning, and meet his eyes.

"I'm sure you had a lot to talk about on the island." He winks at me, and then adds breezily, "Having hated each other's guts beforehand."

I wonder if Ethan is having the same thought I am—that this is a super-weird thing to say, but exactly the thing that someone who is afraid of being busted would say.

"We did," Ethan says, "but it's all good."

"You didn't have to tell Ethan that I'm angry all the time," I say, unable to help myself.

Dane waves this off. "Eh, with you, it's a safe bet. You hate everyone."

This tilts inside me, ringing untrue. For the life of me, I can't think of a single person I hate right now. Except maybe myself, for lying to Mr. Hamilton and ending up in this place, where I'm not sure I'll be able to pay my rent in a month . . . again.

Ethan puts his hand over mine, a silent *Let it go.* And truly, with Dane right now—or ever—arguing hardly seems worth it.

"Where's Ami?" I ask, and Dane shrugs, peeking back over his shoulder at the door. She's fifteen minutes late, and it's disorienting. My sister is the prompt one; Dane is the late one and he's already flagging down the bartender for a second beer.

"So, was this the job offer you got in the airport?" Dane asks once she's gone.

I nod.

"Was it, like, your dream job?"

"No," I say, "but I knew I'd be good at it." I lift the toothpick and swirl the olive in my martini glass. "The best part? I was fired because I saw my new boss in Maui, and we lied to him about being married."

A laugh bursts out of Dane's mouth before he can contain it. He seems to realize I'm being sincere. "Wait. Seriously?"

"Yes, and the wife, Molly, really loved Ethan and invited him to the spouses club and all of that stuff. I think Mr. Hamilton felt uncomfortable trusting me knowing that I'd completely lied my face off for an entire meal with him, and I can't say I blame him."

Dane looks like he has more laughs in him but is wisely keeping them contained. "Why didn't you just tell him you were taking your sister's vacation?"

"That, Dane, is the question of the hour."

He lets out a long, low whistle.

"We can talk about anything else, by the way," I say. "Please."

Dane deftly changes the topic to himself, his workday, how much better he's feeling. How he's gone down a pants size. He has some pretty entertaining stories about explosive diarrhea in public restrooms, but for the most part it just feels like the Dane Show.

The moment Dane pauses to toss a few peanuts in his mouth, Ethan excuses himself to use the men's room, and Dane waves to the bartender for a third beer. Once she leaves again, he turns back to me. "It's wild how much you and Ami look alike," he says.

"Identical, they say." I pick up a straw wrapper and roll

it into a tight spiral, feeling oddly uncomfortable sitting here with just Dane. What's odd is how I used to see the family resemblance in Ethan and Dane, but in this moment, they look nothing alike at all. Is it because I know Ethan intimately now, or is it because he is a good human and his brother seems rotten from the inside?

It's especially uncomfortable because he's still looking at me. Even though I'm not meeting his eyes, I can feel his focus on the side of my face. "I bet Ethan told you all kinds of stories."

And oh. My mind is immediately buzzing. Is he talking about what I think he's talking about?

"About himself?" I deflect.

"About all of us, the whole fam."

Dane and Ethan's parents are two of the most milquetoast people I've ever met in my life—the epitome of Minnesota nice, but also exceedingly dull—so I think both Dane and I know that Ethan wouldn't share many adventures about *the whole fam.* Is it my eternal skeptical filter here that's making me think he's talking about the brother trips being Dane's ideas and, of course, all of his pre-engagement girlfriends?

I look at him over the lip of my martini glass. I am so conflicted. I told Ethan—and myself—that I would let this one go. That Ami is a smart woman and knows what she's getting into. That I am always the buzzkill pessimist.

Dane gets one last freebie, and that's it.

"We all have stories, Dane," I tell him evenly. "You and Ethan have yours. Ami and I have ours. We all have them."

He pops a couple of peanuts into his mouth and grins at me as he chews, mouth open, like he's just outsmarted me. As irritating as he's being, I can tell he's genuinely relieved. If it were anyone else smiling at me like this, I'd feel honored to be so clearly welcomed into the inner circle with just a shift in an expression. But with Dane, it makes me feel slimy, like I'm not supporting my sister by supporting her husband, like I'm betraying her.

"So you like my big brother, huh?" he asks.

The husky quiet of his voice makes me uneasy. "He's all right, I guess," I joke.

"He's pretty great," he says, and then adds, "even if he isn't me."

"I mean," I say, forcing a dorky grin, "who is? Am I right?"

Dane thanks the bartender when she delivers the fresh beer and then takes a foamy sip, still studying me. "You ever want to mix it up, you let me know."

My eyes fly to his face, and I feel the way the blood leaves my complexion in a *whoosh*. There is no way I'm misinterpreting his meaning. "I'm sorry. What?"

"Just a night of fun," he says, breezily, like he hasn't just offered to cheat on his wife with her twin sister.

I tap my chin with a finger, feeling my neck heat, my face flush. It's a struggle to keep my voice even. "You know, I think I'll take an emphatic pass on sleeping with my brother-in-law."

He shrugs like it makes no difference to him—and silently confirming that his vague words meant exactly what I thought they meant—but then his eyes are caught on something over my shoulder. I assume Ethan is walking back, because Dane smiles, tilting his chin. "Yeah," he says as Ethan approaches, "I guess he's all right."

I gape at how casually he returns to our earlier conversation.

"Were you two talking about me?" Ethan asks, lowering onto the stool beside me and pressing his smile to my cheek.

"We were," Dane says. I look at him. There's not even a warning in his expression, not even any fear that I'll say something to Ethan about what just happened. By telling him that we all have stories, by implying that I'm not going to press into his past, have I indicated that I'm okay being eternally complicit somehow?

Dane peeks down at his phone when it vibrates on the bar top next to him. "Oh, Ami is running about an hour late."

I stand, abruptly, robotically. "You know, that's okay. I'm not the best company tonight. Rain check, guys?"

Dane nods easily, but Ethan looks concerned, reaching out with a hand to stop me. "Hey, hey. You okay?"

"Yeah." I run a shaking hand through my hair, looking past him. I feel jittery and gross and somehow like I've done something unfaithful—to Ethan and my sister. I need to get away from Dane and get some air. "I think I just want to go home and wallow for a bit. You know me."

He nods like he does know and releases me with a sympathetic smile.

But I suddenly feel like *I* don't know anything. I am thunderstruck.

That's not entirely true. I know some things. For example, I know I lost my job today. And I know that my sister's husband cheated on her before and is apparently happy to cheat on her again. With her twin. I need to get some clarity and figure out how the hell I'm going to tell Ami about all of this.

chapter **sixteen**

I'm halfway to my car when I hear Ethan's voice calling out across the parking lot. Turning, I watch as he carefully makes his way through the slush and the ice and comes to a stop in front of me.

He didn't bother to put on his coat before following me outside and shivers against the cold. "Are you sure you're okay?"

"I'm not great, honestly, but I'll be fine." I think.

"Do you want me to come back to your place with you?"

"No." I wince, hoping he knows this came out more abruptly than I intended. Attempting to tamp down my anger, I take a deep breath and give him a very wobbly smile; this isn't his fault. I need to talk to Ami. I need to think and make some sense of how Dane had the balls to say something like that to me with his brother just feet away. I need to figure out what the hell I'm going to do for a job, immediately. I scrape the toe of my boot against a patch of ice. "I think I just need to go home and freak out a little on my own."

Ethan tilts his head, gaze roaming my face deliberately. "Okay. But if you need me to come over, just text."

"I will." I pull my lips between my teeth, resisting the urge to tell him to come with me and be my sounding board. But I know that won't work. "I'll be terrible company tonight, but it's still going to be weird sleeping alone in my own bed. You've ruined me."

I can tell he likes this. He takes a step forward and bends to kiss me, deepening it gently, a tiny, sweet taste. When he pulls back, he runs a finger across my forehead. He's so *sweet.* It's started snowing again and the flakes flutter down to land on his shoulders, the back of his hand, the tips of his lashes.

"You left really suddenly," he says, and I'm not surprised that he can't let it go. I'm acting like a maniac. "What happened when I was in the bathroom?"

I take a deep breath and slowly blow it out. "Dane said something kind of shitty."

Ethan leans the tiniest bit away from me. It's such a subtle gesture, I wonder if he even notices that he did it. "What did he say?"

"Why don't we talk about this later?" I ask. "It's freezing."

"You can't just say something like that and then call a rain check." He reaches for my hand, but doesn't squeeze it in his. "What happened?"

I tuck my chin into my coat, wishing I could disappear into it entirely, like a portable blanket fort. "He hit on me."

A blast of wind whips across the front of the building, ruffling the front of Ethan's hair. He's looking at me so intently he doesn't even wince at the cold.

"What do you mean, like . . ." He frowns. "Like, touched you?"

"No." I shake my head. "He suggested Ami and I trade brothers for a little fun." I have the urge to laugh, because saying it out loud makes it sound completely ridiculous. Who the hell does that? Who hits on his brother's girlfriend, who is also his wife's sister? When Ethan doesn't say anything, I repeat it more slowly. "He wanted me to let him know if we ever wanted to *mix it up*, Ethan."

A beat of silence.

Two.

And then Ethan's expression turns quizzical. "'Mix it up' doesn't necessarily mean, like, trade partners."

Stay calm, Olive. I give him a meaningful stare and count to ten in my head. "Yeah. It does."

His expression straightens again, and a hint of protectiveness creeps into his voice. "Okay, granted his sense of humor isn't always appropriate, but Dane wouldn't—"

"I realize this is shocking on a number of levels, but I do know what someone hitting on me looks like."

He steps away, clearly frustrated. With *me*. "I know Dane is immature sometimes and sort of self-centered, but he wouldn't do that."

"Just like he wouldn't lie to Ami for God knows how long while he banged whoever he wanted?"

Even in the dim light, I can see Ethan's face has turned a deep red. "I thought we agreed that we don't know the situation there. It's possible Ami already knows."

"Well, have you asked him?"

"Why would I?" he says, hands waving in front of him like what I'm suggesting isn't just unnecessary, it's preposterous. "Olive. We agreed to let that go."

"That was before he propositioned me while you were in the bathroom!" I stare at him, willing him to have some kind of reaction to this, but he's just closed up on me, his face unreadable. "Have you considered that you've put him on some kind of pedestal—though for the life of me, I can't understand why—and are incapable of seeing he's a *total sleaze*?"

Ethan flinches, and now I feel bad. Dane is his *brother*. My instinct is to apologize, but the words are stuck in my throat, blocked by the enormous relief of finally saying what I think.

"Have you considered you're seeing what you want to see?"

I straighten. "What is that supposed to mean? That I *want* Dane to hit on me?"

He's shaking and I'm not sure if it's from cold or anger. "It means that maybe you're pissed off about losing your job, and you're in the habit of being bitter about everything Ami has that you don't, and you're not objective about any of this."

This feels like a physical punch to my stomach, and I take an instinctive step back.

Flames. On the side of my face . . .

His shoulders fall immediately. "Shit. I didn't mean—"

"Yes, you did." I turn around and keep walking to my car. His footsteps follow across the salted asphalt.

"Olive, wait. Come on. Don't just walk away."

I pull out my keys and fling open the door with so much force, the hinges groan in protest.

"Olive! Just—"

I slam the door and with shaking hands and numb fingers, jam my key into the ignition. His words are drowned out by the sound of the engine struggling to turn over. Finally it catches, and I shift into reverse, backing up. He walks alongside me; hand on the roof of the car as he pleads for my attention. It's so cold I can see my breath in front of my face, but I don't feel a thing. My ears are full of static.

He watches me leave, and in my rearview mirror I see him grow smaller and smaller. We have never been so far from that mountaintop in Maui.

THE DRIVE HOME IS A blur. I alternate between being mad at myself for all of this, terrified about my future income, furious at Dane, sad and disappointed over Ethan, and absolutely heartbroken for Ami. It's not enough to hope that Dane will turn over a new leaf now that he's married—he is a bad guy, and my sister has no idea.

I try not to be dramatic and overthink what Ethan said. I try to give him the benefit of the doubt and imagine how I'd feel if someone accused Ami of doing this. I don't even have to think about it: I'd do anything for my sister. And that's when it hits me. I remember Dane's smiling face at the airport, and my shock today that he would hit on me with his own brother just a few feet away. Dane's confidence in both cases isn't about me or my ability to keep his secret. It was about Ethan and his inability to believe his brother would intentionally do anything bad. Ethan is his ride-or-die.

I consider going to Ami's to wait for her, but if Ami was planning to meet us all at the restaurant, she won't be there anyway. They'd come home together later, too. I certainly don't want to be there when Dane gets back.

I didn't think it was possible, but my mood plummets even more when I pull into my parking lot. Not only is my mom's car there (and parked in my covered space), but so are Diego's and my cousin Natalia's, which means Tía María is probably here as well. Of course.

With my car parked on the other side of the complex, I trudge through the slush and up the stairs to my apartment. I can already hear Tía María's braying laugh—she is my mother's sister and the one closest to her in age, but the two of them could not be more different: Mom is polished and fussy; Tía María is casual and laughs constantly. And whereas Mom has only me and Ami (apparently having twins was plenty for her), Tía María has seven kids, each neatly spaced eighteen months apart. It wasn't until I was in the fifth grade that I realized not everyone has nineteen first cousins.

Although our nuclear family is relatively small compared to the rest of the Torres and Gonzales crew, a stranger would never know that only four of us lived in our house when I was growing up because at least two other people were always there. Birthdays were enormous affairs, Sunday dinners routinely had thirty people at the table, and there was never any place to sulk alone. Apparently not much has changed.

"I'm pretty sure she's a lesbian," Tía María is saying as I close the door behind me. She looks up at the sound and points to Natalia. "Tell her, Olive."

I unwind my scarf from around my neck and stomp the snow from my boots. After the slushy walk through the parking lot, my patience is already thin. "Who are we talking about?"

Tía María is standing at the kitchen counter, chopping tomatoes. "Ximena."

Ximena, the youngest daughter of Mom and Tía María's oldest brother, Tío Omar. "She's not a lesbian," I say. "She's dating that guy, what's his name?"

I look at Natalia, who tells them, "Boston."

I snap, pointing. "That's right. God, what a terrible name."

"It's what you name your dog," Natalia agrees, "not your kid."

I shrug off my coat and toss it over the back of the couch. Mom immediately steps away from the dough she's rolling and crosses the room to pointedly hang it up. Stopping in front of me, she pushes my damp hair off my forehead.

"You look terrible, *mija*." She turns my face from side to

side. "Eat something." Kissing my cheek, she heads back into the kitchen.

I follow, smiling gratefully when Natalia sets a cup of tea down in front of me. For as much as I complain about my family always being in my business . . . having them here is admittedly pretty great. But this also means I can't avoid telling Mom that I was fired.

"A haircut doesn't mean someone's gay, Mom," Natalia says.

Tía María looks up at her incredulously. "Have you seen it? It's all short on the sides and blue on top. She did it right after"—she drops her voice to a whisper—"*the wedding*."

Both Mom and Tía María make the sign of the cross.

"Why would you even care if she's gay?" Natalia motions to where Diego is watching TV on my couch. "Diego is gay, and you don't care about that."

At the sound of his name he turns to face us.

"Diego came out of the womb gay," Tía María says, and then turns to him. "I swear you had copies of *Vogue* under your mattress, instead of dirty magazines."

"Nobody gets porn from magazines anymore, Mom," Natalia says.

Tía María ignores her. "I don't care if she's gay. I just think we should all know so we can find her a nice girl."

"She's not gay!" Diego says.

"Then why did I find a dildo in her sock drawer?" Tía María asks the room.

Diego groans and pulls a pillow over his face. "Here we go."

Natalia turns to face her mother. "She's thirty-three. What were you doing in her sock drawer?"

Tía María shrugs as if this information is irrelevant to the story. "Organizing. It was purple and huge with a little"—she moves her finger in front of her to indicate what she means—"wiggly thing on one side."

Natalia presses her hand to her mouth to stifle a laugh, and I take a sip of my tea. It tastes like sadness and hot water.

My mom stops chopping and sets down her knife. "Why would that mean she's a lesbian?"

Tía María blinks at her. "Because lesbians use those strap-on things."

"Mom, stop," Natalia says. "Lots of people have vibrators. I have a whole box full of them." She waves in my direction. "You should see Olive's collection."

"Thanks, Nat."

My mom picks up a glass of wine and takes a large gulp. "It seems smart to be a lesbian right now. Men are awful."

She is not wrong.

I lean a casual hip against the counter. "So. Why are you

guys cooking at my apartment?" I ask. "And when are you going home?"

Natalia turns off the stove and moves her pot to an empty burner. "Your dad needed some stuff at the house." That's it, that's her entire answer, and in this family, it's plenty: Dad rarely goes to the house—he lives alone in a condo near Lake Harriet—but when he does visit, my mom evacuates the premises immediately. The rare times she feels spunky enough to stick around, she'll commit some pretty petty sabotage. Once, she pulled out his collection of vinyl records and used them as trivets and coasters. Another time, when he stopped by before a weeklong business trip, she put a whole fresh trout under one of the seats in his car and he didn't find it until he got home. It was in August.

"I wish I'd been born a lesbian," Mom says.

"Then you wouldn't have me," I counter.

She pats my cheek. "That's okay."

I meet Natalia's eyes over the top of my mug and fight the laugh that is bubbling up inside me. I worry that if it escapes, it could turn into hysterical cackles that would immediately transition into choking sobs.

"What's with you?" Tía María asks, and it takes me a moment to realize she's talking to me.

"She's probably tired from her new boyfriend," Natalia

sings and does a little sexy dance back over to the stove. "I'm surprised he wasn't with you. We only came in because his car wasn't out front. God knows what we'll see."

They all spin out of control about me and Ethan for a few minutes—

Finally! Se te va pasó al tren!

So perfect, so funny because they hated each other!

Twins dating brothers: is that even legal?—

before I'm able to get them back into orbit. Diego walks into the kitchen and burns himself sneaking something from the frying pan.

"I'm not sure we're still a thing," I warn them. "Maybe we are. We had a fight. I don't even know."

Everyone gasps and a small, dissociated piece of me wants to laugh. It's not like Ethan and I have been together for years. My family just gets so immediately invested. But then again, so did I.

I can't think about things with us being over. It pushes a spike of pain through me.

And wow did I kill the mood. I debate for about three seconds whether I'm going to bother telling them that I also lost my job, but I know I am. If Dane tells Ami, and then Ami talks to one of my cousins and Mom finds out that I got fired and didn't tell her, she will call all of her siblings and before I know it, I will have forty text messages from my aunts and uncles all demanding that I call my mother immediately. Facing it now is going to be terrible, but it's still infinitely easier than the alternative.

"Also," I say, wincing, "I lost my job."

Silence swallows us all. Slowly, very slowly, Mom puts down her glass of wine, and Tía María picks it up. "You lost your job?" Cautious relief takes over her face when she says, "You mean the Butake job."

"No, *Mami*, the one I started today."

Everyone gasps, and Diego comes up, wrapping his arms around me. "*No*," he whispers. "Seriously?"

I nod. "Seriously."

Tía María takes my hand and then glances at Mom and Natalia, eyes wide. Her expression screams, *It is taking everything in me to not call everyone in the family right now.*

But Mom's focus on me remains intense; it's the protective mama-bear expression that tells me she's ready to battle. "Who fired my daughter on her first day of work?"

"The founder of the company, actually." And before she can unleash a tirade about the grave injustice of all this, I explain what happened. She sits down on a barstool and shakes her head.

"This isn't fair. You were in an impossible situation."

I shrug. "I mean, it's actually totally fair. I got a free vacation. I didn't have to lie about it. It's just my luck he showed up, and I got caught."

Natalia rounds the counter to hug me, and I'm swallowing every few seconds just to keep from crying, because the last thing I want is for Mom to worry about me, when—although she doesn't know it—she's going to need to save all her maternal sympathy for Ami.

"Call your father," Mom says. "Have him give you some money."

"*Mami*, I'm not going to ask Dad for money."

But Mom is already looking at Natalia, who picks up her phone to text my father on my behalf.

"Let me talk to David," Tía María says, referring to Tío Omar and Tía Sylvia's oldest son, the owner of a pair of popular restaurants in the Cities. "I bet he has a position for you."

There are some benefits to having an enormous family: you're never on your own to solve a problem. I don't even care if David would have me washing dishes—the prospect of a job is such a huge relief I feel like I'm melting. "Thank you, Tía."

Mom gives her sister a look. "Olive has a PhD in *biology*. You want her to be a waitress?"

Tía María throws her hands up. "You're going to look down your nose at a job? Where's her rent going to come from?"

"No one in this family is too good for any job that helps us pay our bills." I step between them, kissing Tía María's cheek and then Mom's. "I appreciate any help I can get." After Butake, I applied for all the local jobs I'm qualified for anyway, and only Hamilton offered me a position. Right now I'm so exhausted I'm not feeling picky. "Tell David I'll call him tomorrow, okay?"

At this point in the day, I'm running on fumes. With at least one stress settled—the prospect of a job—my body deflates and all at once I feel like I could fall asleep standing. Although the food they're making smells amazing, I know I'll have a fridge full of it tomorrow and am not at all hungry right now. I throw a mumbled "Good night" to them and no one argues when I shuffle down the hall to my bedroom.

Flopping on my bed, I look at my phone. I have a couple of texts from Ethan I'll read tomorrow, but I open my messages with Ami. She texted me about an hour ago.

Holy shit, Ollie! Dane told me about your job!

I just tried to call you!

I'll call you tomorrow.

Okay, sweetie. Love you

Love you too

Dreading the conversation that I'm going to have with my sister tomorrow, I drop my phone onto my bedside table and pull the comforter over my head without bothering to get undressed. I close my eyes and fall into a restless sleep to the sounds of my family in the next room.

chapter **seventeen**

Because the early bird gets the worm or whatever, Ami is at my door before the sun is even fully up. She's clearly already gone to the gym, all swinging ponytail and dewy complexion. She sets a bag with a set of clean scrubs on the back of the couch, which means she's heading to the hospital from here. If the bounce in her step is anything to go by, Dane hasn't said a word about last night.

In comparison—and we are nothing if not consistently on-brand—I'm tired, not yet caffeinated, and I'm sure it shows. I barely slept last night, stressing over paying rent, what I need to say to Ami this morning, and what will happen with Ethan when we finally talk about all of this. I have no plans for today or tomorrow, which is a good thing considering I need to call David and beg for a job.

Once I opened Ethan's texts from last night, I saw there

were only two, and they said, simply, *Call me* and *Headed to bed but let's talk tomorrow*. Part of me is glad he didn't bother trying to apologize in texts because I'm not a huge texter, and another part is mad he didn't even try. I know I need some distance until I talk to Ami, but I've also grown so used to having near constant contact with Ethan and I miss him. I want him to chase me a little, since I'm not the one who messed up here.

Ami comes inside, embraces me tightly, and then bounds into the kitchen for a glass of water. "Are you, like, totally freaking out?"

I'm sure she means the job situation, so when I say, "Um, *yes*," she really has no idea the scope of my anxiety right now. I watch her take down half the glass in a long gulp.

Coming up for air, she says, "Mom says David is going to hire you at one of his restaurants? That's awesome! Oh my God, Ollie, I can come in on the slow nights and it'll be just like when we were kids. I can help with the job search, or your résumé, whatever."

Shrugging, I tell her, "That'd be great. I haven't had time to call him yet. But I will."

Ami gives me a look that is half-amused, half-bewildered that I seem to have forgotten how our family operates. "Tía María called Tío Omar, and Tío Omar got in touch with David, and you're all set."

I laugh. "Oh my God."

She swallows, nodding. "Apparently he has a waitress position at Camelia for you."

Huh. His nicest restaurant. I love my family. "Cool."

This makes Ami laugh in her disbelieving *Oh, Olive* way. " 'Cool'?"

"Sorry," I say. "I swear, I am so emotionally wrecked I can't even get it up to be excited right now. I promise to do better when I talk to David later."

She sets her glass down. "My poor Ollie. Is your stomach feeling better?"

"*My* stomach?"

"Dane said you weren't feeling well."

Oh, I bet he did. And funny thing: as soon as she mentions Dane, my stomach *does* roll over. "Right. Yeah, I'm okay."

Ami tilts her head for me to follow her as she carries her water into the living room and sits on the couch, legs crossed in front of her. "Ethan ended up leaving early, too." She must note the look of surprise on my face because she raises a brow. "You didn't know?"

"I haven't talked to him since I left." I lower myself down beside her.

"Like at all?"

I take a breath. "I wanted to talk to you first."

She frowns, confused. "To me? Is this about how weird he was being?"

"No, I—What do you mean?"

"He was just really quiet, and about twenty minutes after I got there, he said he was going to head out. Dane said he probably had the same bug you had."

I clench my hands into fists, and then imagine what it would be like to slam one of them into Dane's smug face. "Actually, I wanted to talk to you about Dane."

"Dane?"

"Yeah. He . . ." I pause, trying to figure out where to begin. I have gone through this conversation a thousand times, but I still don't have the right words. "Do you remember when Ethan and I first met?"

Ami purses her lips together as she thinks back. "At some picnic or something?"

"The State Fair. Pretty soon after you and Dane started dating. Apparently Ethan thought I was cute, and when he mentioned to Dane that he wanted to ask me out, Dane told him not to bother."

"Wait, Ethan wanted to ask you out? How did he go from that to hating your guts, all in one day?"

"You know, I thought it was because he saw me eating cheese curds." God. Saying it aloud now is mortifying; it sounds so dumb. I know Ami always understood why I thought this—we've both always struggled with our curvy genes, and objectively the world treats thin women differently, but I know now that this is my red button. "I guess he was distant because he was trying not to flirt with me."

Ami laughs like this is a silly joke. "Dane wouldn't say that, honey. He's always hated that you two couldn't get along. He was genuinely so happy when he saw you two at the airport."

"Really?" I ask. "Or is he just saying that because it's what we all want to hear?" I stand from the couch and move to sit on the coffee table in front of her. I take her hand in mine. Our hands are similar in so many ways, but Ami has a glittering diamond on her ring finger.

"I think . . ." I say, still focused on our entwined fingers. This is so hard to say—even to the person I know best in the whole world. "I think Dane wanted to keep me and Ethan apart because he didn't want Ethan to let it slip that Dane was seeing other women when you were first together."

Ami jerks her hand away like she's been shocked. "Olive, that's not funny. Why would you say that?"

"Listen to me. I don't know the exact dates, but Ethan said something in Maui about you and Dane not being exclusive until right before the engagement."

"Ethan said that? Why would he—"

"He assumed you knew. But you and Dane were exclusive the whole time, right?"

"Of course we were!"

I already knew this, but I'm hit with a spike of vindication nonetheless. I *know* my sister.

She stands and walks to the other side of the room. Ami is no longer bouncy and postworkout-giddy. She's quiet, brow furrowed. My sister fidgets when she's anxious, and right now she's tugging on her ring, absently spinning it around her finger.

Being a twin means oftentimes feeling responsible for the other's emotional well-being, and right now all I want is to take it all back, pretend I'm joking and travel back to a time when I knew none of this. But I can't. I may never know what my ideal relationship looks like, but I do know that Ami deserves to be enough for someone, to be loved completely. I have to keep going.

"All the trips they took? Dane let you think they were Ethan's idea, that Ethan had planned them—"

"They *were* Ethan's idea. Like, objectively," she says. "Dane wouldn't plan that kind of thing without talking to me first. Ethan planned stuff to get over Sophie, and because he's single—or *was*"—she lets out a weird, surprised snort—"he just assumed that Dane was free for all the holidays, too."

"Most of these trips were before Sophie, or during." I watch her look for more reasons to explain all this away, and say, "Look, I understand why that's what Dane wanted you to think." I wait until she meets my eyes, hoping she sees that I'm being sincere. "It looks better for him if Ethan is the one who is constantly dragging Dane around the world on these crazy adventures. But Ami, Ethan hates to fly. You should have seen him on the plane to Maui—he could barely keep it together. He gets seasick, too. And seriously, he's such a homebody—like me. I honestly can't imagine Ethan planning a surfing trip to Nicaragua now—like, the idea makes me laugh. Dane was using Ethan as an excuse to go do stuff and to see other women. There's at least one other woman that Ethan mentioned."

"Where the fuck is your tinfoil hat, you psycho?" Ami growls. "I'm supposed to believe that my husband is that manipulative? That he's been cheating on me for what—three years? Do you really hate him that much?"

"I don't hate him, Ami—at least I didn't."

"Do you have any idea how ridiculous this all sounds? Do you have anyone's word besides Ethan's to go by?"

"I do . . . because Dane hit on me last night. At the bar."

She blinks several times. "I'm sorry, *what?*"

I explain what happened, about Ethan going to the bathroom and Dane suggesting we could all swing if the mood happened to strike. I watch as my sister's face, so like my own, goes from confusion, to hurt, to something bordering on rage.

"Holy shit, Olive." She gapes at me. "Why are you like this? Why are you so cynical about *everything*?" She picks up her glass and walks to the sink. Her face is so tight and bleak she looks sick again, and my stomach lurches in guilt. "Why do you always want to see the worst in people?"

I don't even know what to say. I am struck completely mute. In the silence, Ami turns on the water with an aggressive jerk and starts washing out her glass. "Like, are you serious right now? Dane wouldn't hit on you. You don't have to like him, but you don't get to always assume his intentions are terrible, either."

I follow her into the kitchen, looking on as she rinses her glass before filling it with soap and washing it all over again. "Sweetie, I promise you, I don't want to think the worst of him—"

She slams the faucet off and whirls to face me. "Did you tell any of this to Ethan?"

I nod slowly. "Right before I left. He followed me outside."

"And?"

"And . . ."

Her expression clears. "Is that why you haven't talked?"

"He wants to believe his brother is a good guy."

"Yeah. I know the feeling." The seconds tick by, and I don't know what more I can say to convince her.

"I'm sorry, Ami. I don't know what else to say to make you believe me. I never wanted—"

"Never wanted what? To ruin things between Dane and me? Between you and Ethan? That lasted what?" She laughs sharply. "Two whole weeks? You're always so happy to believe everything just *happens* to you. 'My life has turned out the way it has because I'm so unlucky,'" she says, mimicking me in a dramatically saccharine voice. "'Bad things happen to poor Olive, and good things happen to Ami because she's *lucky*, not because she's earned them.'"

Her words carry the vague echo of Ethan's, and I'm suddenly angry. "Wow." I take a step back. "You think I wanted this to happen?"

"I think it's easier for you to believe that when things don't go your way, it's not because of something you did, it's because you're a pawn in some cosmic game of chance. But, news flash, Olive: you end up unemployed and alone because of the choices you make. You've always been this way." She stares at me, clearly exasperated. "Why try when the universe has already decided that you'll fail? Why put any effort into relationships when you already know you're unlucky in love, and they'll end in disaster? Over and over like a broken record. You never actually *try*."

My face is hot, and I stand there blinking, mouth open and ready to respond but absolutely nothing comes out.

Ami and I argue sometimes—that's just what siblings do—but is this what she really thinks of me? She thinks I don't *try*? She thinks I'm going to end up unemployed and alone, and that view of me is only coming out now?

She grabs her things and moves toward the door. "I have to go to work," she says, fumbling to slip the strap over her shoulder. "Some of us actually have things to do."

Ouch. I step forward, reaching out to stop her. "Ami, seriously. Don't just leave in the middle of this."

"I can't be here. I have to think and I can't do that with you around. I can't even look at you right now."

She pushes past me. The door opens and then slams shut again, and for the first time since all this started, I cry.

chapter **eighteen**

The worst thing about crises is they can't be ignored. I can't just walk back to bed and crawl under the covers and sleep for the next month, because at eight in the morning, only an hour after Ami leaves, Tía María texts me to let me know I have to go down to Camelia and talk to David about the waitressing job.

David is ten years older than I am but has a boyish face and a playful smile that helps distract me from the throbbing background impulse to pull all my hair out and fall kicking and screaming to the floor. I've been in Camelia about a hundred times, but seeing it from the perspective of an employee is surreal. He shows me my uniform, where the schedule is taped to the wall in the kitchen, how the flow of traffic moves through the kitchen, and where the staff meets for dinner before the restaurant opens each night.

I have years of waitressing under my belt—all of us do, many of them at one of my cousin David's restaurants—but never at a place this classy. I'll need to wear black pants and a starched white shirt, with the simple white apron around my waist. I'll need to memorize the ever-changing menu. I'll also need to have a training with the sommelier and pastry chef.

I admit to looking forward to these last two things very much.

David introduces me to the rest of the waitstaff—making sure to leave out the part where I'm his baby cousin—as well as the chefs and sous chefs and the bartender, who happens to be there doing inventory. My brain is swimming with all the names and information, so I'm grateful when David turns and tells me to be here tomorrow night for the staff meeting and training, starting at four. I'll be shadowing a waiter named Peter, and when David winks like *Peter is cute*, my stomach twists because I want to be with *my* cute man, the one who won me over with his wit and laugh and—yes, his biceps and collarbones. But I'm pissed at him, and maybe he's pissed at me, and for the life of me I have no idea how this is going to shake down.

David must see some reaction in my face because he kisses the top of my head and says, "I've got you, honey," and I nearly break down in his arms because whether it's luck or generations of effort and attention ensuring it, I have a truly amazing family.

It's only noon by the time I'm back home, and it's depressing to register that I should be halfway into my second workday at Hamilton, meeting new colleagues, setting up accounts. But I admit there is a tiny glimmer in the back of my thoughts—it isn't relief, not exactly, but it's not altogether different from relief, either. It's that I've accepted that it happened—I messed up, I was fired because of it—and that I'm actually okay with it. That, thanks to my family, I have a job that can carry me as long as I need it to, and for the first time in my life I can take the time to figure out what I want to do.

As soon as I finished grad school, I did a short postdoc and then immediately entered the pharmaceutical industry, working as the liaison between the research scientists and medical doctors. I loved being able to translate the science to more clinical language, but I've never had a job that felt like joy, either. Talking to Ethan about what he did made me feel like Dilbert in comparison, and why should I spend my entire life doing something that doesn't light me on fire like that?

This fresh reminder of Ethan makes me groan, and although I know he's at work, I pull out my phone and send him a quick text.

I'll be home tonight if you want to come over.

He replies within a few minutes.

I'll be there around seven.

I know he isn't the most emotionally effusive guy, but the tone of his last three texts sends me into a weird panic spiral, like it's going to take more than a conversation to fix whatever is going on with us, even though I didn't do anything wrong. I have no idea what his perspective is on any of this. Of course I hope that he believes me, and that he apologizes for last night, but a tight lead ball in my stomach warns me that it might not go that way.

Looking at my watch, I see that I have seven hours until Ethan gets here. I clean, I grocery shop, I nap, I memorize the Camelia menu, I stress-bake . . . and it only eats up five hours.

Time is inching along. This day is going to last a decade.

I can't call Ami and ramble about any of this, because I'm sure she's still not speaking to me. How long is she going to keep this up? Is it possible that she'll believe Dane indefinitely, and I'll have to eat my words even though—again—I haven't done anything wrong here?

I put the menu down on my coffee table and sprawl on the carpet. The possibility that this rift between me and Ami could become permanent makes me light-headed. It would probably be a good idea for me to hang out with someone for distraction, but Diego, Natalia, and Jules are all at work, Mom will only worry if she knows what's going on, and calling anyone else in my family will just result in fifteen people showing up on my doorstep with sympathy dinner later when Ethan and I are trying to hash things out.

Thankfully he doesn't make me wait. He comes over right at seven, holding takeout from Tibet Kitchen that smells so much more appealing than the pizza I'd ordered for us to share.

"Hey," he says, and gives a little smile. He ducks, like he's going to kiss my lips, but then makes a detour at the last second, landing on my cheek instead.

My heart drops.

I step back, letting him in, and it suddenly feels too warm in my apartment; everything seems too small. I look everywhere but at his face, because I know if I look at him and get the sense that things between us really aren't okay, I'm not going to be able to keep myself together for the conversation we need to have.

It's so weird. He follows me into the kitchen, we make up plates of food, and then we sit on the floor in the living room, on opposite sides of the coffee table, facing each other. The silence feels like a huge bubble around me. For the past week, Ethan has practically lived here. Now it feels like we're strangers all over again.

He pokes at his rice. "You've barely looked at me since I got here."

The response to this dries up in my throat: *Because you kissed my cheek when you walked in. You didn't pull me against you, or get lost in a long kiss with me. I feel like I barely had you, and now you're already gone.*

So instead of answering aloud, I look up at him for the first time and try to smile. He registers the failed effort, and it clearly makes him sad. An ache builds and expands in my throat until I'm honestly not sure I'll be able to get words around it. I hate this somber dynamic more than I hate the fact that we're fighting.

"This is so weird," I say. "It would be so much easier to be snarky with each other."

He nods, poking at his food. "I don't have the energy to be snarky."

"Me either." I really just want to crawl across the floor and into his lap and have him tease me about my bra being too small or how I couldn't stay away from him long enough to finish my dinner, but it's like Dane and his fratty face are just parked here in between us, keeping us from being normal.

"I talked to Dane last night," he says right then, adding, "late. I went over there late."

Ami didn't mention this. Did she even know that Ethan stopped by last night?

"And?" I say quietly. I have no appetite and basically just push a piece of beef around the plate.

"He was really surprised that that's how you took what he said," Ethan says.

Acid fills my stomach. "What a shock."

Ethan drops his fork and leans back on both hands, staring at me. "Look, what am I supposed to do? My girlfriend thinks my brother hit on her, and he says he didn't. Does it matter who is right here? You're both offended."

At this, I am incredulous. "You're supposed to believe me. And it absolutely matters who's right here."

"Olive, we've been together for like two weeks," he says helplessly.

It takes a few seconds for me to be able to unscramble the pile of words that falls into my thoughts. "I'm lying because our relationship is new?"

Sighing, he reaches up, wiping one hand over his face.

"Ethan," I say quietly, "I know what I heard. He propositioned me. I can't just pretend like he didn't."

"I just don't think he meant what you thought he did. I think you're primed to think the worst of him."

I blink back down to my plate. It would be so easy to choose to make peace with Ethan and Ami and just say, "You know what? You're probably right," and just let it be, because after all this, of *course* I'm primed to think the worst of Dane, and I could easily give him a wide berth for the rest of time. But I can't do that. There are too many red flags—why am I the only one who can see them? It's not because I am a pessimist or look for the worst in people; I know that isn't true about me, not anymore. I fell for Ethan on that island, after all. I'm excited about a job at Camelia so that I have time to really think about what I want my life to look like. I'm trying to fix all the parts of me that aren't working because *I know I have a choice in how my life goes*—that it isn't all luck—but as soon as I try to be proactive, it's like no one wants to *let* me.

And why isn't Dane here with Ethan, trying to make things right with me? Actually, I know why: He is so sure that no one will believe me, that everyone will think, *Oh, Olive is just being Olive. Just believing the worst about everyone*. My opinions are so inconsequential because in their eyes I'm always going to be the pessimist.

"Have you talked to Ami?" he asks.

I feel the way heat crawls up my neck and across my face. The fact that my twin is on Ethan and Dane's side here is truly killing me. I can't even admit it out loud, so I just nod.

"You told her about him dating other people before they were exclusive?" he asks. I nod again. "And about yesterday?"

"Yeah."

"I thought you weren't going to say anything to her," he says, exasperated.

I gape at him. "And I thought Dane wouldn't hit on his wife's sister. I guess we've both disappointed you."

He stares at me for a long beat. "How did Ami take it?"

My silence clues him in that Ami didn't believe me, either. "She didn't know about the other women, Ethan. She thinks Dane has been committed since day one."

Ethan looks at me pityingly and it makes me want to scream. "So you're not going to be able to move past this?" he asks.

My jaw actually drops. "Which part? My sister's husband cheating on her before they were married, your brother hitting on me, or my boyfriend not believing me about any of it?"

His gaze turns back to me, and he looks apologetic but unwavering. "Again: I don't believe his intent was what you think it was. I don't think he'd hit on you."

I let him hear the shock in my voice. "Then you're right," I say. "I'll have a hard time moving past this."

When he leans forward, I think he's going to dig into his plate, but instead he pushes to stand. "I really like you," he says quietly. He closes his eyes and drags a hand through his hair. "I am crazy about you, actually."

My heart twists, painfully. "Then take a step back and look at this situation from a different angle," I plead. "What do I have to gain from lying about Dane?"

We've had so many disagreements, and they all seem so hilariously minor in hindsight. The cheese curds, the airplane, the Hamiltons, Sophie, the Skittle dress. I get it now—that all of those were opportunities for us to have contact with each other. This is the first time we've been at a true impasse and I know what he's going to say before he even gets the words out.

"I think we should probably break up, Olive. I'm sorry."

chapter **nineteen**

It's the quiet before the dinner rush, and I'm doing the final check of my section. Natalia is the fourth family member this week to just happen to stop by Camelia at exactly four o'clock. She said she wanted to say hi to David because she hasn't seen him in forever, but I know that's bullshit because Diego—who came by yesterday to hassle me using a similarly flimsy story—said both David and Natalia were at Tía María's less than a week ago.

As much as the size and presence of my family can feel oppressive at times, it's the greatest comfort I have right now. Even if I pretend to be annoyed that they're constantly checking up on me, they all see through it. Because if it were any of them struggling—and it has been, many times—I would find a reason to drop by at four o'clock wherever they work, too.

"*Mama*, when we're sad, we eat," Natalia says, following me with a plate of food as I adjust the placement of two wineglasses on a table.

"I know," I tell her. "But I swear, I can't eat anymore."

"You're starting to look like a bobble-headed Selena Gomez." She pinches my waist. "I don't like it."

The family knows Ethan broke up with me, and that Ami and I are "arguing" (although there's nothing active about it; I called her a few times after our big blow-up, and two weeks later she has yet to return any of my calls). In the past ten days, I've been bombarded with well-meaning texts and my fridge is completely packed with food that Mom brings daily from Tío Omar, Ximena, Natalia, Cami, Miguel, Tío Hugo, Stephanie, Tina—almost as if they've made a Feed Olive calendar. My family feeds people; it's what they do. Apparently my missing Sunday dinner for two weeks in a row—because of work—has gotten the entire family on high alert, and it's driving them all crazy not knowing what's going on.

I can't blame them; if Jules, or Natalia, or Diego went into hiding, I'd be out of my mind worried. But it isn't my story to share; I wouldn't know how to tell them what is happening, and according to Tío Hugo, who came by yesterday to "Um, get a business card for an insurance agent from David," Ami won't talk about it, either.

"I saw Ami yesterday," Natalia says now, and then pauses

long enough for me to stop fussing with the table settings and look up at her.

"How is she?" I can't help the tight lean to my words. I miss my sister so much, and it's wrecking me that she isn't speaking to me. It's like missing a limb. Every day I get so close to caving, to saying, "You're probably right, Dane didn't do anything wrong," but the words just won't come out, even when I test the lie out in front of the mirror. It sticks in my throat, and I get hot and tight all over and feel like I'm going to cry. Nothing all that terrible even happened to me—other than losing my job, my sister, and my boyfriend in a twenty-four-hour period—but I still feel a kind of burning anger toward Dane, as if he slapped me with his own hand.

Natalia shrugs and picks a piece of lint off my collar. "She seemed stressed. She was asking me about someone named Trinity."

"Trinity?" I repeat, digging around in my thoughts to figure out why the name sounds familiar.

"Apparently Dane had a few texts from her, and Ami saw them on his phone."

I cover my mouth. "Like sexy texts?" I am both devastated and hopeful if this is true: I want Ami to believe me, but I'd rather be wrong about all of it than have her go through that pain.

"I guess she just asked if he wanted to hang out, and Dane was like 'Nah, I'm busy' but Ami was pissed that he was texting a woman at all."

"Oh my God, I think Trinity was the girl with the mango butt tattoo."

Natalia grins. "I think I read that book."

This makes me laugh, and the sensation is like clearing away cobwebs from a dark corner of a room. "Ethan mentioned someone named Trinity. She—"

I stop. I haven't told anyone in my family about what Ethan told me. I could try to blow Dane's entire cover story if I wanted, but what good would that do? I don't have any proof that he was seeing other women before he married Ami. I don't have any *proof* that he propositioned me in the bar. I just have my reputation as a pessimist, and I don't want my entire family looking at me the way Ethan did when he registered that even my twin sister thinks I'm making this all up.

"She what?" Natalia presses when I've fallen quiet.

"Never mind."

"Okay," she says, fired up now, "what is going on? You and your sister are being so weird lately, and—"

I shake my head, feeling the tears pressing in from the back of my eyes. I can't do this before my shift. "I can't, Nat. I just need you to be there for Ami, okay?"

She nods without hesitation.

"I don't know who Trinity is," I say, and take a deep breath, "but I don't trust Dane at all anymore."

AFTER MIDNIGHT, I DRAG MY bag from my locker in the back room and sling it over my shoulder. I don't even bother to look at my phone. Ami isn't texting, Ethan isn't calling, and there's nothing I can say in reply to the forty other messages on my screen every time I look.

But halfway to my car, it chimes. It's a brief flurry of bells and rotors and change falling: the sound of a jackpot. Ami's text tone.

It's ten below outside, and I'm in a black skirt and thin white button-down, but I stop where I am anyway and pull my phone from my bag. Ami has sent me a screencap of Dane's text list, and there are the usual suspects—Ami and Ethan and some of Dane's friends—but there are also names like Cassie and Trinity and Julia. Ami's text says,

Is this what you were talking about?

I don't know how to answer. Of course my gut tells me that those are all women Dane has slept with, but how would I know? They could be work colleagues. I bite my lip, typing with frigid fingers.

I have no idea who they are.

I don't have a list of names. If I did, I would have shown it to you.

I wait for her to start typing again, but she doesn't, and I'm freezing, so I climb into my car and crank the heat as high as it will go.

But about three blocks from my apartment complex, my phone chimes again, and I pull over with a sharp jerk of my steering wheel.

Dane left his phone here yesterday.

I spent like two hours trying to guess his passcode, and it's fucking "1111."

I bite back a laugh and stare at the screen hungrily: she's still typing.

I sent myself all the screenshots.

All the messages from these women are asking the same thing—whether Dane wants to hang out. Is that code for a booty call?

I blink at the screen. Is she serious?

Ami, you know what I think already.

Ollie what if you were right?

What if he's cheating on me?

What if he's been cheating on me this whole time?

A fracture forms right down the middle of my heart. Half of it belongs to my sister, for what she's about to go through; the other half will always keep beating for myself even when no one else will.

I'm sorry Ami. I wish I knew what to say.

Should I answer one of the texts?

I stare at the screen for a beat.

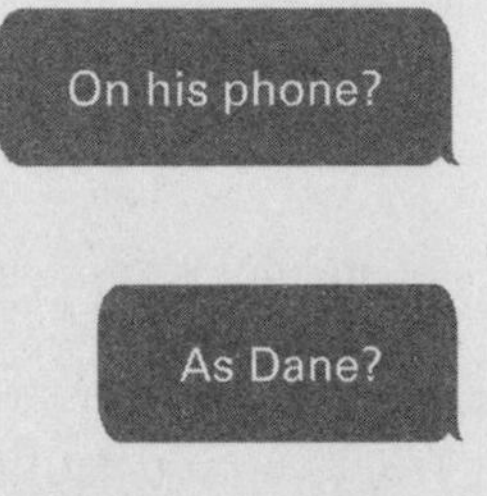

Yes.

I mean, you could.

If you don't think you'll get an honest answer from him.

I wait. My heart is in my throat, clawing its way up.

I'm scared.

I don't want to be right about this.

I know, honey.

For what it's worth, I don't either.

I'm going to do it tonight.

I take a deep breath, close my eyes, and let it out slowly. Somehow, being believed at last doesn't feel nearly as good as I'd hoped it would.

I'm here if you need me.

ALTHOUGH I'D HAD TWO MONTHS of unemployment not too long ago, I spent most of that time hunting for jobs or helping Ami prepare for the wedding, so now, keeping busy during the day has become so much more important. Because if I don't, I think about Ethan. Or Ami.

I don't hear from her the entire next day, and there's a knot in my stomach the size of Texas. I want to know how things went with Dane last night. I want to know whether she's replied to the texts or confronted him, and what happened. I feel protective, and worried for her, but there's literally nothing I can do, and I can't call Ethan, either, because we all know he's on the Dane Train until the end of the tracks.

Given that I'm off tonight, getting out of my apartment—and my head—becomes a priority. I dread going to the gym, but whenever I get in front of the punching bag, I'm amazed how much better I feel. I've started walking dogs at the local Humane Society and have a new golden retriever buddy named Skipper that I'm considering bringing home for Mom as a surprise—whether it would be a good surprise or a bad one I'm not sure, which is why I'm still considering it. I help a few of my neighbors shovel their walkways, go to a talk on art and medicine at the Walker Art Center, and meet Diego for a late lunch.

He hasn't heard from Ami today, either.

It's strange to realize that as soon as I got off the career treadmill, my life suddenly started to feel like mine again. I feel like I can look up for the first time in a decade. I can breathe. There's a reason Ethan didn't know much about my job: I never talked about it. It was what I did, not who I was. And even though many of my breaths ache—because I miss Ethan, I do, I miss him so much it hurts—not having the weight of a corporate job on my shoulders is an unbelievable relief. I never knew I was this person. I feel more myself than I've ever been.

Ami calls at five, when I've just walked in my front door and am making a beeline for the lint roller; Skipper is a shedder, even in early February. I haven't heard her voice in two weeks, and I can hear the way my own shakes when I answer.

"Hello?"

"Hey, Ollie."

I leave a long, quiet pause. "Hey, Ami."

Her voice comes out thick and strangled. "I'm really sorry."

I have to swallow a few times to get past the clog of emotions in my throat. "Are you okay?"

"No," she says, and then, "but yes. Do you want to come over tonight? I made lasagna."

I chew my lip for a few beats. "Is Dane going to be there?"

"He'll be here later," she admits. "Please Ollie? I really want you to be here tonight."

There's something about the way she's said it that makes me feel like it's more than just sister-reconnecting time. "Okay, I'll be over in twenty."

I LOOK AT MYSELF IN the mirror every day, so it shouldn't be so jarring to see Ami standing on her porch waiting for me, but it is. We've never gone two weeks without seeing each other—even in college. I was at the U, she was at St. Thomas, and even in the busiest week, we still saw each other at dinner on Sundays.

I wrap my arms around her as tight as they'll go and squeeze even tighter when I can tell she's crying. It feels like that first inhale after holding my breath as long as I can.

"I missed you," she says through a sob into my shoulder.

"I missed you more."

"This sucks," she says.

"I know." I pull back, wiping her face. "How are you?"

"I'm . . ." She trails off, and then we sort of stand there, grinning at each other through the telepathy because the answer is obvious: *My wedding was ruined by food poisoning, I missed my honeymoon, and now my husband may be cheating on me.* "I'm alive."

"Is he home?"

"Work." She straightens, taking a deep breath and pulling herself together. "He'll be home around seven."

She turns and leads me inside. I love their house—it's so open and bright, and I'm grateful that Ami has such a strong decorating sense because I assume if it was left up to Dane, the decor would be a lot of Vikings purple, dart boards, and maybe some hipster leather couches and a craft cocktail cart that he'd never use.

Ami moves to the kitchen, pouring us each a big glass of wine.

I laugh when she hands mine to me. "Oh, so it's that kind of night."

She nods, smiling even though I can tell there's nothing happy happening in her body right now. "You have no idea."

I still feel like I have to tiptoe around the topic, but I can't help but ask, "Did you take his phone last night? What's the latest?"

"I did." Ami takes a long drink and then looks at me over the rim of her glass. "I'll tell you all about it later." She tilts her head, indicating that I should follow her into the family room, where she's already got our plates of lasagna set up on two TV trays.

"Well, this looks comfy," I tell her.

She curtsies, flops down onto the couch, and hits play on *The Big Sick*. We missed it in the theater and kept meaning to watch it, so there's a sweet little ache that rises in my throat knowing that she waited to see it with me.

The lasagna is perfect, the movie is wonderful, and I almost forget that Dane lives here. But then an hour into the movie, the front door opens. Ami's entire demeanor shifts. She sits up, hands on her thighs, and takes a deep breath.

"You okay?" I whisper. Am I here for moral support

while she confronts her husband? I can't decide whether that will be fantastic or excruciating or both.

I hear Dane drop his keys on the counter, shuffle through the mail, and then call out, "Hey, babe."

"Hey, honey," she calls back, brightly, falsely, and it is so incongruous with the bleak way she looks at me.

My stomach drops in a weird burst of anticipatory stress, and then Dane is there in the doorway. He sounds surprised and displeased. "Oh. Hey, Olive."

I don't bother turning around. "Go to hell, Dane."

Ami chokes on her wine and then looks at me, eyes shining with amusement and tension. "Honey, there's lasagna in the oven if you want some."

I can feel him still looking at the back of my head—I know he is—but he just stands behind me for a few more seconds before saying quietly, "Okay, I'll grab some and leave you two to it."

"Thanks, hon!" Ami calls out.

She glances at her watch and then reaches for the remote, turning the volume down. "I'm so nervous, I'm nauseated."

"Ami," I say, leaning in, "what's going on?"

"I texted them," she says, and my jaw drops. "I'm screaming inside." I see it, too—the tightness around her eyes, the way I can tell she's holding back tears. "I had to do it this way."

"Do what exactly, Ami?" I ask.

But before she can answer, the doorbell rings.

Ami's attention shoots over my shoulder, toward the door leading to the kitchen, and we listen as Dane walks across the tile entryway to answer it. Slowly, so slowly I can see she's shaking, Ami stands.

"Come on," she says quietly to me, and then she calls out to Dane with a calm clarity I can't believe, "Who's at the door?"

I follow Ami out just as Dane is frantically trying to guide a woman back outside, and my blood pressure drops.

Did she text the women as Dane, and invite them here?

Oh my god.

"Who is it, honey?" Ami repeats, innocently.

The woman pushes past Dane. "Who's that?"

"I'm his wife, Ami." Ami stretches out her hand. "Which one are you?"

"Which *one* am I?" the woman repeats, too thunderstruck to return Ami's handshake. She glances at Dane, and her face pales, too. "I'm Cassie."

Dane turns, ashen, and stares at my sister. "Babe."

For once, I see Ami's jaw twitch at the pet name, and I want to shoot a rocket of joy into the sky because I *knew* she hated it and just pretended to like it! Twin powers for the win!

"Excuse me, Dane," Ami says sweetly, "I'm in the middle of introducing myself to one of your girlfriends."

I can see the panic in his eyes. "Babe, this totally isn't what you think."

"What do I think it is, *babe*?" she asks, eyes wide with faux-curiosity.

Another car pulls into the driveway, and a woman slowly emerges, taking in the scene in front of her. She looks like she just got off work: she's wearing nurse's scrubs and her hair is in a bun. It occurs to me that this is not how you dress for someone you're trying to impress; it's how you dress for someone you've known for a long time and are comfortable around.

I can't help but glare at Dane. What a complete dirtbag.

Ami looks at me over her shoulder and says to me, "That must be Trinity."

Oh my God. My sister is currently blowing up Dane's game, and she doesn't even need a checklist to do it. This is nuclear-level madness.

Dane pulls Ami aside, leaning down to meet her eyes. "Hey. What are you doing, hon?"

"I thought I should meet them." Her chin shakes, and it's painful to watch. "I saw the messages on your phone."

"I haven't—" he starts.

"Yeah," Cassie says quietly. "You have. Last week." She looks at Ami, then at me. "I didn't know he was married. I swear I had no idea."

She turns and makes her way back to her car, passing the

other woman, who's stopped several yards away. I can tell from Trinity's expression that she's figured out what's happening here.

"You're married," she says flatly, from a distance.

"He's married," Ami confirms.

Trinity looks back at Dane when he sits down on the doorstep and puts his face in his hands. "Dane," she says. "This is so fucked up."

He nods. "I'm sorry."

To her credit, Trinity looks directly at Ami. "We haven't been together in a while, if that helps."

"What's 'a while'?" Ami asks.

Trinity lifts a shoulder, drops it. "Five months or so."

Ami nods, breathing deep and fast, struggling to not cry.

"Ami," I say, "go inside. Lie down. I'll be in in a second."

She turns and quickly dodges Dane's outstretched hand as she passes. A car door slams down at the street and my heart lurches—how many more women are going to show up tonight?

But it isn't another woman. It's Ethan. He's coming from work, wearing fitted gray pants and a blue dress shirt, looking good enough to climb.

I'm shell-shocked by what's happening and trying to keep my shit together so I can be strong for Ami, but I still feel like I've been turned inside out at the sight of him.

"Oh," Ami says from the door, loud enough for everyone to hear. "I invited Ethan, too, Ollie. I think he owes you an apology." And then she quietly closes the front door behind her.

Trinity meets my eyes and gives me a dry smile. "Good luck with this." Looking down at Dane, she says, "I thought it was weird that you texted me to come over after disappearing months ago." She gnaws her lip, looking more disgusted than upset. "I hope she leaves you." With that, she climbs into her car and pulls out of the driveway.

Ethan has stopped a few feet away to watch this interaction, his brows furrowed in recognition. He turns his attention to me. "Olive? What's going on here?"

"I think you know what's going on here."

Dane looks up, eyes red and swollen. Apparently he'd been crying behind that hand. "Ami invited them here, I guess." He lifts his hands, defeated. "Holy shit, I can't believe what just happened."

Ethan looks at me again and then back to his brother. "Wait. So you really were . . . ?"

"Just a couple times with Cassie," Dane says.

"And Trinity about five months ago," I add helpfully. This moment is in no way about me and Ethan, but I can't help giving him my best *I told you so* face.

Dane groans. "I'm such an idiot."

I can see when Ethan realizes what he's hearing. It's like an invisible fist punches him in the chest, and he takes a step back before looking up at me with the clarity he should have had two weeks ago.

God, it should be satisfying, but it isn't. Nothing about this feels good.

"Olive," he says quietly, voice thick with apology.

"Don't," I say. I have a sister inside who needs me and have zero time for him or his worthless brother. "Take Dane with you when you go."

Turning, I walk back into the house and don't even look back at Ethan as I close the door behind me.

chapter **twenty**

It's a few hours before I get—and ignore—a call from Ethan. I can only assume he's been busy dealing with Dane, but I am also dealing with Dane, just less directly: I am packing up all of his clothes. And I can feel the intensity of Ami's desire to get him out of the house because for maybe the first time in her life, it doesn't even occur to her to look for a coupon before she sends me off to buy a giant stack of boxes at Menards.

I didn't want to leave her alone while I ran out, so I called Mom, who brought Natalia, Jules, Diego, and Stephanie, who apparently texted Tío Omar and his daughter Tina to bring more wine. Tina and Tío Omar also brought cookies—along with a whole carload of cousins—so, faster than you can say *Good riddance, dirt-bag*, there are twenty-two of us working on packing up every personal trace of Dane Thomas and putting each box in the garage.

Exhausted but accomplished, we all land on whatever empty, flat surface we can find in the living room, and it already feels like we have jobs: mine is to cuddle Ami; Natalia's is to keep her wineglass full; Mom's is to rub her feet; Tío Omar's is to refresh the plate of cookies every now and then; Jules and Diego are handling the music; Tina is pacing the room, detailing precisely how she's going to castrate Dane; and everyone else is cooking enough food for the next month.

"Are you going to divorce him?" Steph asks, carefully, and everyone waits for Mom to gasp . . . but she doesn't.

Ami nods, her face in her wineglass, and Mom pipes up, "Of *course* she's going to divorce him."

We all stare at her, stunned, and finally she sighs in exasperation. "*Ya basta!* You think my daughter is dumb enough to get tangled up in the same stupid game her parents have been playing for two decades?"

Ami and I look at each other, and then burst out laughing. After a heavy beat of incredulous silence, the entire room follows suit, and finally even Mom is laughing, too.

In my pocket, my phone rings again. I peek but don't get it hidden again fast enough because Ami catches a peek at my contact photo for Ethan on the screen before I can decline the call.

Tipsy now, she leans into me. "Aw, that was a good picture. Where did you take that?"

It's honestly a little painful to recall that day, when Ethan and I rented the hideous lime-green Mustang and drove along the Maui coastline, becoming friends for the first time. He kissed me that night. "That was at the Nakalele blowhole," I tell her.

"Was it pretty?"

"It was," I say quietly. "Unbelievable, really. The entire trip was. Thank you, by the way."

Ami squeezes her eyes closed. "I am so glad Dane and I didn't go."

Staring at her, I ask, "Seriously?"

"Why would I regret missing it now? We would have had even more good memories ruined. I should have known it was a bad omen when literally everyone but you and Ethan got sick at the wedding." She turns her glassy eyes up to me. "It was a sign from the universe—"

"*Dios*," Mom interjects.

Diego holds up a finger. "*Beyoncé*."

"—that you and Ethan are the ones who should be together," Ami slurs. "Not me and Dane."

"I agree," Mom says.

"So do I," Tío Omar calls from the kitchen.

I hold up my hands to stop them all. "I don't think Ethan and I are going to happen, guys."

My phone rings again, and Ami stares right at me, eyes suddenly clear. "He's always been the good brother, hasn't he?"

"He's been the good brother," I agree, "but not the best boyfriend or the best brother-in-law." I lean forward, kissing her nose. "You, on the other hand, are the best wife, sister, and daughter. And you are very loved."

"I agree," Mom says again.

"So do I," Diego says, lying across our laps.

"So do I," a chorus calls from the kitchen.

THE GOOD BROTHER CONTINUES TO call me a few times a day for the next several days, and then transitions to texts that say simply,

I'm sorry.

Olive, please call.

I feel like such an enormous jerk.

When I don't respond to any of them, he seems to take the hint and stops trying to get in touch with me, but I'm not sure if that's better or worse. At least when he was calling and texting I knew he was thinking about me. Now he might be focused on moving on, and I'm so conflicted over how that makes me feel.

On the one hand, screw him for not having my back, for enabling his brother to be a terrible boyfriend/husband, for being obstinately obtuse about a serial cheater. But on the other hand, what would I do in the same situation to protect Ami? Would it be hard to see her as sketchy the same way it was hard for Ethan to see Dane?

On top of that, Ethan was so perfect in all other respects: witty, playful, infatuated, and stellar in bed—it honestly feels so crappy to lose my boyfriend because we disagreed with a fight that didn't even involve us, really, rather than because we weren't a good fit.

We were a great fit. Our ending—by contrast—still seems so jagged and unfinished.

About a week after Dane leaves, I move out of my apartment and into Ami's house. Ami doesn't particularly want to be alone, and it works for me, too: I like the idea of saving to buy a place of my own or having some extra in the bank for an adventure once I figure out what kind of adventure I want to have. I see all these choices unrolling in front of me—career, travel, friends, geography—and despite things being insane and hard and messy, I don't think I've ever liked myself more than I do now. It's the strangest feeling to be proud simply because I'm taking care of me and mine. Is this what it's like to grow up?

Ami is so oddly, constitutionally solid that once Dane picks up his stuff from the garage and officially moves out, she seems mostly fine. It's almost as if the knowledge that he is trash is enough for her to get over him. The divorce doesn't seem like a wild good time, but she plugs ahead through her Divorce Checklist with the same calm determination with which she sent in the thousand sweepstakes entries to win the honeymoon.

"I'm going to have dinner with Ethan tomorrow," she says out of the blue while I make us pancakes for dinner.

I flip one badly, and it folds in half, batter oozing onto the lip of the pan. "Why would you do that?"

"Because he asked me," she says, like it's obvious, "and I can tell he feels bad. I don't want to punish him for Dane's sins."

I frown at her. "That's big of you, but you know you could still punish Ethan for Ethan's sins."

"He didn't hurt me." Ami stands to refill her glass of water. "He hurt you, and I'm sure he wants to own that, too, but that's between the two of you, and you have to answer his calls first."

"I don't *have* to do anything where Ethan Thomas is concerned."

Ami's silence leaves my words to echo back to me, and I

realize how they sound. So unforgiving but . . . familiar. I haven't felt like that version of myself in so long, and I don't like it.

"Well," I amend, "tell me how dinner goes, and I'll decide if he deserves a phone call."

FROM WHAT I CAN TELL, Ami and Ethan had a great time at dinner. He showed her photos from our Maui trip, ate a sufficient amount of the blame for Dane's past behavior, and generally charmed her senseless.

"Yeah, he's really good at being charming over dinner," I tell her, aggressively unloading the dishwasher. "Remember the Hamiltons in Maui?"

"He told me about that," Ami says, and laughs. "Something about being invited to a club where they look at labia in mirrors." She drinks from her wineglass. "I didn't ask for clarification. He misses you."

I try to pretend like this doesn't absolutely thrill me, but I'm sure my sister sees straight through that nonsense.

"Do you miss him?" she asks.

"Yes." There's no purpose in lying. "A lot. But I opened my heart to him, and he pinched it." I close the dishwasher and lean against the counter to face her. "I'm not sure if I'm the kind of person who can open back up again."

"I think you are."

"But if I'm not," I say, "then I think that means I'm smart, right?"

Ami smiles at me, but it's her new, restrained smile and it wrecks me a little. Dane killed something in her, some optimistic, innocent light, and it makes me want to scream. And then the irony hits me: I don't want to let Ethan make me cynical again. I like *my* new optimistic and innocent light.

"I want you to know I'm proud of you," she says. "I see all the changes you're making."

My life feels like mine again, but I didn't know I needed her to acknowledge it. I take her hand, giving it a little squeeze. "Thank you."

"We're both growing up. Holding some people accountable for their choices, letting other people make amends for theirs . . ." She lets the sentence trail off and gives me a little grin. Very subtle, Ami.

"Wouldn't it be weird for you if Ethan and I got back together?" I ask.

She shakes her head and quickly swallows another sip of wine before saying, "No, actually, it would make me feel like everything that happened in the past three years happened for a reason." Ami blinks away, almost like she doesn't want to admit this next part but can't help herself. "I'm always going to want there to be a reason for it."

I know now that it's a waste of my time looking for reasons, or fate, or luck. But I've definitely come to embrace choices in the past month or so, and I'm going to have to figure out which one I'll make where Ethan is concerned—do I forgive him, or do I walk away?

THE NIGHT THAT A CHOICE is put directly in front of me, the unexpected and terrible happens: I am happily working a dinner shift when Charlie and Molly Hamilton are seated in my section.

I can't blame the hostess, Shellie, because how would she know that this is perhaps the most awkward dining party she could give me? But the moment I approach the table and they look up, we all fall into a corpse-level silence.

"Oh," I say. "Hi."

Mr. Hamilton does a double take over the top of his menu. "Olive?"

I enjoy waitressing so much more than I ever expected, but I admit I don't enjoy the tiny wince that snags his shoulder when he registers that I'm not just coming up to his table to say hello, but I am in fact here to serve his dinner. This is going to be awkward for all of us.

"Mr. Hamilton, Mrs. Hamilton, good to see you." I smile, nodding to each of them. Inside, I am screaming like a woman being chased with a chainsaw in a horror movie. "I'm supposed to be serving you this evening, but I expect that we would all feel more comfortable if you were put in someone else's section?"

Mr. Hamilton gives me an easy, generous grin. "I'm okay with this if you are, Olive."

Ah, but there's the kicker: I am not.

Molly looks at him, brows pulled low. "I think she's trying to say she would be more comfortable not having to serve the man who fired her on her *first day of work*."

My eyes go wide. Is Molly Hamilton on Team Olive here?

I smile again at her, then him, struggling to keep a bit of professional distance. "It will just take a moment to get you set up. We've got a beautiful table right by the window for you."

With pinpricks all down my neck—and Molly's hissed "Are you pleased with yourself now, Charles? You are still trying to fill that position!" echoing in my ear—I hustle over to Shellie, tell her the situation, and she quickly shuffles a few reservations around.

They're moved, given a free appetizer, and I exhale an enormous breath. Dodged that bullet!

But then I return to my section to find that Ethan Thomas is seated at the table in their place.

He's alone and wearing a gaudy Hawaiian shirt with a vibrant plastic lei, and when I approach the table, mouth agape, I realize that he's brought his own glass: a plastic fluted cocktail cup with a giant $1.99 sticker on it.

"What in God's name am I seeing?" I ask, aware that at least half of the diners and much of the restaurant staff is watching us.

It's almost like they all knew he'd be here.

"Hi, Olive," he says quietly. "I, um . . ." He laughs, and seeing him nervous does wiggly, protective things to me. "I was wondering whether you served mai tais here?"

I say the first thing that comes to mind: "Are you drunk?"

"I'm trying to grand-gesture. For the right person. Remember when we had delicious mai tais?" He nods to the cup.

"Of course I remember."

"That day, I believe, was the day I fell in love with you."

I turn and glare at Shellie, but she won't meet my eyes. The kitchen staff scurries back into the kitchen. David pretends to be engrossed in something on an iPad near the water pitchers, and if I didn't know better, I'd think that was Ami's flash of dark hair darting down the hall to the bathroom.

"You fell in *love* with me?" I whisper, handing him a menu in a pathetic attempt to make it look like there's nothing to see here.

"I did," he says. "And I miss you, so much. I wanted to tell you how sorry I am."

"Here?" I ask.

"Here."

"While I'm working?"

"While you're working."

"Are you just going to repeat everything I say?"

He tries to wrestle his smile under control but I can see how much this exchange lights him up inside.

I try to pretend it doesn't do the same to me. Ethan is *here*. Ethan Thomas is grand-gesturing in an ugly shirt, with a fake mai tai glass. It's taking my brain a little time to catch up to my heart, which is currently jackhammering away beneath my breastbone.

It's beating so hard, in fact, that my voice shakes. "Did you coordinate with the Hamiltons for maximum effect here?"

"The Hamiltons?" he asks, and turns to follow my eyes over to their table. "Oh!" Ducking, he glances up at me, eyes comically wide. As if there's anywhere to hide in that shirt? Oh, Ethan. "Wow," he whispers. "They're here? That is . . . a coincidence. And awkward."

"*That's* awkward?" I look with meaning at his bright shirt and his Day-Glo green cup in the middle of the classy, muted dining room of Camelia.

But instead of looking embarrassed, Ethan straightens, growling a quiet "Oh, you're ready for awkward?" He reaches up to begin unbuttoning his shirt.

"What are you *doing*?" I hiss. "Ethan! Keep your clothes—"

He shrugs out of it, grinning, and words immediately

fall away. Because beneath his Hawaiian shirt he's wearing a shiny green tank top that strongly resembles . . .

"Tell me that's not," I say, biting back a laugh that is so enormous, I'm not sure I'm big enough to contain it.

"It was Julieta's," Ethan confirms, and looks down at his chest. "We had it made out of her dress. Yours is, presumably, still intact in your closet."

"I burned it," I tell him, and he looks like he's going to vehemently protest this decision. "Okay, fine, I didn't. I planned to." I can't help but reach out and touch the slippery satin. "I didn't realize you were attached to it."

"Of course I am. The only thing better than you in that dress was you out of it." Ethan stands, and now everyone is really looking at him. He's tall, hot, and wearing a shiny green tank top that leaves nothing to the imagination. Ethan is in great shape, but still . . .

"That really is a terrible color," I say.

He laughs, giddy. "I know."

"Like, it says a lot that even someone as cute as you can't pull it off."

I watch his smile turn into something heated and seductive. "You think I'm cute?"

"In a gross way."

He laughs at this, and it honestly sends a sharp pang through my chest how much I love that smile, on this face. "Cute in a gross way. Okay."

"You're the worst," I growl, but I'm grinning and don't pull away when he slides his hand to my hip.

"Maybe so," he agrees, "but remember what I told you about my penny? How it isn't so much that the penny itself is lucky, but it reminds me of times when good things happened?" He gestures to the shirt and waggles his eyebrows. "I want you back. Olivia."

"Ethan," I whisper, and dart my eyes around, feeling the pressure of everyone's attention on us, still. This moment is starting to feel like a reconciliation, and as much as my heart and lungs and lady parts are on board for that, I don't want to roll over the deeper issue here, which is that what he did by ignoring my truth wasn't okay. "You really hurt me. We had this rare, awesome honesty, and so when you thought I was lying, it was really hard."

"I know." He bends so that his lips are right near my ear. "I should have listened to you. I should have listened to my own instincts. I'm going to feel shitty about that for a long time."

There are two responses in me. One is a joyful *Okay then, let's do this!* and the other is a fearful *Oh hell no*. The first feels breezy and light, the second feels comforting and familiar and safe. As good as it feels to be careful, and to risk boredom and loneliness over heartache, I don't particularly want comfortable and safe anymore.

"I guess you deserve another chance," I tell him, only inches away from his kiss. "You do give a great massage."

His smile comes to rest on mine and the entire restaurant erupts. All around us, people stand from their chairs and I look up, realizing that men in the corner were Dad and Diego in wigs, and the table of women in the back was Mom, Tía María, Ximena, Jules, and Natalia. The woman in the hallway to the bathroom really was Ami, and the restaurant is filled with my family, who are all standing and clapping like I'm the luckiest woman alive. And maybe I am.

Looking over, I see the Hamiltons near the window, standing and clapping, too. I suspect that they didn't just show up here tonight—that Ami got them here so they could see that what they endured with us in Maui resulted in something enduring between me and Ethan here tonight—but in the end it doesn't matter.

I don't think I've ever imagined happiness like this.

Luck, fate, determination—whatever it is, I'll take it. I pull Ethan down to me, feeling the slippery slide of his tank top under my hands and my laugh echoing into our kiss.

epilogue

TWO YEARS LATER

ETHAN

"Man, he is *out*."

"Is he drooling?"

"He's a cute sleeper. But deep, wow. I bet people drew on his face in college."

"Not usually this deep." A pause. I try to open my eyes but the fog of sleep is still too heavy. "I'm tempted to lick his face to wake him up. Would that be mean?"

"Yes."

Many have said that my girlfriend and her sister are so similar that even their voices sound the same, but after two years with her, I can distinguish Olive's easily. Both voices are soft, with an almost imperceptible accent, but Olive's is huskier, slightly scratchy around the edges, like she doesn't use it much. Always the listener with most people; the observer.

"Lucas?" It's Ami's voice again, wavy and slow, as if coming through water. "Can you carry him off the plane if we need to?"

"Doubtful."

I am jostled. A hand comes up to my shoulder, sliding up my neck to my cheek. "Ethannnnn. This is your faaaaather. We are laaaaanding."

It isn't my father, in fact; it's Olive, speaking through her fist directly into my ear. I drag myself out of sleep with intense effort, blinking. The seat in front of me comes into blurry focus; the surface of my eyes feel syrupy.

"He lives!" Olive leans over into my field of vision, and grins. "Hi."

"Hi." I lift a heavy hand and rub my face, trying to clear the fog.

"We're almost on the ground," she says.

"I swear I just fell asleep."

"Eight hours ago," she tells me. "Whatever Dr. Lucas gave you worked well."

I lean forward, looking past Olive in the middle seat and Ami on the aisle to where Ami's new boyfriend—and my longtime friend and physician, Lucas Khalif—sits on the other aisle seat. "I think you gave me a dose for a horse."

He lifts his chin. "You're a lightweight."

I fall back against the seat, preparing to close my eyes again, but Olive reaches for me, turning my face to the window so I'll look. The view sucks the breath out of my throat; the intensity of color is like a slap. I missed this the first time we came to Maui, spending the entire flight pretending to not look at Olive's boobs through my anxiety haze, but below us, the Pacific Ocean is a sapphire, resting on the horizon. The sky is so blue it's nearly neon; only a handful of wispy clouds are brave enough to block the view.

"Holy shit," I say.

"Told you." She leans in, kissing my cheek. "You okay?"

"Groggy."

Olive reaches up and tweaks my ear. "Perfect, because first up is a dip in the ocean. That'll wake you up."

Ami dances in her seat, and I glance at my girlfriend as she takes in her sister's reaction. Ami's excitement is infectious, but Olive's is nearly blinding. Things were hard for her for a long time after losing her job, but it also gave her a clarity she'd never had before. She realized that, while she loved science, she didn't particularly love her job. While waiting tables at Camelia, she served a woman who ran a nonprofit health advocacy center. After a long meal peppered with intense, enthusiastic conversations while Olive worked a busy dinner shift, Ruth hired Olive as her community education coordinator, in charge of speaking at schools, church groups, retirement communities, and businesses about the science behind vaccines. She gets to geek out all over the Midwest about the flu vaccine now.

When she found out where the National Community Health Awareness winter conference would be this year—Maui—we knew it was fate: We owed Ami a trip to the island.

The landing gear lowers; the plane crosses the coastline and then sweeps over the lush landscape of the island. I glance down my row to where Ami has reached across the aisle to hold Lucas's hand. It's fitting that her first time in Maui should be with someone who adores her with as much devotion as he does.

And it's fitting that this time Olive and I are headed to Maui, I've got a real ring in my pocket.

DAY TWO AND IT TOOK some convincing to get Ami to agree to go zip-lining. For one, it wasn't free. And also, zip-lining essentially requires jumping from a platform, trusting the harness, and flying through the air while hoping there really is a platform on the other side. For a woman like Ami, who relishes keeping a stranglehold on all of the variables possible at any given moment, zip-lining isn't ideal.

But it's one of the few things Olive and I didn't get to do on our first trip, and my girlfriend would hear no dissent.

She did the research for the best location, bought the tickets, and now ushers us up to the platform for our first jump with a no-nonsense wave of her hand.

"Step right up," she says.

Ami peers over the edge of the platform and then immediately takes a step back. "Wow. It's high."

"That's a *good* thing," Olive reassures her. "It would be way less fun to do this from the ground."

Ami stares flatly at her.

"Look at Lucas," Olive says. "Lucas isn't scared."

He finds himself the object of all of our attention right as he's adjusting himself in the harness.

Lucas gives her a little salute but I tilt my head. "Lucas probably isn't scared because Lucas regularly goes skydiving."

"You're supposed to be on my team," Olive growls. "Team Listen-to-Olive-Because-This-Will-Be-Fun-Damn-It."

"I'm always on that team." I pause and give her a winning smile. "But is it a good time to suggest a better team name? Or no."

She stares me down, and I fight a smile because if I told her right now that with her blue shorts and white tank top, and the blue harness and yellow helmet they've given her, she looks like Bob the Builder, she would murder me with her bare hands.

"Look, Ami," she says, and her mouth curls into a delighted grin, "I'll go first."

The first drop is 50 feet above a ravine with a platform 150 feet away. Two years ago, Olive would have waited until everyone was safely on the other side before taking her turn, certain her bad luck would snap the cord or break the platform and end with us all crumpled on the forest floor. But now I watch as she stands behind the gate, following instructions to wait until her lead is strapped to the pulleys, and then steps out onto the platform. She hesitates for only a moment before taking off in a running leap and sailing (screaming) through the tops of the trees.

Ami watches her go. "She's *so* brave."

She doesn't say it like it's an epiphany; she just says it like it's a fact, something we've all always known about Olive, a core quality. And it's true, of course, but these little truths, finally being spoken aloud, are tiny, perfect revelations, dropped like jewels in Olive's palm.

So even though Olive didn't hear this, it's still awesome to see Ami looking after her twin in wonder like this, like she's still figuring things out about this person she knows as well as she knows her own heart.

THE LAST LINE OF THE day is one of the biggest in Hawaii—nearly 2800 feet from platform to platform. The best part is there are two parallel lines; we can ride it in tandem. As we make our way to the top, I remind her where to keep her hands and to angle her wrists the opposite direction that she wants to turn.

"And remember, even though we're starting side by side, I'll probably make it there faster because I weigh more."

She stops, looking up at me. "Okay, Sir Isaac Newton, I don't need a lesson."

"A what? I wasn't giving one."

"You were mansplaining how gravity works."

I go to argue but her brows go up as in *Think before you speak,* and it makes me laugh. She's not wrong.

Leaning in, I press a kiss to the top of her yellow helmet. "I'm sorry."

She scrunches her nose and my eyes follow the movement. Her freckles were the first thing I noticed about her. Ami has a few, but Olive has twelve, scattered just across the bridge of her nose and over her cheeks. I had an idea of what she looked like before we met—obviously I knew she was Dane's girlfriend's twin—but I wasn't prepared for the freckles and how they moved with her smile, or the way adrenaline dumped into my veins when she pointed that smile at me and introduced herself.

She didn't smile like that at me again for years.

Her hair is curly from the humidity and coming loose from her ponytail and even dressed like Bob the Builder, she's still the most beautiful thing I've ever seen.

Beautiful, but also very suspicious. "That apology was easier to extract than I expected."

I run my thumb over a strand of her rebellious hair and push it back from her face. She has no idea how good my mood is right now. I'm struggling to find the right moment to propose, but I'm enjoying every second more than the one that came before it; it makes it hard to choose how and when to do this. "Sorry to disappoint," I say. "You and your arguing kink."

With a blushing eye roll, she turns back toward the group. "Shut up."

I bite back my smile.

"Stop making that face."

I laugh. "How do you know I'm making a face? You're not even looking at me."

"I don't have to look at you to know you're doing that derpy heart-eyes thing."

I bend to whisper in her ear. "Maybe I'm making a face because I love you, and I *like* when you're argumentative. I can show you just how much I like it when we get back to the hotel."

"Get a room." Ami shares a commiserating look with Lucas as he's strapped into the pulley.

But then she turns and meets Olive's gaze across the platform. I don't need to understand secret twin telepathy to know that Ami isn't just happy for her sister, she's elated.

Ami isn't the only one who believes Olive deserves every bit of bliss this world has to offer. Seeing that tiny, salty woman crack up or melt or light up like a constellation gives me life.

Now I just have to get her to agree to marry me.

I THINK I'VE FOUND MY moment when four nights in, we're given a sunset that's so surreal it feels computer generated. The sky is this layered parfait of pastels; the sun seems reluctant to disappear entirely, and it's one of those perfect progressions where we can watch it slowly diminish in size until it's nothing but a tiny dot of light and then—poof. It's gone.

It's right then that I hold my phone up, snapping a selfie of Olive and me on the beach. The sky is a calming purple-blue. Her hair is blowing across her face, we're both a little tipsy. Our feet are bare, toes digging in the warm sand, and the happiness in our expressions is palpable. It's a great fucking photo.

I stare down at it, spinning a little inside. I'm so used to seeing our faces together, so used to how she fits against my shoulder. I love her eyes and her skin and her smile. I love our wild moments and our quiet ones. Love fighting and fucking and laughing with her. I love how easy we look side by side. I've spent the last few days agonizing over when to propose, but it occurs to me that this is when I do it: in this quiet space, where we're just us, having a perfect night. Ami and Lucas are down the beach a ways, walking in the lapping waves, and so it feels like we have this little stretch of sand entirely to ourselves.

I turn to her; my heart is a thunder inside me. "Hey, you."

She grins at the phone, taking it from me. "This is cute."

"It is." I take a deep breath, steadying myself.

"Caption this photo," she says, oblivious to my internal mayhem, my mental preparation for one of the biggest moments of my life.

"Um . . ." I say, a little thrown but thinking as I try to play along.

And then she bursts out laughing. "Here's one: 'She said yes!' " She leans into me, cracking up. "Oh, my god, this is a good picture of us but this is exactly the kind of vacation photos people in Minnesota put on their mantel in shell-encrusted frames to remind themselves of the sunshine when we are in the deepest pit of winter." She hands the phone back to me. "How many Minnesotans do you think get engaged on the beach? Eighty percent? Ninety?" Shaking her head, she grins at me. "What total—"

And then she stops, her gaze moving over my face. It feels like a wad of cotton has lodged itself in my throat. Olive claps a hand over her mouth as realization draws her eyes comically wide. "Oh. Shit. Oh, Ethan. Oh, *shit*."

"No, it's okay."

"You weren't, were you? Am I that big an asshole?"

"I—but no. I don't—it isn't. Don't worry."

She gapes at me, eyes wide with panic as it becomes clear her sarcasm wasn't that far off the mark. "I am such a dick that I've broken your brain."

I don't know whether to be amused by this destroyed attempt at proposing or bummed. It did seem like the perfect moment; I felt like we were on the same page and then—nope. Not even a little.

"Ethan, I'm so—"

"Ollie, it's okay. You don't know what I was going to say. You think you do, but you don't." Based off her unsure look, I add, "Trust me. It's all good."

I lean in, kissing her, trying to get her to let go with a gentle bite to her lower lip, a growl that has her softening beside me, opening her mouth to let me feel her. It escalates until we're both a little out of breath, wanting to take it to the next place where clothes come off and bodies come together, but although it's getting dark, it isn't *that* dark or that empty out here on the beach.

When I pull back and smile at her like everything is fine, I can sense the skepticism lingering in her posture, how she holds herself carefully like she doesn't want to make a wrong move. Even if Olive thinks I was going to propose, she still hasn't said anything like *I would say yes, you know* or *I was waiting for you to ask*, so maybe it's a good thing I didn't manage to get the words out. I know that her view of marriage has been marred by her parents and by Ami and Dane, but I also like to think that I've changed her views on long-term commitment. I love her wildly. I want this—want to marry her—but I have to accept the reality that it isn't what she wants, and we can live just as happily together forever without that ceremony binding us.

God, my brain is a blender all of a sudden.

She lays down in the sand, pulling me gently back so that she can curl on her side, her head to my chest. "I love you," she says simply.

"I love you, too."

"Whatever you were going to say—"

"Sweetheart, let it go."

She laughs, kissing my neck. "Okay. *Fine*."

We need a new subject, something to help us limp away from this crash.

"You really like Lucas, don't you?" I ask. It had taken Ami almost a year to start dating again after the divorce. Dane held out hope that she'd take him back and that they could work things out, but I didn't blame her for not wanting to try. My brother didn't just lose Ami's trust in all this; he lost mine, too. Things between us have slowly gotten better, but we still have a long way to go.

"I do. He's good for her. I'm glad you introduced them."

I didn't think Olive would ever welcome another guy into her sister's life. She was protective at first, but at dinner one night, Lucas—doctor, adventure seeker, and widowed father of the most adorable four-year-old I've ever seen—won her over.

"Ethan?" she says quietly, pressing small kisses up my neck and along my jaw.

"Hmm?"

She holds her breath and then lets it out in a shaky exhale. "I saw the ugliest dress the other day."

I wait for her to continue, admittedly confused, but finally have to prompt her. "Trust me, I'm riveted. Tell me more."

She laughs, pinching my waist. "Listen. It was this horrific orange. Sort of fuzzy? Like, velvet, but not. Something between velvet and felt. Velvelt."

"This story keeps getting better."

Laughing again, she bares her teeth against my jaw. "I was thinking we could get it for Ami. As payback."

I turn my face to hers. Up close she's only individual features: enormous brown eyes, full red mouth, high cheekbones, gently sloping nose. "What?"

She rolls her eyes and growls. When she speaks, I see her bravery; it's the same Olive who blindly jumped from a platform to sail through the forest. "I'm saying . . . maybe if we got married she would have to wear the ugly dress this time."

Struck dumb, all I can manage is, "You want to get married?"

Suddenly unsure of herself, Olive pulls back. "Don't you?"

"Yes. Totally. Absolutely." I trip over my words, gathering her back close to me. "I didn't think—from earlier—I thought you weren't—"

She looks directly at me, chin up. "I do."

Olive slides over onto me, cupping my face. "I think my joke earlier was totally Freudian. I thought maybe you would. But then we've been here a few days and you didn't. And then I was like, why shouldn't I do it? There's no rule book that it has to be the man."

I reach into my pocket and pull out the tiny box. "It's true—it doesn't have to be me, and you can totally get down on one knee to propose, but just so you know, I don't think this ring would fit me."

She squeals, rising to her knees to take the box. "For me?"

"I mean, only if you want it. I can go ask someone else if you—"

Olive shoves me, laughing. If I'm not mistaken, her eyes are a little misty. She opens the box and slides her hand over her mouth when she sees the delicate band lined with a halo of diamonds, the emerald-cut stone cradled in the center. I'll admit, I'm proud of myself—it is a pretty great ring.

"Are you crying?" I ask, grinning. Drawing intensely positive emotion out of this woman makes me feel godlike.

But of course Olive would never admit to happy tears. "No."

I squint at her. "You sure?"

"Yes." She valiantly works to clear her eyes.

"I mean"—I lean in for a closer look—"it looks like you might be."

"Shut up."

Gently, I kiss the corner of her mouth. "Will you marry me, Oscar Olivia Torres?"

Her eyes close and a tear breaks loose. "Yes."

Smiling, I kiss the other side of her mouth and then slide the ring on her finger. We both look down at it. "Do you like it?"

Her voice shakes. "Um. *Yeah.*"

"Are you usually better at making conversation than you are with me?"

She laughs, tackling me. The sand is still warm at my back, and this little bundle of fire is hot all along my front and I burst out laughing, too. What a ridiculous, silly, mistake-ridden proposal that was.

It was absolutely perfect.

acknowledgments

Ahhh, what a fun ride this one was! No book is *easy* to write, but even if this one wasn't easy, it was a total blast. One of the best things about writing as a team is the opportunity we get to make each other laugh. *The Unhoneymooners* offered plenty of such opportunities, and it meant our days drafting this were spent laughing at the computer screen. Not too shabby for a day job.

We always give ourselves permission to draft fast, edit later, and partly that's because it's easier to fix than create. But in reality, we have the luxury of working this way because we have fantastic editors. Kate Dresser and Adam Wilson—you two are so incredibly good at this. Thank you for always making sure our books are as strong as they possibly can be and for being hilarious and good-hearted humans in the process. We say it all the time but we feel very lucky to be able to do this with you.

Our agent is Holly Root and she is the best of the best—saavy, intuitive, level-headed, and totally lovable. Thank you, Holly, for the past eight years of ninjaness.

Thank you to our PR rep and precious, Kristin Dwyer. *You did so good, girl* is starting to feel like an understatement, but at the end of the day it will always remain true because you always do so good. Above and beyond, every time.

Thank you to our Gallery Books team: Carolyn Reidy, Jen Bergstrom, Jen Long, Aimee Bell, Molly Gregory, Rachel Brenner, Abby Zidle, Diana Velasquez, Mackenzie Hickey, John of the Mustache Vairo, Lisa Litwack, Laura Cherkas, Chelsea Cohen, the amazing sales force (we heart you), and anyone who has helped our books get into the hands of readers. We are so grateful for every single one of you.

Huge gratitude to our pre-readers Yesi Cavazos, Arielle Seleske, Gabby Sotelo, and Frankie O'Connor, and also to those in the CLo & Friends group for helping us in our goal to write an authentic Mexican-American family. Your feedback was so fantastic and we hope we made you proud. It goes without saying that anything we got wrong or any opportunity we missed is entirely on us. You are all so wonderful!

To all the booksellers and librarians out there, not every hero wears capes! (I mean, maybe you sell books while wearing a cape and that's amazing, but even if you don't, you're still #1 in our book.) Books are life, they are brain food, they bring joy, and relief, and connection. Doing what you do, and getting books you love into the hands of readers is such a gift to the world, and we are grateful to you beyond words.

To the bloggers, reviewers, readers: what we have is a symbiotic relationship. We couldn't do this without you, and there is not a day that goes by when we don't think about this. Thank you for your support, encouragement, and time spent reading our words. Every time you recommend a book of ours to a friend, an angel gets their wings. Or a puppy gets tummy rubs. Or a hedgehog gets a mealworm. Bottom line: good things happen in the universe. We heart you.

To our families: we love you all so much but you know that. What you really need to hear is our thanks for putting up with us. Living with a writer often means you're asking them a question and they're staring off into space, trying to figure out what the hell comes next in the book. You handle that with grace and patience (and also it works out for you, too, because we're working from home so there's rarely an excuse why we can't also throw some dinner in the Instant Pot).

Christina, this was your year. Your voice, your humor, and your ability to flesh out a story: it's all back and ready to blast off into all the fun things we have coming up next. I know I say it all the time, but I'm so proud to be able to do this with you.

Lo, the way you put words together still astounds me. There are times I read something you've sent me and I find myself just staring at the computer, wondering where in the world you came up with an idea or phrase. If I didn't also know you're the most loving, generous, loyal friend ever I would really hate your guts. Ha! I kid. Mostly. Thank you for letting me do this with you. I love you.

Don't miss the next novel from *New York Times* bestselling author Christina Lauren

TWICE IN A BLUE MOON

Coming in October 2019 from Gallery Books!

From the *New York Times* bestselling author of *The Unhoneymooners* and the "delectable, moving" (*Entertainment Weekly*) *My Favorite Half-Night Stand* comes a modern love story about what happens when your first love reenters your life when you least expect it. . . .

Sam Brandis was Tate Jones's first: Her first love. Her first everything. Including her first heartbreak.

During a whirlwind two-week vacation abroad, Sam and Tate fell for each other in only the way that first loves do: sharing all of their hopes, dreams, and deepest secrets along the way. Sam was the first, and only, person who Tate—the long-lost daughter of one of the world's biggest film stars—ever revealed her identity to. So when it became clear her trust was misplaced, her world shattered for good.

Fourteen years later, Tate, now an up-and-coming actress, only thinks about her first love every once in a blue moon. When she steps onto the set of her first big break, he's the last person she expects to see. Yet here Sam is, the same charming, confident man she knew, but even more alluring than she remembered. Forced to confront the man who betrayed her, Tate must ask herself if it's possible to do the wrong thing for the right reason . . . and whether "once in a lifetime" *can* come around twice.

With Christina Lauren's signature "beautifully written and remarkably compelling" (Sarah J. Maas, *New York Times* bestselling author) prose and perfect for fans of Emily Giffin and Jennifer Weiner, *Twice in a Blue Moon* is an unforgettable and moving novel of young love and second chances.

chapter **one**

JUNE

FOURTEEN YEARS AGO

Nana turned to inspect the hotel room. Behind her, the curtains drifted closed with a whisper. With her dark, sharp eyes, she surveyed the cream and red decor, the generic paintings, and the television she no doubt found gaudily perched on the otherwise beautiful dresser. Never in my life had I been in a room this fancy, but her gaze, as it touched everything, read, *Given the cost, I expected more.*

Mom had always described this expression as *pruney*. It fit. My grandmother—only sixty-one—totally looked like a piece of soft, dried fruit when she got mad.

As if on cue, she grimaced like she'd just smelled something sour. "Our view is the *street.* If I wanted to stare at a street

I could have stayed in Guerneville." She blinked away from the dresser to the telephone on the desk, moving toward it with purpose. "We aren't even on the right side of the building."

Oakland, to New York, to London, landing just over an hour ago. For the longest leg, our seats were in the middle of a group of five, on the bulkhead row, where we were flanked on one side by a frail older man who fell immediately asleep on Nana's shoulder and a mother with an infant on the other. By the time we were finally situated in the room, I just wanted a meal, and a nap, and a tiny patch of quiet away from Nana the Prune.

Mom and I lived with Nana since I was eight. I knew she had it in her to be a good sport; I'd seen it every day for the past ten years. But right then we were far from home, way out of our comfort zone, and Nana—owner of a small-town café—detested spending her hard-earned money and not getting exactly what she was promised.

I nodded to the window as a very European black taxi zoomed by. "It *is* a pretty great street, though."

"I paid for a view of the *Thames.*" She ran a blunt fingertip down the list of hotel extensions, and my stomach clenched into a ball of guilt at the reminder that this vacation was way more lavish than anything we'd ever done. "*And* Big Ben." The tremble of her hand told me exactly how quickly she was calculating what she could have done with that money if we'd stayed somewhere cheaper.

Out of habit, I tugged at a string on the hem of my shirt, wrapping it around my finger until the tip pulsed. Nana batted my hand away before she sat at the desk, heaving an impatient breath as she lifted the phone from its cradle.

"Yes. Hello," she said. "I'm in room 1288 and I have brought my granddaughter all the way here from—yes, that's correct, I am Judith Houriet."

I looked up at her. She said Judith, not Jude. *Jude* Houriet baked pies, served the same regular customers she'd had since she opened her café at nineteen, and never made a fuss when someone couldn't afford their meal. *Judith* Houriet was apparently much fancier: she traveled to London with her granddaughter and certainly deserved the view of Big Ben she'd been promised.

"As I was saying," she continued, "we are here to celebrate her eighteenth birthday, and I specifically booked a room with a view of Big Ben and the Tham—yes." She turned to me, stage-whispering, "Now I'm on *hold.*"

Judith didn't even sound like my nana. Was this what happened when we left the cocoon of our town? This woman in front of me had the same soft curves and stout, worker's hands, but wore a structured black jacket I knew Jude could barely afford, and was missing her ubiquitous yellow gingham apron. Jude wore her hair in a bun with a pencil dug through it; Judith wore her hair blown out and tidy.

When whoever was on the other end returned, I could tell it wasn't with good news. Nana's "Well that's unacceptable," and "I can *assure* you I am going to complain," and "I expect a refund of the difference in room rates," told me we were out of luck.

She hung up and exhaled long and slow, the way she did when it had been raining for days, I was bored and testy, and she was at her wits' end with me. At least this time, I knew I wasn't the reason behind her mood.

"I can't tell you how grateful I am," I said quietly. "Even in this room."

She blew out another breath and looked over at me, softening only slightly. "Well. We'll see what we can do about it."

Two weeks with Nana in a tiny hotel room, where she was sure to complain about the poor water pressure or the too-soft mattress or how much everything cost.

But two weeks in *London*. Two weeks of exploring, of adventure, of cramming in as much experience as I could before my life got small again. Two weeks seeing sights I'd only ever read about in books, or seen on TV. Two weeks watching some of the best theater productions anywhere in the world.

Two weeks of not being in Guerneville.

Dealing with a little pruney was worth it. Standing, I lifted my suitcase onto my bed, and began unpacking.

AFTER A SURREAL WALK ACROSS Westminster Bridge and past the towering Big Ben—I could actually *feel* the chimes through the center of my chest—we ducked into the darkness of a small pub called The Red Lion. Inside, it smelled of stale beer, old grease, and leather. Nana peeked in her purse, making sure she'd brought enough cash for dinner.

A few figures lurked near the bar, yelling at the television, but the only other people there for a meal at five in the evening were a couple of guys seated near the window.

When Nana spoke—strong voice, clear American accent saying, "A table for two, please. Near the window."—the older of the two men stood abruptly, sending the table screeching toward his companion.

"Across the pond as well?" he called out. He was around Nana's age, tall and broad, dark-skinned with a shock of salt-and-pepper hair and matching mustache. "We just ordered. Please, come join us."

Nana's dread was apparent; it settled across her shoulders in a gentle curve.

She waved away the host, taking the menus from his hand and leading us both to their table by the window.

"Luther Hill." The older man stretched out his hand to Nana. "This is my grandson, Sam Brandis."

Nana gingerly shook his hand. "I'm Jude. This is my granddaughter, Tate."

Luther moved to shake my hand next, but I was hardly paying attention. Sam stood at his side and just looking at him sent an earthquake rattling down my spine, the way the chimes of Big Ben had reverberated along my bones earlier. If Luther was tall, Sam was a redwood, a skyscraper, wide as a road.

He ducked a little to pull my attention from the expanse of his chest, giving me a smile that I imagined must be cultivated to reassure people that he wasn't going to break their hand when he shook it.

He pressed his palm to mine and squeezed, carefully. "Hi, Tate."

He was gorgeous, but just imperfect enough to seem . . . perfect. His nose had been broken at some point, and healed with a small bump near the bridge. He had a scar through one of his eyebrows and one on his chin—a tiny, indented comma below his lip. But there was something about the shadow he cast, the solid weight of him, and the way he came together—his soft brown hair, wide-set green-brown eyes, and full, smooth mouth—that made my pulse seem to echo in my throat. I felt like I could stare and stare at his face for the rest of the night and still find something new in the morning.

"Hi, Sam."

Nana's chair screeched dissonantly across the wooden floor, and I snapped my gaze to where Luther was helping her into her seat. Only two weeks prior, I ended a three-year relationship with Jesse—the only boy in Guerneville I'd ever considered worthy of affection. Boys were the last thing on my mind.

Weren't they?

London wasn't supposed to be about boys. It was about being in a place with museums, and history, and people who were raised in a city rather than in a tiny, damp, redwood-lined river town. It was meant to be about doing every last thing Nana has ever dreamed of doing here. It was about having one fancy adventure before I ducked back into the shadows and began college in Sonoma.

But it seemed Sam didn't get the mental memo that London wasn't about him, because although I'd looked away, I could feel the way he was still watching me. And was still holding my hand. In unison, we looked down. His hand felt heavy, like a rock, around mine. Slowly he let go.

We sat together at the cramped table—Nana across from me, Sam to my right. Nana smoothed the linen tablecloth with an inspecting hand, pursing her lips; I could tell she was still mad about the view and barely containing the need to voice it to someone else, to hear them confirm that she was right to be up in arms over this injustice.

In my peripheral vision I caught Sam's long fingers as they reached out and engulfed his water glass.

"Well now." Luther leaned in, pulling a whistling breath in through his nose. "How long have you been in town?"

"We just landed, actually," I said.

He looked at me, smiling beneath his bushy, old-man-pornstache. "Where you all from?"

"Guerneville," I said, clarifying, "about an hour north of San Francisco."

He dropped a hand on the table so heavily that Nana startled and his water rippled inside the glass. "San Francisco!" Luther's smile grew wider, flashing a collection of uneven teeth. "I've got a friend out there. Ever met a Doug Gilbert?"

Nana hesitated, brows tucking down before saying, "We . . . no. We've not met him."

"Unless he drives up north for the best blackberry pie in California, we probably haven't crossed paths." I said it proudly, but Nana frowned at me, like I'd just given them some scandalously identifying information.

Sam's eyes gleamed with amusement. "I hear San Francisco is a pretty big city, Grandpa."

"True, true." Luther laughed at this, at himself. "We have a small farm in Eden. Vermont, just north of Montpelier. Everyone knows everyone there, I suppose."

"We sure know how that is," Nana said politely before surreptitiously peeking down at the dinner menu.

I struggled to find something to say, to make us seem as friendly as they were. "What do you farm?"

"Dairy," Luther told me, smile encouraging and bright. "And since everyone does it, we also do a bit of sweet corn and apples. We're here celebrating Sam's twenty-first birthday, just three days ago." Luther reached across the table, clutching Sam's hand. "Time is flying by, I tell you what."

Nana finally looked back up. "My Tate just graduated from high school." A tight cringe worked its way down my spine at the way she emphasized my age, glancing pointedly at Sam. He might have been twice my size, but twenty-one is only three years older than eighteen. Going by her expression you'd think he'd been practically middle-aged. "She's starting college in the fall."

Luther coughed wetly into his napkin. "Whereabouts?"

"Sonoma State," I said.

He seemed to be working on a follow-up question, but Nana impatiently flagged down the waiter. "I'll have the fish and chips," she ordered, without waiting for him to come to a full stop at the table. "But if you could put them on separate plates, I'd appreciate it. And a side salad, no tomatoes. Carrots only if they aren't shredded."

I caught Sam's eye and registered the sympathetic amusement there. I wanted to explain that she owns a restaurant but hates eating out. She's picky enough to make her food perfect, but never trusts anyone else to do the same. After he gave me a small smile, we both looked away.

Nana held up a hand to keep the waiter's attention from turning to me yet. "And dressing on the side. Also, I'll have a glass of chardonnay and an ice water. *With ice.*" She lowered her voice to explain to me—but not so quietly that everyone didn't hear it too: "Europeans have a thing about ice. I'll never understand it."

With a tiny grimace, the waiter turned to me. "Miss?"

"Fish and chips." I grinned and handed him my menu.

The waiter left, and a tense, aware silence filled his wake before Luther leaned back in his chair, letting out a roaring laugh. "Well now. I guess we know who the princess is!"

Nana became a prune again. Great.

Sam leaned forward, planting two solid arms on the table. "How long you here for?"

"Two weeks," Nana told him, pulling her hand sanitizer out of her purse.

"We're doing a month," Luther said, and beside him, Sam picked up a piece of bread from the basket at the center of the table and wolfed it down in a single, clean bite. I worried they'd ordered a while ago, and our appearance had really delayed the delivery of their meal. "Here for a couple weeks as well," Luther continued, "then up to the Lake District. Where are you staying in London?"

"The Marriott." My voice carried the same reverence I'd use to tell him we were staying in a castle. "Right on the river."

"Really?" Sam's eyes darted to my mouth and back up. "So are we."

Nana's voice cut in like a razor: "Yes, but we'll be moving as soon as we can."

My jaw dropped open, and irritation rose in a salty tide in my throat. "Nana, we don't—"

"Moving hotels?" Luther asked. "Why on earth would you leave that place? It's beautiful, historic—It's got a view of everything you could possibly want."

"Our room doesn't. And in my book, it's unacceptable for us to pay what we're paying for two weeks only to look at a row of parked cars." She immediately handed the water glass back to the waiter when he put it in front of her. "Ice, please."

She's tired, I reminded myself and drew in a deep, calming breath. *She's stressed because this is expensive and we're far away from home and Mom is alone there.*

I watched the waiter turn and walk back toward the bar;

I was mortified by her demands and her mood. A tight, leaden ball pinballed around inside my gut, but Sam laughed into another sip of his own water, and when I looked at him, he grinned. He had my favorite kind of eyes: mossy green backlit by a knowing gleam.

"This is Tate's first trip to London," Nana continued, apparently ignoring the fact that it was her first trip there, too. "I've been planning this for years. She should have a view of the river."

"You're right," Sam said quietly, and didn't even hesitate when he added: "You should take our room. Twelfth floor. We have a view of the river, the London Eye, and Big Ben."

Twelfth floor. Same as us.

Nana blanched. "We couldn't possibly."

"Why not?" Luther asked. "We're barely ever there. The better views are outside, when you're out and about."

"Well of course we won't be sitting in the *room* the entire time," Nana protested defensively, "but I assumed if we're paying—"

"I insist," Luther broke in. "After dinner, we'll trade rooms. It's settled."

"I DON'T LIKE IT." NANA sat by the window while I shoved all my clothes back in my suitcase. Her purse on her lap, and the packed suitcase at her feet told me she'd already decided to trade rooms, she just needed to make a show of protest. "Who offers to give up a view of the river and Big Ben for a view of the street?"

"They seem nice."

"First, we don't even know them. Second, even with *nice* men you don't want to be obligated."

"Obligated? Nana, they're trading hotel rooms with us, not paying us for sex."

Nana turned her face toward the window. "Don't be crude, Tate." She fingered the organza curtain for a few quiet beats. "What if they find out who you are?"

There it was. Reason number one I'd never traveled east of Colorado before today. "I'm eighteen. Does it even matter anymore?"

She started to argue but I held up a hand, giving in. It mattered so much to Nana that I stayed hidden; it wasn't worth pushing back.

"I'm just saying," I said, zipping up my bag and rolling it toward the door. "They're being nice. We're here for two weeks, and glaring at that street will drive you crazy. Which means it will drive me crazy. Let's take the room." She didn't move, and I returned a few steps closer to her. "Nana, you know you want the view. Come on."

Finally she stood, saying, "If you'd be happier with it," before leading me out. We fell silent as our suitcases rolled dully behind us, wheels rhythmically tripping over the seams in the sections of thick carpet.

"I just want your vacation to be perfect," she said over her shoulder.

"I know, Nana. I want yours to be perfect too."

She hiked her JCPenney purse higher on her shoulder and I felt a pang of protectiveness. "It's our first trip to London," she said, "and—"

"It's going to be amazing, don't worry." The café did well for a café in a small town, but it was all relative; we'd never been rolling in cash. I couldn't even fathom how long it took her to save for all this. I mean, I'd seen her itinerary and it was packed: museums, Harrods, shows, dinners out. We were going to spend more in two weeks than Nana probably spent in a year.

"I'm already so excited to be here," I said.

Sam and Luther emerged from their room: Luther was rolling a bag behind him, and Sam had a duffel slung over his shoulder. Once again I experienced a weird physical leap inside at the sight of him. He seemed to completely fill the hallway. He'd pulled a worn blue plaid shirt over the T-shirt he wore earlier, but at some point took off his green Converse and padded his way down the hall only in socks. It was oddly scandalous.

Sam lifted his chin in greeting when he saw me, and smiled. I don't know if it was the smile or the socks—the hint of being undressed—but a shiver worked its way down my spine.

I'm here for museums and history.

I'm here for the adventure and experience.

I'm not here for boys.

Sam was right there, four, three, two feet away. He

blocked out the ambient light coming in from a row of narrow windows—I barely came up to his shoulder. Was this what it felt to be a moon, orbiting a much larger planet?

"Thanks again," I mumbled.

"Are you kidding?" His eyes followed me as we passed. "Anything to make you smile."

THE NEW ROOM WAS EXACTLY the same as our old one, except for one important detail: the view. Nana unpacked, hanging her clothes in the narrow closet, lining her makeup and lotions on the wide granite counter. Against the swirling black and cream, her drugstore blush and eye shadow palettes looked dusty and faded.

Within only a few minutes she was in bed, beginning her ritual of foot cream, alarm setting, reading. But despite the time difference and long flight, I was still buzzing. We were in London. Not just down the freeway in Santa Rosa or San Francisco—we were actually across an entire *ocean*. I was exhausted, but it was in that speedy, jittery way where I didn't want to sleep. In fact, I didn't think I ever wanted to sleep again. I knew if I got into bed now my legs would wrestle with the sheets anyway: hot, cold, hot, cold.

Anything to make you smile.

I hated to admit it, but Nana was right: the view was spectacular. It made me itch to slip out like a shadow into the night and explore. Right there, just outside the window was the Thames and Big Ben, and just below was a manicured garden. The grounds were dark, spotted with tiny lights and fluttering shadows; it looked like a maze of lawn and trees.

"Think I'll sit outside and read for a bit," I said, grabbing a book and trying to hide how jittery I felt. "Just in the garden."

Nana studied me over the top of her reading glasses, practiced hands rhythmically rubbing in hand cream. "By yourself?" I nodded, and she hesitated before adding, "Don't leave the hotel. And don't talk to anybody."

I kept my tone even. "I won't."

The real directive remained unspoken in her eyes: *Don't talk about your parents.*

So my answer remained in mine: *When have I ever?*